ENDURE

ALSO BY SARA B. LARSON

Defy
Ignite

ENDURE

⊰ A DEFY NOVEL ⊱

SARA B. LARSON

SCHOLASTIC PRESS
New York

All rights reserved. Published by Scholastic Press, an imprint of Scholastic Inc.,
Publishers since 1920. SCHOLASTIC, SCHOLASTIC PRESS, and associated logos
are trademarks and/or registered trademarks of Scholastic Inc.

The publisher does not have any control over and does not assume any
responsibility for author or third-party websites or their content.

This book is a work of fiction. Names, characters, places, and incidents are
either the product of the author's imagination or are used fictitiously, and any
resemblance to actual persons, living or dead, business establishments, events,
or locales is entirely coincidental.

Library of Congress Cataloging-in-Publication Data

Larson, Sara B., author.
Endure : a Defy novel / Sara B. Larson. — First edition.
pages cm
Sequel to: Ignite.
Summary: Alexa and King Damian are engaged to be married, but the kingdom of
Antion is besieged, their friend Rylan is a prisoner of the enemy, and Alexa has not
told Damian that she is at the mercy of the evil Rafe, bound to obey one command
of his choosing — but now Alexa must travel deep into enemy territory and
confront an army of black sorcerers to rescue Rylan.
ISBN 978-0-545-64490-7 (jacketed hardcover : alk. paper) 1. Magic — Juvenile
fiction. 2. Kings and rulers — Juvenile fiction. 3. Rescues — Juvenile fiction.
4. Conspiracies — Juvenile fiction. 5. Adventure stories. [1. Magic—Fiction. 2. Kings,
queens, rulers, etc. — Fiction. 3. Rescues — Fiction. 4. Conspiracies — Fiction.
5. Adventure and adventurers — Fiction.] I. Title.
PZ7.L323953En 2016
813.6—dc23
[Fic]
2015015932

10 9 8 7 6 5 4 3 2 1   16 17 18 19 20

Printed in the U.S.A.   23
First edition, January 2016

Book design by Elizabeth B. Parisi

*For my parents, who taught me to dream and then told me
to never give up. Thank you will never be enough for
everything you've done for me.*

*And for everyone who has lost someone they love —
look to the sky and remember.*

⊰ PREFACE ⊱

Damian

MY FATHER TAUGHT me that the only way to ensure your subjects' loyalty is to make them fear you. He used cruelty and terror as tools to ensure his power. My mother, on the other hand, taught my brother and me something entirely different: A king — a *good* king — must be who his people *need* him to be.

I live by her words.

For the grieving woman, I am compassionate, I am kind. To the generals who lead my armies, I am firm and absolute. To the daughters of the royal court, I am courteous but, of necessity, aloof.

I've spent a lifetime practicing, becoming who I must be to survive. Hiding in plain sight, always acting, always playing a part. There are times when I fear that I'll lose *me*, my *true* self, in the haze of the facade. But that fear doesn't matter to anyone besides myself. It doesn't build homes for the orphans and women left broken by my father's reign of terror. It doesn't put Antion back together, or stop us from getting dragged into another unwanted war. The only thing that counts is that I carry on and do what I must.

So that is what I do.

Until night falls and I lie in my bed, with the weight of a kingdom bearing down on me, trying to breathe under the pressure of

1

all that I hope to do, all that I want to accomplish — all that I fear. And that is when the smell of gardenia mixed with the coppery tang of blood comes to haunt me.

The memory of my mother is both happiness *and* terror intertwining into a tangle of comfort and horror. I try to erase the bad with the good. Her arm draped around my shoulder at night, a comfortable weight. The remnants of her gardenia perfume in my nose, with Victor on her other side. Her voice flowing over us along with the blanket of darkness as night fell. She started all of her stories with "Once, a long time ago . . ." Her Blevonese accent made her words different, almost magical. She painted pictures for me and Victor, holding us in the protective wings of her arms, curled up together on her massive bed. Her stories always ended well, sending us off into dreams, warm in the comfort of happily ever after. But her gentle life ended in a tapestry of blood, at the hands of my father. Nightmares drenched in dark, dripping crimson have been my constant companion ever since.

My story, if someone were to tell it, would begin with her voice.

Once, a prince was born. He was a second son, who worshipped his older brother as all younger sons do — even if it was in secret most of the time. His mother adored both of her children. She told them stories; she showed them sorcery. She was magic, to this young prince. And when he found that he, too, could do strange and wonderful things, she taught him to hide his secret from everyone — even his brother. The same brother who teased him mercilessly, but was the first to stand up to anyone else who dared look sideways at the young prince. She taught him that magic was a death sentence in the world his father had created. It became a marvelous game to him — one that he was determined to win, even if he wasn't quite sure what the prize was. She promised that when he got older, she would tell him all the secrets of her people and the magic they both wielded.

When they were together, they were happy.

And then his father, the king, took her away. One moment his mother was looking at him, all her secret pleadings and advice swimming in the tears that glistened in her eyes, and the next she was gone. Murdered. No one could stand up to the king, not even his own sons. The older brother held the young prince in his arms that night. In the dark silence where once had been their mother's voice and touch, they sobbed as though they were still children, even though they were halfway grown into men.

War started. The prince's life was never the same.

And then his brother was taken from him, too.

One by one, the prince lost every person he had ever loved, until he was completely alone, save for a healer who hid deep in the palace with his half brother — to bring him the bloodroot that suppressed his abilities, concealing his secret to save his life.

The prince had no choice except to change. He buried who he truly was and pretended to be someone else. He grew; he became an adult. He continued to pretend, but inside he dreamed — and he plotted.

Until the day a young woman joined his personal guard — a girl pretending to be a boy. He knew her secret, as all sorcerers had the ability to sense a person's true identity — male, female, sorcerer or not. He feared for her, thinking that Iker, the black sorcerer working for the king, would know and punish her. But nothing happened — at least at first. She proved her ability time and again, and the black sorcerer left her alone. For months and months, the prince watched her and found himself dreaming of things that could never be. She had suffered; she had endured loss; she wore sadness like a second skin. But she still had her brother — her twin, Marcel.

For the first time in years, the prince yearned to be his true self instead of the persona he'd been forced to adopt to protect himself from his father's machinations. He fought the urge to let his defenses down with her. He didn't dare. Too much rested on his shoulders.

And then her brother died and Iker made his move, choosing her to guard his door day and night. The prince realized his father suspected him — and Iker was using the girl as a way to manipulate and threaten him.

Unbeknownst to anyone except a very select few, the prince had put a plan into action — a dangerous plan to try and overthrow his father and stop the atrocities against the people of Antion and the war that never should have started. And that prince . . . he decided to risk everything when he came out in the dead of night to speak with his guard. When slowly, carefully, he let her see him for who he truly was.

And together, they remade the world into something brighter. Together, they brought back hope to the people of Antion. Together, they gave his kingdom freedom.

That is how my mother would have told my story. I wonder if she knows the ending — if she still watches me. If she's proud of the man I've tried to become, or the king I am.

We succeeded, Alexa and I. Despite my fear, I let myself love her. And together we beat Iker and my father. The young prince who never should have inherited the throne was suddenly the king of Antion.

But once again threats amass all around us, attempting to tear us apart — to rip my kingdom to pieces. I refuse to let them succeed. I will raise Antion from the depths of depravation my father drove us into. And I will not lose *her*, no matter the cost.

I am Damian, the king of Antion, and no one will ever take someone I love from me again and live.

4

⇥ ONE ⇤

Alexa

DAMIAN PACED IN front of the large window overlooking the courtyard, his crown nestled in his dark hair, the afternoon sunshine gilding everything in the library. General Tinso's missive lay open on the desk, his threat of war hanging in the air, heavy and unfathomable. The same foreboding I'd felt before, that much more was happening around us than we realized, pressed down on me, along with the guilt of what I still had to tell him.

"I can't let you go after him," Damian said at last, his voice tight with frustration. "I know you're his best chance, but I need you, too. Especially if I can't stop another war from beginning."

"I know." I stood by his desk, watching him, trying to decide when — and how — to tell him. I *had* to go after Rylan. Not just to save my friend, but also to find some way to kill Rafe and free myself from his control.

Finally, he stopped and turned to me, bruise-like circles underneath his brilliant blue eyes, the exhaustion and worry of the last few days etched onto his face. The shadow of stubble darkened his jaw, a sure sign of his distraction. I'd never seen him anything other than clean-shaven, except on our trek through Antion to Blevon, when he was pretending to be a hostage. "I'm the king; I'm supposed to know what to do to save my people from more death. I've *already* done so much. I spent years figuring out how to stop Iker and my father." His expression was so bleak. He closed his eyes briefly and shook his head. "Was it all for nothing?"

"No, not for nothing." I hesitantly stepped toward him. He'd been so full of hope this morning when I'd returned to the palace, when we'd gone to visit Jax and seen for ourselves that Lisbet had healed him from the wounds and illness he'd suffered in the jungle. But then General Ferraun had shown up, demanding an audience with him immediately — alone. Damian had reluctantly left me, with a promise that he would send for me the moment he was done.

Once I'd reassured myself that Jax was truly well, Lisbet had sent me back to my room, forcing me to rest. She'd come with me, removing the stitches Tanoori had given me to heal my back. I'd been shocked to fall asleep as soon as she left, but horrible night-mares had plagued me, until I'd bolted up in bed, yanked from sleep by a knock on my door. Damian was in his library and wished to see me.

When I'd entered the room, it was to find a different man from the one who'd run to meet me outside the palace walls in the pale light of dawn. He'd turned to me, and the expression on his face had sent a shiver down my spine. Gone was the hope I'd seen this morning, replaced by something darker, wilder.

They attacked again, he'd told me. *General Ferraun just received word.* Another village completely destroyed — everyone killed except for one woman, half-crazed with grief, sent to bring word of the massacre. *If I don't start fighting back, they are going to kill us all and leave me the king of a graveyard. They are leaving me no choice. And thanks to my father, we have no sorcerers to defend ourselves, except for me and Eljin — if he'll even fight against his own people. No matter what I do, my people will die.*

And then he'd begun to pace, while I stood near his desk, watching. Aching to help him, to comfort him, to prevent this war from happening, and not knowing how.

As I slowly neared Damian, he watched me, silent. Finally, I stopped in front of him, tipping my head back to look up at him. I reached up to cup his jaw, and he closed his eyes, turning to press a kiss into the palm of my hand. "It wasn't for nothing," I repeated. "And we can't give up now. Bring your people here. Send out notices for the villages and towns to evacuate, to bring all the food and supplies they have and come to Tubatse, to the palace. Gather every weapon left in Antion and make your enemies come to you, rather than roaming freely through the jungle, murdering your people in their homes."

"And give them one big target to destroy?" Damian's eyes were bleak. "General Ferraun and I have discussed every option we can think of. People are already panicking and flocking to Tubatse. There isn't enough space to house them all, or food to feed them. Families are living on the streets, too terrified to go back to their homes, fearing that their villages will be next."

"I understand what you're saying, but our army is depleted," I argued. "We don't have enough men to send patrols through the jungle. If we bring as many people here as we can, at least we can set up a perimeter. We will have a *chance* to fight."

"And we will all die." Damian turned to look away, out the window. Probably trying to hide the hopelessness from me, but I saw it. I saw the defeat in his eyes.

"Stop it. Right now." I grabbed his hand and squeezed it tightly. "You *can't* give up. If you do, you're right, we will all die."

He continued to stare out the window.

"Damian." My voice was sharp, and he finally looked back at me. "We've beaten insurmountable odds before. Do you remember what you told me this morning? Together, we can do anything, right?"

He nodded, a muscle tightening in his jaw.

"We won't let Antion die. I promise."

Damian's eyes roamed over my face with such a desperate need lurking in their depths that it sent a responding surge of emotion through my belly and down into my legs. This was the one thing I *could* do — I could love him. I could hold him and tell him everything was going to be fine, even if we both knew it was a lie. He had just bent toward me, his lips inches from mine, when there was a knock at the door. He was motionless for a long moment, and then finally straightened and called out, "Enter."

I stepped back and turned to the door.

Deron entered the library and smiled at Damian. "Sire, I bring good news. Eljin is awake and asking for you."

⇥ TWO ⇤

*E*LJIN WAS PROPPED up in bed, shirtless, with a huge bandage wrapped tightly around his ribs. Tanoori sat on the other side of his bed, holding an open book in her lap. She smiled when we entered. I couldn't stop staring at Eljin. Seeing him alive and awake made my legs weak with relief. Though Lisbet had assured us he would live, I hadn't quite believed her. Not after the amount of blood he'd lost. Because of me.

Though he was sitting up, he was still obviously unwell — not completely healed yet. But to even see him like this was a miracle, after what had happened last night. He was pale, and his mask was missing, exposing the scars on his face. I'd never thought about covering my own scars the way he did, until that very moment, when it struck me how similar we were after my battle with Iker. Subconsciously, I reached up to touch my own striated skin, but quickly dropped my hand when I noticed him watching me.

"I can't tell you how good it is to see you awake," Damian said as he strode across the room to clasp Eljin's hand.

"And I, you," he responded, a small smile quirking his thin lips. I'd only seen him with his mask off once before, when I'd ripped it from his face with my sword while sparring at his father's castle in Blevon. It struck me that I'd never seen him smile before.

9

For some reason, that realization made my heart feel strangely heavy.

"My life was never in danger. She needed a living king to make her a queen," Damian said, disgust in his voice.

"She got to us all in the end." Eljin looked up at Damian with understanding in his eyes. "There is nothing to be ashamed of."

"Except for Alexa," Tanoori pointed out.

Guilt twisted in my gut as I realized I still hadn't told Damian — or anyone else — that although *Vera* hadn't succeeded in putting me under her control or killing me, the same was not true of her brother. I'd bargained with Rafe, offered to let him give me one order in exchange for Jax's life. A huge risk that had ended with me being forced to protect him from any and all threats, a command that still burned through my mind, making me unable to harm him in any way. At least Vera was gone — killed by Damian, who had somehow managed to fight through her command to murder me — and her control had perished with her. But Rafe still lived. And so did his power over me. "Damian, you broke through her control. I didn't think that was even possible." I forced away the thoughts of Rafe and the secret I still harbored.

He glanced back and gave me a small half smile. "The whole time I was under her control, I kept getting horrible headaches. When she commanded me to kill you, somehow, deep down I knew I shouldn't do it, but my head felt like it was going to split in two when I tried to resist."

"Maybe it was your mind trying to fight back." Tanoori mused.

We were all silent, until I said, "Well, regardless of how you did it, I'm just glad you did."

"So am I." Damian's eyes met mine across the room, and I had to suppress a shiver of fear. If he hadn't found the strength or the power or whatever it was that broke Vera's control over his mind, I wouldn't be standing here right now.

There was a knock at the door, and then a messenger poked his head in.

"Your Majesty, the general asked me to find out if you're ready to assemble the meeting yet?"

The hint of a smile on Damian's face slid away. "Yes, of course. Tell him to meet us in the throne room in ten minutes."

The messenger boy nodded, bowed, and exited.

Damian reached over and squeezed Eljin's shoulder. Something passed between them, a look I couldn't decipher, and then the man I loved stood up, replaced by the king I served. A curtain had fallen over his face, the expression he wore when he was trying to conceal his emotions. He turned to me, and when he spoke, his voice was carefully controlled. "Come, Alexa, it's time to decide what must be done." He looked over at Tanoori. "You may come, too, if you wish. This concerns all of us."

She looked down at Eljin, and he nodded. "Go. I'll be here when you get back."

Tanoori stood up, her gaze still lingering on him, but he'd already turned his head to the side and closed his eyes.

Without another word, we followed Damian out of the room to face whatever meeting he and the general had planned.

⊰ THREE ⊱

*D*AMIAN PAUSED TO look out over those who had gathered — only the select few who knew the truth of what had happened, or most of it anyway — and then resumed pacing. Tanoori's hands were clutched in the folds of her skirt as she gazed up at the king, as did Lenora, the girl who had given me her nightgown and helped me so that I could get to Damian when Vera had taken control of the palace, even though I had been forced to take her to the breeding house before Damian dispatched his father. I wasn't sure why she was here, but Tanoori had insisted that she bring her.

Maybe she was hoping Lenora could help calm the people's fears if she knew how much the king cared about them. Word of General Tinso's letter declaring war again had circulated the palace in record time, and the unrest of Damian's subjects had even reached the guards' ears, from what Deron told me as we waited for everyone to gather for the meeting. He said whispers of where the king's true loyalty lay — of what he would do if he must fight his mother's people — were building strength. And yet others wanted answers to what had happened to Vera. They wanted to know what power she had wielded, and what she had done to all of them.

My hand rested on the hilt of my sword. Though all those gathered were close allies, and friends, I still felt on edge. Nervous that a new threat could attack at any moment — and I refused to be caught off guard. Rafe had ensured that I couldn't hurt *him*, but at least he hadn't made it so I couldn't protect Damian, as long as Rafe wasn't the one threatening his life.

Despite my own turmoil, I was careful to keep my face blank, to hide the pain and guilt that festered deep inside, squirming through my muscle and bone, surging through my blood like a parasite. I had to tell Damian the truth of what had happened, and soon. We also needed to talk to Eljin as soon as possible. Alone. I wanted answers about Blevon — about *Sì Miào Chán Wù*, the temple in Blevon, and *Rén Zhùsas*, the three powerful sorcerers who lived there, whom Eljin had mentioned petitioning for help if things went badly with Vera and Damian. Rafe's words in the jungle rose back up, taunting me. He'd claimed that Dansii knew the secrets Blevon had worked so hard to keep to themselves — he'd hinted that Dansii had power beyond even what the Blevonese were capable of or knew to be possible.

The time for secrets had passed. Eljin had to see that. I'd *make* him see it.

And there was also the problem of the man in the dungeons. I hadn't told anyone what he'd said and done to me yet. The one who called himself *Manu de Reich os Deos*.

And of course, Rylan. I had to get him back. I had to go after him, whether Damian wanted me to or not — it was my fault he was injured and captured by Dansii.

I felt as though we were being pulled in too many directions without knowing where the true threat — or purpose of the attacks — lay. We needed to make a plan and *do* something.

When I glanced up, Damian was watching me. Our eyes met, and for a brief moment, the mask he wore slipped, and I could see the fear lurking beneath his collected exterior. But in the blink of an eye it was gone, and he looked away.

It didn't seem real that just this morning I'd come stumbling out of the jungle to find him standing on the wall, watching for me in desperation, fearing the worst after Jax had shown up at the palace in the middle of the night, sick and alone, save for one of Rafe's men. It almost seemed a dream that Jax truly was back and that Lisbet had healed him of the jungle fever he'd caught.

The door closest to Damian opened, and Lisbet came in, holding Jax's hand. She'd healed his body, but her power didn't extend to reversing the emotional damage his abduction had caused. Jax clung to Lisbet as they walked over to where Tanoori and Lenora stood. He hadn't left her side since waking up in his room, healed from his ordeal the night before. As I watched Damian's half brother cower against Lisbet, pressing as close to her as he could physically get, I couldn't help the sadness that washed over me. Yet another child's innocence shattered by the ravages of war. Thankfully, he hadn't been forced to face death — but he'd come close. Lisbet had an arm wrapped around him, but her face was also turned up to Damian, waiting with everyone else. The empty space next to her was all too evident, since Eljin was still in bed healing.

"I suppose we'd better get started." Damian finally spoke.

I felt, more than saw, Deron stiffen next to me, preparing himself for whatever was to come. I, too, found myself looking to

Damian, wondering what he was planning on saying. He hadn't told me about a meeting. General Ferraun stood near Lisbet and Jax, his shoulders stiff beneath his uniform's golden epaulettes, which denoted his rank. The rest of the guard flanked the king, in our usual positions, even though this wasn't a formal proceeding. Tanoori and Lenora were to my right, huddled together.

"You are all people I trust — or people who are trusted by those whom I trust." He glanced at Lenora, standing next to Tanoori. "We are under siege, and I want nothing more than to protect my kingdom — my people — from further harm. I might be the king of Antion, but I admit that I'm struggling to decide what is best. That's why you're here. To help me and General Ferraun make a decision. We need help. We need *your* help."

I'd spent so much of my life training to protect Damian, but after falling in love with him, that desire extended to more than just his physical safety. And now, as I watched him, that urge to shield him from hurt swelled within me so strongly, I had to force myself to remain still, rather than stepping toward him and taking his hand in mine. He stood tall, his expression as calm and confident as ever, despite his words to the contrary. Even as he admitted to needing help, he still managed to exude the power and surety that would comfort his subjects. But I knew him well enough to see the truth lurking in his eyes.

"Sire, if I may speak." Tanoori lifted up her hand, and Damian nodded, gesturing for her to continue. "You've assigned me to take care of the other women and babies from . . . from . . ."

"Yes," Damian interjected when Tanoori couldn't seem to come up with a word or name to describe the breeding house his

15

father had sentenced them to, just for the crime of being orphans. "And you've done a remarkable job."

"Thank you." Tanoori inclined her head. "But some of the women — including myself — wish to do more with our lives."

"As is to be expected, but I don't see the relevance to the current situation," Damian said.

"We wish to fight, Your Majesty," Lenora burst out, stepping up next to Tanoori, her shoulders thrown back and chin raised. "We wish to learn to defend ourselves and help you defeat the enemies that are threatening Antion."

Damian's eyebrows lifted, and I heard a few of the guards around us murmuring in disbelief.

"Impossible," General Ferraun responded before Damian could speak again. "I don't have time to assign my men to teach *women* how to wield a sword. They'd be better off mending uniforms, preparing bandages, doing all that needs to be done to support the men who will be fighting this war."

"Are you implying that women can't learn how to fight?" Lenora turned on the general, clearly affronted by the condescending tone in his voice. "What about Alexa? Isn't *she* an example of just how capable a woman can be?"

"There are plenty of women who wish to stay here and do the very things you suggest," Tanoori added, her tone more placating. "But some of us wish to do more. We don't ever want to feel helpless or incapable of protecting ourselves again."

"Even if I could be convinced that you girls were capable of learning how to fight, I already told you I don't have enough men, or time, to do it!" The general's face was turning red in his irritation. "This is no game — we have a *war* to deal with!"

16

"You think we don't know that?" Lenora practically shouted back.

"*Enough.*" Damian's voice rose over them all, and everyone immediately fell silent, turning to look at the king. He took a deep breath through his nose, his lips tightening into a thin line as he deliberated. "How many women feel this way, Tanoori?" he finally asked.

When the general began to protest, Damian held up a hand, and General Ferraun's mouth snapped shut again.

"As I said," Tanoori began, "most of the women still wish to stay here, and to help in other ways. Especially those with babies or who are pregnant. But there are probably six or seven of us who wish to learn to fight."

Damian was silent for a long moment again, and then he nodded once, a brief jerk of his head. "We are short on men, but we can spare one or two to teach you at least basic sparring and defensive skills, and then you can continue to practice amongst yourselves until you are up to par with the other soldiers. If you wish to fight, I will not stop you. We need all the help we can get, and I know from personal experience that a woman is just as capable as a man, with the right training." He gave me a grim smile of acknowledgment, and I bowed my head slightly in return.

"Thank you, Sire." Tanoori also bowed her head, as did Lenora. "We are fast learners; it won't take much time away from your men at all. I promise." This was addressed to the general, whose lips were pursed together in displeasure. But he, too, nodded curtly.

"As the king wishes," was all he said.

"Now that we have that settled, if we could please return to the topic at hand."

From where I stood, directly next to Damian, I could see the vein along his temple standing out, a sure sign that he had a headache. But he hid it well as he surveyed those before him.

"We have more than one major problem that we need to address, and I'm hoping that you might offer input or insight to help us find some solutions." He turned to General Ferraun. "Were you able to get any information from the Dansiian prisoners?"

"I interrogated the man you asked me to. Not only did he refuse to concede any information, he made threats against you. . . ."

When he trailed off, Damian stiffened next to me. "And?" he prompted.

"And others who are close to you," General Ferraun admitted, his eyes flitting to me and then back to the king.

Damian's hand clenched into a fist, a wave of hot rage emanating from him, but my body ran cold as I thought of Manu, the terrifying man in the dungeons who had come to the palace with Vera. I'd gone to interrogate him myself, against Damian's wishes, and he had somehow forced a horrible vision into my mind — a vision of Damian being killed. He'd made me hear things, see things, even *feel* things, that weren't really happening. He'd threatened Damian; he'd claimed that the "true king," *his* king — King Armando — would destroy us all. That Armando would use me, and when he was done with me, he'd kill me. I'd meant to tell Damian about it, but with everything else that had happened . . .

"I have sentenced him to death by beheading tonight to set an example for the other Dansiians," the general continued quickly. "We will not be getting anything useful out of him, and I have a bad feeling about that man. I learned long ago to trust my instincts.

I know that you wish to avoid bloodshed if possible, but I strongly urge you to agree to my sentencing."

"Done. The sooner he's dead, the better," Damian growled. General Ferraun's eyebrows lifted in surprise at the king's vehemence. "The rest of the Dansiians must be interrogated as soon as possible. They were close to Vera, perhaps they could —"

"Damian, I have to tell you something," I interrupted. "The man in the dungeons, he —"

I was cut off by a shriek from the hallway, followed by the thud of a body.

"What was that?" Jerrod said in alarm from the other side of Damian.

And then the door closest to us flew open. "Your Majesty! He's com —"

Whatever the soldier standing guard had been about to say was cut off when a sword impaled him from behind, thrusting out through his belly, then disappearing again. With an agonized scream that faded to a gurgle, the man slumped to the ground, dead.

And standing behind him, holding the bloody sword, was the man in the black-and-white robes who called himself *Manu de Reich os Deos.*

⊰ FOUR ⊱

*H*OW DID HE escape?" someone shouted over the dull roar of blood in my ears.

There was no time to worry that I'd tried to warn them too late about what he'd done to me in the dungeons. I unsheathed my sword, along with the rest of the guard. The general did as well, rushing to stand in front of Tanoori and Lenora. Lisbet had already grabbed Jax's hand and was running to the back of the room, to the other door. I had a glimpse of his eyes growing wide with terror before she pulled him away.

"Ah, the would-be king and his pathetic entourage of subjects and advisors." Manu stepped over the body and moved forward into the room, his pace slow and deliberate. His eyes met mine across the expanse, and his lips curled into a hideous imitation of a smile. "Did you tell your lover about our little visit in the dungeons yet?"

"Your little *what*?" Damian whirled on me.

"Apparently not." Manu laughed, a maniacal crow of glee. He paused before moving within striking range of the general or anyone else.

"When did you talk to him?" Barely controlled anger flashed in Damian's eyes. "I gave strict orders to keep you away from this man."

"Now's not exactly the best time to be having this conversation," I hedged, pointing my sword at Manu, who stood still, watching us.

"He's just an old man. He poses no true threat," General Ferraun said.

"An old man who managed to escape your dungeon and make it all the way up here without being stopped," Manu countered. "An old man whom you are all so afraid of, no one has made the first move yet."

"You're no sorcerer," Damian said. "So whatever you did to escape must have been impressive indeed, but I guarantee you are no match for me and my guard."

"Not a sorcerer? Hmmm . . . maybe not the kind you are familiar with, it's true. But the king I serve — the *true* king — dreams of a new world and a new breed of sorcery. And I am at his side, helping to create it for him." He reached into his robe and withdrew a small vial with a dark red liquid inside of it. "Behold, the power of The Summoner."

"Stop him!" I shouted, lunging forward, but it was too late. He threw the bottle to the ground, where it exploded. The minute the liquid hit the air, it turned into a dark vapor that swirled and grew, larger and larger. It was as though he'd unleashed a storm in the middle of the throne room. It hid Manu from view, then expanded to the general, Tanoori, and Lenora, billowing toward the rest of us. Someone screamed, but I couldn't tell who it came from.

"Damian!" I cried out. "Run! Leave this place!"

There were more screams from within the depths of the black cloud as it swirled to where the first few members of the guard had begun to back up, bumping into one another in their haste to get away but still trying to protect the king, with swords raised.

Damian lifted his hands, and the ground began to tremble. But an earthquake would do nothing to stop whatever evil Manu had unleashed on us. I grabbed his arm. "Damian, *go*," I shouted, shoving him behind me and lifting my sword. "Captain, get him out of here!"

"No, I'm not leaving you!" Damian yanked free of Deron's grasp, but the captain of the guard was bigger and stronger than the king. He wrapped both arms around Damian, trapping his arms at his sides, and physically forced him away from me, dragging him down the stairs with the help of Mateo and Asher, who had to grab his legs as he thrashed and shouted, cursing them and me, as his men rushed him away.

The ground began to shake again, as Damian continued to fight against his own guard.

"Alexa!" He roared. "No!"

He managed to get an arm free and slammed his elbow into Deron's shoulder, then he thrust his hand out and sent Asher flying back to slam into the ground with a thud. "ALEXA!"

And then the cloud reached me, and he was gone.

At first nothing happened. I tightened my grip on my sword and lifted it up higher in preparation. I could hear more screaming — both male and female — turning my blood to ice in my veins.

And then someone rushed toward me through the darkness.

My eyes widened in shock when I saw Iker lifting his hands to hurtle another ball of his unholy fire at me. I threw my body to the side, slamming into the railing and flipping over it, falling to the ground with a bone-jarring thud. How could he be back? I'd seen him die. I'd *killed* him.

Iker leaped over the railing as if it were nothing, landing nimbly in front of me, then he rolled his head and his face changed, becoming Rafe. I barely kept myself from screaming as he stalked forward through the darkness.

"Look at me, Alexa," he said, his voice hissing all around me, burning through me. "You're *mine* now. *You will do whatever I say.*"

There was more screaming from behind me. Or in front of me. I couldn't tell where I was anymore as I scrambled backward on my hands and feet, reaching for my sword, which had come out of my grip when I fell.

"You will kill him. *You* will kill *all* of them," Rafe shouted, as Damian stepped forward out of the darkness, followed by Rylan. My fingers brushed the hilt of my sword, and I grabbed it, lurching back up onto my feet, even though I was strangely dizzy. The darkness and Rafe's grinning, laughing face swam before me as I stumbled forward.

"No," I whispered.

"Oh yes. You will be marvelous. You'll kill everyone I tell you to." Rafe shoved Rylan toward me. "You already started the job with this one!"

"NO!" I rushed forward, thrusting my sword into Rafe, but he popped into nothing, and my momentum carried me forward, until I tripped over something and nearly fell. I choked back a scream when I looked down at the charred body of Papa.

This isn't real. This can't be real. Some part of my brain attempted to convince me, but as I tried to escape the sight of my father lying there dead, I tripped over another body — this time my mother. And next to her was Marcel, his face pale and drawn, just as he'd looked when he'd fallen beside me in the jungle. Blood coated his neck, chest, and stomach.

But that didn't make sense — he'd been killed by an arrow, not a sword.

There was a shout from behind me. Struggling to control my horror and confusion, I lifted my sword and spun around to see Damian rushing toward me with his own sword lifted, his eyes blank.

"And now you will die," Damian said, a sneer curling his lips.

My whole body trembled and my head ached as I stepped back. "No. This isn't real. You aren't real!" I remembered the way Rafe had disappeared when I'd tried to attack him, and instead of continuing to retreat, I stopped and lifted my sword. *"You aren't real!"*

"Are you quite sure about that?" Damian laughed scornfully. He lunged at me, and when I lifted my sword to parry his attack, the sound of steel on steel clanged through the darkness.

That was no mirage — that was a *real* sword. Had Damian escaped the guard? Could Manu be controlling him?

With a gasp that was half dread, half desperation, I continued to block his assault. There was more screaming, but it sounded as though it were coming from somewhere far away, echoing through the swirling darkness as if we were in a cave or a tunnel. Damian continued to smile, his eyes terrifyingly empty as he attacked again and again. How did this happen? Was Rafe back? Had he done this?

I choked on a sob as I deflected his hits again and again.

"Come on, Alexa. You're supposed to be better than this. I admit, I'm disappointed," Damian mocked, his voice not quite ringing true for some reason. "You're making this too easy."

But then I heard something else. My name, being shouted, a terrified, desperate sound — a voice I'd know anywhere. But that was impossible, because I was fighting him in front of me. How could he be shouting for me from somewhere else?

I shook my head, trying to clear my hazy, confused thoughts. I could barely breathe as Damian with the blank eyes pressed his advantage and managed to nick my forearm with his blade before I spun out of reach. I tripped and nearly fell over a body, but when I glanced down, it wasn't Papa or Marcel on the ground — it was General Ferraun, lying in a pool of blood, his eyes open, unseeing.

With a gasp, I jerked up my head, and Damian's features blurred for a second and then snapped back into focus. The cloud had lightened slightly; I could see shards of daylight again, and understanding suddenly struck me. This was not Damian. It was some sort of illusion — or hallucination. But if it wasn't Damian . . . who was it?

"Don't quit on me now," not-Damian taunted, swiping his sword toward my abdomen, but I jumped back just in time to avoid being gutted.

"I never quit."

"Good. Because I don't, either." He pressed his advantage on me, his lips pulled back in a snarl. I realized he was herding me toward the door. "My king wants you alive, but that doesn't mean you have to be functional. Perhaps even a simple vial of your blood would be sufficient, since I may have no other option."

"Alexa!" I heard Damian's voice again from behind me, closer now.

"No, Sire, you can't go after her!" someone else shouted.

"I will not fail," not-Damian growled, and finally clarity rushed in. I realized who I was fighting. My grip on my sword tightened, despite the blood running down my wrist and dripping off my hand. I leaped forward with a cry of rage. Not-Damian's eyes widened, but so did his grin. He met my attack with a sudden increase in skill. Had he been toying with me?

I moved as fast as I could, as the cloud grew thinner and thinner around us, and slowly Damian's features began to melt away from the man I fought, revealing eyes with abnormally large pupils and thin silver irises.

"You made a mistake," I grunted, as I parried another hit from him and took a step back.

"Oh?" he lunged forward again, aiming for my sword arm, but I deflected him and spun around, slicing my sword through the air so quickly it whistled as it arced toward his body. He barely managed to block me, then used his sword to push me away and lunged toward me once more, aiming for my stomach. "I think not. You left me no choice except to attack now. But I never make mistakes."

"Yes, you do," I shouted as I jumped back, just enough to let his blade slide by me. Before he completely missed, I grabbed his wrist with my free hand and twisted him around, using his own momentum to propel him past me. Before he could react, I spun and impaled him from behind. The same way he'd killed our man only minutes before. "It was a *huge* mistake to think *you* could ever beat *me*."

With a swift motion, I pulled my sword back, and he crumpled to the ground, just as the last of the fog cleared away, revealing the real Damian standing a few feet away, staring at me, his face pale, Deron and Mateo at his side, still holding him back.

Our eyes met. I wanted nothing more than to have him rush to me and take me in his arms, but he stood still, watching me, motionless.

When I looked down to see Manu lying next to the general, the adrenaline drained out of my body, leaving me trembling as I remembered I'd seen other bodies in my hallucination. Which meant . . .

Dread pounded within me as I slowly turned. When I saw what was behind me, a sob tore through me. Lenora lay on the ground, her throat slit, her eyes open and unseeing. And beyond her was Oliver, one of the newer guards. Jerrod knelt beside him, his sword bloody.

Jerrod looked up at us, his face drained of color. He kept shaking his head over and over. "I . . . I didn't know. I thought . . . it wasn't him. I swear I thought it was —" His voice broke and he stood up abruptly, throwing his sword to the ground with a clatter, and rushed from the room.

"Jerrod!" I shouted, stepping forward to follow after him, but someone grabbed my arm.

"Let him go."

I looked up to see Damian staring down at me, his eyes haunted. His gaze moved past my face, down to my sword hand. "You're hurt."

"Just a scratch." My whole body was beginning to shake.

"What happened?" His voice was low and controlled. He was trying to hide his emotions from me.

27

"It . . . it was terrifying. Some sort of sorcery that made me hallucinate. I saw . . . I saw . . ." Flashes of what I'd seen surged up: Iker, Rafe, my family lying dead around me — when it was really my friends and allies. The acid in my stomach surged up into my throat.

I turned away from Damian to look back at the general and Lenora. Tanoori now knelt beside her friend. She held Lenora's limp hand in hers, pressing it to her tear-streaked cheeks.

Pulling free from Damian, I walked over to where Lenora lay, silent and still. When I touched Tanoori's shoulder, she jumped and looked up at me with wild eyes.

"It's all right, it's just me. It's over now." I tried to comfort her, even though the remnants of horror still lingered in my own veins, making my legs weak beneath me as I knelt beside Tanoori.

"I heard her screaming. I heard her . . . but I thought I was in that . . . that place again. I thought the men were coming for me." Tanoori's voice cracked, and she crumpled into my lap, her shoulders shaking with sobs. "I couldn't save her. I couldn't . . . I couldn't . . ."

"We need Lisbet," I heard Damian say from behind me. "She's going into shock, and there are others who are injured. Mateo, you and Asher go find help to prepare the bodies. We will honor them tonight at sunset."

"Yes, Your Majesty," the other guards murmured, but I didn't look up. I just wrapped my arms around Tanoori and held her, trying to hold back my own tears.

❧ FIVE ☙

I T SEEMED AS though almost the entire palace had gathered in
the courtyard, but despite the mass of people, there was a hush
as Deron lit the torch and slowly moved his way down the funeral
pyres. There were more than three — Manu had left a trail of bodies on his way to the throne room, starting with the new keeper of
the keys, found with his throat slit in the cell Manu had been
locked in. First one, then another, and another, and another, down
the row until Deron finally reached General Ferraun's. I stood
next to Damian in a clean uniform, my forearm wrapped because
there hadn't been a chance for Lisbet to heal it yet. She'd been too
busy taking care of Jerrod and Tanoori, sedating them both with
an herbal concoction because they were so distraught.

She'd also worked on Eljin a bit more, healing him enough
that he was able to get up and move around. But he'd chosen to sit
with Tanoori until the time came for the funerals. Now he stood
beside me, his mask still missing. Two scarred sentinels beside our
stoic king.

Damian had hardly said a word since the attack. He stood
stiffly now, staring at the flames as they rose higher to meet the
last dying streaks of sunlight across the sky of Antion, above
the massive palace wall and the jungle beyond it. His face had set

into a stony facade, reminding me more of the Damian I had once known — or thought I'd known, before he revealed his true self to me. The firelight flickered across his face, sending his eyes into shadow, making the gold of his crown flare in the falling darkness. With a shiver, I looked forward again. The sight of the burning pyres was almost too much; it brought back the memory of another night, another time I'd stood here, watching the flames take away all that remained of someone I loved.

Damian suddenly unsheathed his sword and lifted it up in front of his face, pointing it high, to the stars that had begun to flicker above us. The scrape of hundreds of swords being pulled from their scabbards sounded around us as I, the rest of the guard, and all the soldiers gathered did the same. Tears burned my eyes as the smoke billowed up into the oncoming night.

Only I was close enough to see how Damian's hand trembled slightly and the way a muscle in his jaw ticked.

General Ferraun had been his ally and friend — the man who had taught him how to fight. There were very few people in Damian's life who he felt he could trust, and now one of the most important ones — his head general — was gone.

Finally, he lowered his sword, and again, we all followed his lead.

I'd expected him to say something, and everyone else seemed to also as they looked up at their king. But he continued to stare forward, silent. The only sounds in the heat-drenched night were the occasional cry from a baby and the hiss and pop of the flames that consumed the wood of the pyres and the bodies of the slain. The choking smell burned my nose. I longed to escape, to leave the death and loss far behind me. But there was no true escape for any of us. I surveyed the people in front of me, the women in fine dresses standing next to soldiers in tattered uniforms, a few scattered children, their hands clutched in a father's or mother's. All of us, from the poorest soldier to the richest members of the royal court, had slept with war as our bedmate, with death as a constant threat, for most of our lives.

The women from the breeding house — Lenora's friends, their cheeks wet with tears — huddled together, some cradling babies in their arms. Which of them had hoped to learn how to fight? If Lenora *had* been trained, would her body still be on that burning pyre? Or would she have been able to protect herself, as she'd wished? Whatever it was that Manu had created, it had unleashed our worst nightmares upon everyone trapped in it. What — or who — had she believed killed her?

Tears slipped over my own cheeks, and I swallowed hard to keep myself from breaking down entirely. It seemed as though the death, the pain, the fear and loss would never end.

"No more." Damian finally spoke, but it was a mutter. A quiet, cold statement. His sword clanged as he roughly shoved it into the scabbard at his side, then he turned on his heel and strode back into the palace.

A murmur went through the crowd, a stunned, unhappy ripple of whispers.

I stood there shocked for a moment, until Eljin said, "You'd better go after him."

I met his concerned gaze in the falling darkness and then spun on my heel and rushed after the king.

I caught up to Damian in the grand entrance, just beyond the massive palace doors, which had been repaired after the fight with

Iker and his father, when they'd been burned down. He was rushing toward the stairs, his long strides eating up the ground. I reached him just as he stepped up onto the first stair and grabbed his arm, but he yanked it free and whirled on me, his expression fierce, his eyes lit with fiery anger.

I stumbled back, shocked. "What's wrong?" I knew he was upset about General Ferraun's death, but as he glared down at me, he looked *furious*, not sad.

"What's *wrong*?" He shook his head and pressed his lips together, until they were little more than a thin line of anger.

Without another word, he spun and rushed away, taking the stairs two at a time. The doors behind us banged, and I glanced back to see Deron and a few other guards looking at me questioningly, but I shook my head.

"Make an announcement that the king is feeling unwell but will address his subjects tomorrow, when he's had time to process the shock of the events of this day. Station the guard at the bottom of the stairwells leading to this wing, and don't let anyone up. He needs some space," I instructed, making Deron's eyebrows lift.

"Who made you captain?" Asher groused.

"Maybe she thinks she can boss us around since she's going to be a queen now," Leon piped up from behind Deron.

"Enough," Deron thundered. "You heard Alexa. Do as she said."

Our eyes met across the expanse, and he nodded, his expression grim. Something was very, very wrong. Damian was a consummate actor. He never let his emotions show like this.

I turned and ran up the stairs after him.

When I hit the landing of the second floor, it was just in time to see him turn the corner into his rooms and to hear the echo of his door slamming shut.

"Damian!"

I ran down the hallway and tried the handle, only to find it locked. "Damian!" I pounded on the door, my throat tight with fear. When he didn't answer, I pounded even harder. "Damian, please let me in! You're scaring me!"

The door suddenly swung open, and I stumbled into his room. It was dark; there was no moon visible through the skylight. He turned and walked away, through the outer chamber and into his actual bedroom. I followed him, my heart thudding against my rib cage.

"How does it feel?" he asked, his voice low, once I closed his bedroom door behind me. He stood a few feet away, a tall, shadowed figure in the nighttime.

"Feel?" I echoed, confused and unaccountably nervous.

"Yes. How does it feel to be scared for someone you love?"

"You know very well what it feels like." The humidity was stifling, making it hard to breathe. Or maybe it was the anger in his voice that made my lungs tighten, stealing my air.

"Yes, I do." He spun away from me, shoving his hands into his hair and crossing the room to kick the chair behind his desk. My eyes widened. I hadn't seen him like this in so long — not since he'd stopped the act of playing the spoiled, petulant royal brat he'd portrayed for so long. "You nearly died today," he said to the empty fireplace, his back to me. The anger was suddenly gone from his voice. In the darkness, his shoulders sagged.

And I finally realized what was going on — he *was* mad. At me.

⇥ SIX ⇤

No, I didn't. He barely even hurt me." I hurried over to Damian to put my hand on his shoulder, but he flinched and moved away from my touch. I pulled back, hurt and confused.

"Only because he couldn't get to you fast enough!" Damian slammed his fist against the wall and then turned to face me, his eyes wild in the dim light, his hair askew. "Tanoori told Eljin what it was like. She told him what that poisonous vapor did to you all. What did you see in there? Who did you think you were fighting?"

He searched my face, his expression stony, brooking no patience with lies.

"You," I whispered, my heart in my throat. "I thought I was fighting you again."

"Then I was right. You almost died."

"No, I wasn't —"

"You were going to *let* me kill you rather than hurt me the other night. And that's what would have happened again, if that cloud hadn't begun to dissipate before it was too late. You *weren't* actually fighting me, but you thought you were, so you would have given up rather than hurt me. The only difference was that

34

man wouldn't have made himself stop like I did." Damian spoke in a rush, stepping closer to me. "And he would have killed you."

I stared up at him, struck silent. "But he didn't," I finally repeated quietly.

"You *pushed* me away. You had them *drag* me out of there — away from you." He lifted one hand as though he wanted to stroke my face, but he paused before actually touching me, his fingers shaking in the space between us. "How could you do that to me? I had to threaten them with their *lives*, as their king, to get Deron to let me go back in. I had to use my sorcery against my own men." He closed his hand into a fist and let it drop to his side. "It made me sick to do it, but I was sure I'd lost you. And I was sure that when I finally reached you, I would find a corpse, instead of my fiancée."

"I'm your *guard*, Damian! It's my job to protect you! When are you going to learn that and stop risking yourself for me?"

"When are *you* going to learn that you are *not* just my guard?" Damian finally touched me, but it was no gentle caress of a lover. He grabbed my shoulders, his fingers digging in to my muscle and bone. "You are to be my *queen*."

"I —"

"I *love* you, Alexa." He cut me off, his voice urgent and tinged with hopelessness. "You're all I have, and yet you throw your life around as though it were worth nothing, and I can't take it. I can't take the thought of losing you."

"Damian, I'm —"

But then his mouth covered mine, stopping my words with his kiss. He crushed me to him, his lips hungry and desperate. I clung to him, my own fear and love surging through my body at his touch. His hands twisted in my tunic, pulling it up to expose the skin of my back. When his fingers brushed my spine, skimming the scars from the wounds Lisbet had healed, I shivered. A want I could barely understand swelled through me, making me feel both weak and strong at once. I threaded a hand through his hair, pushing against him, molding my body to his. He backed me up until I was pressed against the wall. He kissed my jaw, moving down my neck. I couldn't breathe as his hands kneaded their way up my back, pushing my shirt up higher, exposing my stomach so I could feel the fabric of his tunic against my skin.

And then he suddenly pulled away, stumbling back a step. "Not like this," he said, his voice hoarse.

I stared at him, gasping for air. With a shake of his head, he turned away and walked over to the fireplace, putting one hand on the mantle and running the other through his hair, his head hanging down.

Shakily, I pushed myself away from the wall and straightened my tunic, my lips stinging from his kiss. I slowly advanced on him until I was close enough to wrap my arms around him from behind. He dropped the hand from his hair to weave his fingers through mine, pressing my arms more firmly against his abdomen.

"I can't lose you," he whispered. "I know you only just realized who *I* am in the last few months. But I've loved you for years."

Tears burned in my eyes as I pressed my face to his back and breathed in his scent.

"I watched you train for hours upon hours upon hours. I watched you with your brother. I saw your courage every minute of every day that you risked discovery protecting me — a spoiled, rotten brat — and your brother. Marcel loved you so much, and I couldn't help but love you, too. I never thought there would be a chance to tell you that. Much less for you to actually love me in return."

"Which is why you were so quick to believe me when I told you I didn't trust you and couldn't be your queen," I said quietly, my lips moving against the cloak he still wore over his clothes.

"Yes." He finally pushed away from the mantle and turned to me, his eyes roaming over my face. "And that's why I can't let you go after Rylan."

The tears I'd been trying to hold back spilled over, slipping down my cheeks. "How did you know?"

He simply said, "Because I know *you*."

I opened my mouth to protest, but he rushed on, lifting his hands to brush away my tears and cup my face.

"You're so brave, and I love that about you. But you're also reckless. You don't think about the consequences. How could you go down there to the dungeons to see that man when you knew I didn't want you to?" The hurt in his eyes lashed at my heart, but I just shook my head.

"Because I had to know. I thought I could get answers out of him."

"And did you? Did you find out anything? Or did you just give him a target?" I could tell he was struggling not to get angry again.

"He . . . he called himself *Manu de Reich os Deos*. He told me about his king and said that there is much more to all of this than we realize. And he made me see . . . things."

"What kind of things?"

I just shook my head. If I told him now, he'd burst out in anger again for sure.

Damian's jaw clenched when I didn't answer. "He could have killed you then. If he was able to kill a man as huge as the keeper and escape, he could have done the same to you. I don't know why he didn't." Damian shook his head angrily and jerked away from me. "I know that you think you're helping, but do you have any idea what it would do to me if you died?"

I was silent, trying to swallow back my guilt. When I'd decided to interrogate him, I hadn't thought there was a chance Manu would be able to hurt me — not until he made me see that horrifying vision in the dungeons. When he'd made me think, for a moment, that he'd killed Damian. He'd told me that I *would* die, when the time was right, but that his king wasn't done with me. He'd told me I needed to learn a lesson. But apparently his sudden death sentence had changed things.

"And that's why I must forbid you from going after Rylan." Damian moved over to the window, standing by the drapes Eljin and I had emerged from after using the secret passageway from my room to Damian's to get to him and Vera. "I know you care about him. That you probably even love him. And it's not in your nature to leave it to someone else to help those you love."

"It's not only that —"

"Let me finish, please." Damian held up a hand, and I obediently fell silent. He turned to face me but didn't move, leaving the distance between us. "I know that you love him. But you also love me . . . don't you?"

I nodded, my eyes burning.

"I know this makes me selfish, but I'm asking you — *pleading* with you — if you love me at all, stay here. Help me figure out what is happening and help me avoid war. Stay where I know you are safe. I will send a contingent of men after Rafe to get Rylan back. I won't let them get away. They can't have gotten far yet. He'll be back by the end of the week."

A terrible, gnawing pain seized my stomach, clutching my belly and making me feel ill. But how could I fault him for this request? He was right; I'd risked myself so many times — often against his will — and so far, I'd been lucky. I'd survived. But maybe next time I wouldn't.

"If you're going to force me to choose you or him, I choose you, Damian," I said, even as my heart broke at the thought of Rylan out there in the jungle, wounded by *my* sword, trapped with Rafe. "I'll stay here, if that is what you wish."

Damian nodded, but he still looked miserable. "I'm sorry, Alexa. I'm so sorry."

I hesitantly stepped toward him, and when he didn't stop me, I wrapped my arms around him, burying my face in his shoulder so he couldn't see my tears. "Don't be sorry for needing me," I said against his tunic, my voice muffled. "I need you, too."

His arms came around me, clutching me to him. "I don't know what to do," he admitted, sounding so lost, so afraid. "I don't know how to save my kingdom."

There was nothing I could say to him that wasn't an empty promise, so I just held him more tightly. We stood there, wrapped in each other, trying to push our fears away, until I remembered Deron and the other guards, waiting for word about their king, and pulled back slightly.

"I should go. The guard is . . . concerned. I need to tell them that you're all right."

Damian stared down at me and then nodded. "Of course. Please send them my apologies for my inexcusable behavior."

"You're the king, Damian. You can act however you want."

He was silent for a long moment and then made a noise that was somewhere between a sigh and a mirthless laugh. "Regardless, I would appreciate it if you sent them my apologies."

"Of course," I said, feeling as though we were still off balance for some reason. As though the weight of Rylan's absence, and Damian's asking me to stay with him, had tilted the ground we stood on, leaving us on unsure footing.

Damian lifted his hand, and this time, he stroked the skin along my jaw with the back of his fingers, sending a shudder of need through me. "Thank you," he whispered.

I stared up at him, silent, waiting. But then he let his hand drop and turned away without kissing me.

Unaccountably cold, despite the ever-present humidity and sweltering heat of the jungle, I turned and left Damian standing by his window, looking out at the now-dark courtyard.

⇥ SEVEN ⇤

*T*HE PALACE WAS quiet; the hush of nightfall and sleep silenced everything but the sound of my boots on the stone floor. I'd told Deron and the rest of the guard to take up their normal positions, that Damian had been upset by the loss of General Ferraun, Lenora, and so many good men and that he would be fine by the morning. I knew him well enough to know that was true — or at least, he would resume his act of *seeming* fine, even if he wasn't.

Damian had stayed in his room, presumably having gone to bed. I was certain he was actually pacing, worrying, and trying to figure out what to do next. Though it wasn't my night to be on duty, I wasn't able to sleep, either. So instead, I was trying to find answers.

When I reached Eljin's room, I knocked softly on the shut door.

There was the sound of someone moving and then the door cracked open, revealing a sliver of Eljin, holding up a sword. When he saw it was me, he relaxed and opened the door wider.

"To what do I owe this honor? A visit from the future queen of Antion." Eljin gestured for me to sit in the chair next to his bed, and he sat down across from me on his mattress.

"So, you've heard."

"Tanoori filled me in," Eljin confirmed. "Congratulations. We could all use some happiness to focus on right now."

"How is Tanoori?"

Eljin grimaced. I was still unused to seeing him without his mask. I wondered if he couldn't find another, or if something had changed and he'd decided to stop wearing it completely. I secretly hoped the latter — it was comforting in a strange, horrible way to have someone else as disfigured as I not act ashamed of his scars any longer.

"She's . . . upset. Lenora was a close friend. And whatever was in that vial caused some fairly horrific results — as you know. She hasn't been able to calm down, so my aunt gave her something to help her sleep. She's resting now."

It took me a moment to remember that Lisbet was General Tinso's sister, and therefore Eljin's aunt. But that reminded me that we didn't know what had happened to the general — what had caused him to write that missive declaring war on Antion, after he'd fought so hard side by side with Damian to create peace between the two kingdoms. Had anyone told Eljin about the letter, or our suspicions about his father?

"Whatever it is they're doing in Dansii, it's not right. It goes against the rightful laws of using sorcery, and it will not go unpunished. Whether by us, or by the Unseen Power, abominations are not tolerated forever."

"What do you mean?" I asked. "What laws? What power?"

Eljin rubbed one hand over his face, drawing my attention to the dark bruises beneath his eyes. Though it was a complete miracle that he was alive right now, he obviously still wasn't completely

42

well yet. "I told you that all Blevonese sorcerers go to our temple when they reach a certain age."

"Yes, *Sì Miào.* . . ."

"*Sì Miào Chán Wù.*" Eljin nodded. "Part of the vows we take state the ways in which we'll use the sorcery we have been gifted with."

I was silent, hoping he'd continue. He looked at me appraisingly, his lips pursed together.

"I assume you've never heard of the first sorcerers?"

When I shook my head, he sighed.

"Sorcery has not always been a part of our world," Eljin began. "The temple I told you about — the one that the *Rén Zhǔsas* guard — it is no ordinary building. And I fear that what Armando is after lies within its walls."

My pulse kicked up a beat, and I had to keep myself from leaning forward, to urge him to speak faster.

"This information is sacred to our people. But . . . things are escalating. I'm concerned . . . that is . . ." Eljin's voice was gruff, and he had to stop to clear his throat. "It's the only reason I can think of that would entice Armando to try to get to Blevon."

I was silent for a moment, and then I spoke. "Eljin, Dansii knows. Rafe told me. They know your secrets."

Eljin sucked in a sharp breath, his eyes widening. "That's not possible."

"I think it is. You have to tell us — you have to put us on even footing if we want to have any hope of winning this war," I insisted.

He shook his head, but before he could speak, I rushed on.

"We can't win a war we don't understand. Please, Eljin. The time for secrecy has passed."

When Eljin looked at me again, his eyebrows were drawn together, his expression somewhere between desperation and hopelessness. "I don't know what to think anymore. I don't know what is right."

I was silent, letting him mull it over for a moment — to let Rafe's claims sink in.

He closed his eyes and let his head drop. "If Dansii truly does know . . . if they have captured my father and are forcing him to declare war on us again . . . the future is dire indeed." There was a long moment of silence. When Eljin met my gaze, the look in his eyes chilled me. "I believe they're trying to get us to continue to fight each other so that Armando and his sorcerers can sweep right on past us and break into the temple."

So he did know about his father. I almost reached out to lay my hand on top of his, but he sat so stiffly, no longer looking at me, that I didn't dare. It wasn't my place to offer him comfort.

"Perhaps you had better find out what we are facing. To beat your enemy, you must know him. You must *understand* him. And if this knowledge has been passed down through the kingship and sorcerers of Dansii, then Antion is the only one left ignorant," Eljin said.

"We are also the only ones left barren, stripped of sorcery, thanks to King Hector." I wondered how different my life would have been if Hector hadn't had every sorcerer in Antion put to death. If he hadn't been intent on starting a war with Blevon and crushing our people with his vile acts in the name of battle.

Eljin was silent for a long time, most likely warring within himself. Trying to decide if he could really share his knowledge with me. Finally, he shut his eyes and swallowed once, hard.

"As you know, our temple is called *Sì Miào Chán Wù*, which means 'Temple of Awakening to Truth,'" he began, and I held my breath, hoping he'd continue. "It's called that because when a sorcerer goes there, he or she is taught the truth of how sorcerers came to be, and the sacred oath our people made.

"Hidden deep inside the temple is the original source of our power, a small waterfall with water the color of gold. Mokaro, a former king of Blevon, found it many hundreds of years ago with his brother, Delun, long before you or I were born. He and his brother were hiking through the Naswais Mountains behind their castle. Mokaro was on a spiritual quest, praying for answers on how to strengthen his kingdom and protect his people, and his brother had accompanied him to protect him in his weakened state. Mokaro was led deep into the heart of the mountains, where he found the waterfall.

"He felt drawn to the strange water and, when he approached it, he heard a voice, telling him to drink from it — but only once. He was warned that the consequences of drinking from it again would be dire. When King Mokaro drank from it, he fell to the ground, unconscious. His brother, who hadn't heard the voice, also drank from the water, and he, too, fell unconscious on the ground. Mokaro had a dream where the voice spoke to him again — the Unseen Power — and told him he had been given a gift to protect his people. This king was a good man, and he swore he would only use this power for good. He and Delun awoke as sorcerers, and they returned to the castle.

"King Mokaro and Prince Delun kept their secret until the day Mokaro realized his sons had been born with the same power given to him. This king took his sons to the waterfall and told

45

them what had happened there many years before. While they were there, the Unseen Power's voice came again — only this time, all three of them heard it. The voice charged King Mokaro and his sons with the duty of protecting the well. The king had the temple constructed around it, hidden deep in the mountains, and had the pathway to the temple guarded day and night.

"Years passed without incident, until Mokaro's sons began to grow into men and their powers grew stronger. Prince Delun was a well-intentioned man, but he had a weak heart and was prone to jealousy. He only had the power to manipulate water and earth. He couldn't use his power to fight, as his brother, the king, and his nephews, the princes of Blevon, could. Unhappy with his gift, he began experimenting."

Eljin stared ahead unseeingly, lost in the story, his voice almost mournful. I trembled with a strange, unnameable emotion that was part fear and part sorrow as he continued.

"Through his experiments, Delun found ways to increase his power, but it came at a horrible cost. He became the first black sorcerer. He gathered some followers behind his brother's back. Over the years, his jealousy had twisted his love for his brother into hatred and bitterness, until one night, he led an attack on the castle. He hoped to kill King Mokaro, who was now very elderly, and take possession of the temple and the fountain of power.

"Mokaro and his sons fought Delun, the black sorcerer, but they were no match for his unholy power and the fire he wielded. Many Blevonese died that day, including the elderly queen and one of King Mokaro's grandsons. King Mokaro and his sons retreated to the mountain, hoping to draw Delun and his followers away from the castle and their people. When they reached the temple,

46

they began praying to the Unseen Power for help. Delun and his men had nearly reached the temple in pursuit of King Mokaro and his sons, when the king and princes of Blevon were able to join their power together and cause a massive earthquake. The ground beneath Delun split open before he could summon his fire and kill them. The king watched as his brother and his men fell deep into the earth and were buried, leaving the king and the temple safe.

"The darkness was stopped, at least for a time. But Blevon paid a price for Delun's abominations. My kingdom once had a very temperate climate; it was warm year-round, with no harsh weather. Our lands were verdant and lush — not quite like Antion, but close. However, the black sorcerer's deeds on our soil cursed our kingdom, making the ground turn harder; the seasons grew harsher. It snowed for the first time in Blevon that year."

"So the rumors about a curse on your kingdom are true," I interrupted, my chest tight; I was enthralled and horrified by his story. It finally explained why the weather, vegetation, and land in Blevon were so different from Antion's.

Eljin shook himself as if coming out of a trance and glanced at me sharply. Maybe he'd forgotten I was even there. Finally, he nodded. "Yes. They are true."

After a brief pause, he continued. "Shortly after the battle in which he lost his wife and grandson and had to kill his own brother, King Mokaro had another vision. In this vision, he was warned that any sorcerer who delved into black sorcery forfeited their soul to Adhakka, the father of demons. Mokaro made a vow that he and his descendants would never dishonor the gift given to them by calling upon the power of the demons. A promise and a curse were placed upon him: If anyone of his lineage began to use black sorcery, they would lose their power — and their life — and they would become *Diūsh*."

"What is *Diūsh*?" I interrupted again.

"It means 'lost.'"

"Lost . . . as in you'd lose your power?" I imagined that would be an unwelcome result, but not enough to deter every person in Blevon from experimenting.

"Worse. It means to be cursed. To die, but not be dead. To wander aimlessly through the *Jiān* — the Inbetween — forever. It means to lose your soul."

"The Inbetween?" I was ashamed of how little I knew of Blevonese beliefs or history. Why hadn't Papa told me any of this? There was no religion in Antion — at least not in my lifetime; King Hector had forbidden it along with sorcery. But I had always believed in my heart that there was a higher power, that Something was there, even if it didn't seem like it. I'd heard Mama and Papa praying at night when they thought we were asleep, pleading with a force or power I'd never learned about, in the darkness.

But they'd never told us *any* of this, and I couldn't help feeling as though they'd betrayed me somehow. Especially Papa.

"The Inbetween is a place of complete darkness, where those who commit the worst crimes known to this world are cursed to reside."

"So all black sorcerers are condemned to this fate when they die?" I couldn't help but think of Iker, and I hoped he was paying for the heinous crimes he'd perpetrated in Antion.

"I can't say for certain what happens to those from Dansii. But any sorcerer from Blevon who delves into such practices will endure that fate, yes. And not just *when* he or she dies. Because of the curse, if any Blevonese sorcerer even attempts black sorcery, he *immediately* dies, and his soul is banished to spend eternity in the Inbetween."

I took a deep breath, understanding finally falling into place. "Which is why you promised Damian there was no way the black sorcerers could be from Blevon."

"Yes."

"But why not just tell him this? Why not tell everyone? Then the accusations against your kingdom would end."

Eljin looked at me hard and long. "Because when Blevonese sorcerers are given all this information, we are sworn to protect it with our lives. If all the people in our world knew about the power the golden waters hold, what do you think would happen? And if the sorcerers in Dansii were to know what would happen to a Blevonese sorcerer if they attempted any sort of black sorcery, what could they do with that knowledge?"

I grimaced, imagining the catastrophic results. "So why don't the sorcerers in Dansii die immediately from attempting black sorcery?"

"We don't know. Some believe that one of the sorcerers who had followed Delun escaped the battle and fled to Dansii. Supposedly, he murdered the king and offered him as a sacrifice to the demons who empower black sorcerers, and in return, the demons kept him alive, saving him from the curse of instant death and banishment to the Inbetween. He then took the throne for himself."

I shuddered at the thought of that sorcerer killing and sacrificing the king in order to get greater power. Perhaps that was the reason why — perhaps the demons protected them in Dansii because they were too far away from the Unknown Power in Blevon for the curse to take hold of them. Eljin's story also made me wonder about the sorcerers who had once lived in Antion. What had they been like — and how many had there been before Hector had them all murdered? Had they been part Blevonese, as Damian was? Or had any native Antionese ever been granted such power?

When I spoke again, I changed the subject slightly. "Well, that explains why there could be no black sorcerers from Blevon. But it doesn't explain why the Blevonese army wouldn't use a black sorcerer from Dansii to help them, if they wished."

"Because of the other part of the curse. Mokaro was also warned that if black sorcery breached the sacred ground of the temple again, all power would be stripped from the world. *Every* sorcerer would be destroyed."

My mouth fell open. "So if Armando brings his black sorcerers to attack the temple, to try to gain access to the fountain . . . *every* sorcerer in the world will *die?*" My thoughts immediately flew to Damian.

"Yes, if he manages to breach the temple walls, that is what we believe will happen."

A dark abyss of hopelessness opened before me. If what he was telling me was true, what chance of saving our people did Damian have?

"But Mokaro was also given a promise," Eljin continued. "So long as he and his sorcerer descendants proved themselves worthy by using their power to protect, heal, and fight the evil brewing in Dansii — even giving their lives to protect the temple if necessary — they would be strengthened and given even greater power in their time of need."

"Enough to stop Dansii?"

"I don't know." Eljin lifted one shoulder, his mouth pressed together.

"At least if Dansii does make it all the way to the temple and begins to attack, it gives your people the upper hand. It gives them hope."

"Hope is a fragile thing."

"But powerful."

Eljin tilted his head in acknowledgment. "And now I have given you my burden — the fear and hope of what may come. Mokaro was instructed to only share his visions with Blevonese sorcerers within the protection of the temple walls. All of those who fight for Blevon in our armies are told just enough to understand that accepting help from a black sorcerer, or giving one support, would have catastrophic results for our kingdom and our sorcerers. But that's all they're told. They don't know the details.

"In telling you all of this, I have broken my oath."

His hands were clenched in the folds of his tunic, and he stared down at his feet, not meeting my gaze. I couldn't fathom what it had cost him to tell me the secrets of his people. But what he'd shared with me was invaluable.

"Thank you, for telling me," I said quietly.

"Don't thank me," he barked, suddenly angry. "I broke my oath. I may very well become *Diūsh* now when I die."

I drew back, shocked. "I don't believe that. You're helping us, so we can help your people."

He was silent for a long moment, his teeth clenched.

"Alexa," he spoke to the ground, "we must stop Armando. We can't let him reach the temple."

"If he does make it there — if he can't be stopped — and if he

51

somehow reaches the fountain and drinks from it . . . what will happen?"

Eljin finally looked at me, his expression bleak. "I don't know."

"But . . . you said if your people continue to use their sorcery for good, that their power will be increased. The Unseen Power promised . . . it won't let you all be destroyed, will it?"

Eljin shook his head. "I don't know. No one knows for sure who or what the Unseen Power is; the voice has never revealed itself to anyone besides King Mokaro and his sons. For all we know, they might have made it all up."

"If you truly believed that, why didn't you just tell me and Damian all this before?"

Eljin didn't respond. Instead, he lay back on his bed and rolled away from me. "You have the answers you wanted. Now go. I need to rest."

I sat there for a moment, shocked by his sudden coldness, and then abruptly stood. "Of course, I'm sure you're exhausted."

He didn't respond.

Chilled, I quietly left Eljin, shutting his door behind me. He was right; he'd given me the answers I'd asked for, but he'd broken an oath to do it. And I'd never seen him so defeated before.

"Alexa! There you are. I've been looking for you everywhere."

I whirled around to see one of the palace messenger boys hurrying down the hallway. He stopped in front of me and held out a sealed parchment.

"I have a message for you."

Hesitantly, I reached out and took it from him.

"Who is it from?"

"I'm not sure. It was given to me by one of the perimeter guards with the instructions that it had to reach you tonight."

I glanced down at the seal. It was an unfamiliar bird with a sharp beak in a nosedive. For some reason I had to quell a tremble in my hand as I tore it open and unfolded the note.

My dearest Alexa,

I am sad to report that your unfortunate decision to flee camp has had more dire consequences than you may have anticipated. Your fellow guard and friend is not healing well from the wounds you inflicted on him. I am regrettably unskilled in the art of healing, and my healer was one of the men you killed. Out of the graciousness of my heart, I am rushing him back to my king, where we will hopefully arrive in time to do something about this situation.

I am only doing this because I know you care for the young man. I am counting on you to use your head. If you wish to see him alive, you will come back for him — alone. If I discover that even the smallest force from Antion is following us, I will kill him myself. I've already envisioned just how I'd do it. You'd be proud of how creative I've become.

His fate is in your hands.

Yours,

Rafe

Trying to breathe past the sudden knot in my chest, I jerked my head up to question the boy who had brought this to me, only to see an empty hallway.

He was gone.

⇥ EIGHT ⇤

*I*PACED IN MY room for an hour, trying to build the courage to go in to Damian. My stomach was a mess of acid and indecision. I'd *promised* him. I'd told him I'd stay — that I chose him.

But Rafe's note changed everything.

How had the missive been brought to the palace? Had Rafe come here?

Unease clawed at my chest. The black sorcerers in Dansii were inexplicably untouched by the curse placed on Blevonese sorcerers. They had somehow created Rafe and Vera — twin monsters able to control others with their words and eye contact, *and* other sorcerers couldn't sense them the way they normally could. The man calling himself *Manu de Reich os Deos* had used some sort of potion to induce hallucinations of our worst fears come to life. He'd made me hallucinate just by looking into his eyes.

What other heinous surprises did they have in store for us?

Steeling my will, I made my decision. I didn't want to face the other members of the guard, or explain why I was going to see Damian in the middle of the night, even though we were engaged. Instead, I hurried over to the wall and searched along the wooden panels until I found the knot that opened the secret passage between our rooms. A gust of hot, dusty air hit me as I stepped through, into the darkness. Instead of turning back for a torch, I felt along the wall sightlessly until I reached the opening for Damian's room.

When I stepped out of the passageway into the curtains, a sudden, unexpected surge of panic hit me. The last time I'd done this, I'd emerged to see him kissing Vera. I'd nearly killed Eljin, and Damian had nearly killed *me*, before turning his sword on Vera and killing her instead.

I took a deep breath, reminding myself that she was gone. That Damian was himself. When I walked out, he wouldn't attack me.

Pushing the curtain aside, I hesitantly moved forward into his room and immediately noticed him standing beside his desk, staring down at something in his hand, the light of the moon painting his olive skin and dark hair with a silver sheen.

The floor creaked beneath my foot, and his head jerked up, his hand closing into a fist. When he saw it was me, he relaxed infinitesimally. "Alexa," he breathed. "What are you doing here?"

"I had to talk to you. Something's . . . happened."

"What is it? Are you hurt?" Damian set down the object in his hand and strode over to me. "What's wrong?"

"I'm fine — it's not me," I reassured him as he grabbed my arms and stared down at me, searching my face. With him standing so close, his warm breath touching my cheeks and lips, the heat from his body only inches from mine, I could barely make myself continue. I had to hurry, or I might not have the strength to tell him.

"Rafe sent me a message tonight."

"*What?*"

"A palace messenger boy brought me this." I pulled the parchment out from where I'd stuffed it in my belt.

Anger flashed across Damian's face, but he took the note and walked over to the window, holding it out in the moonlight, and quickly scanned it. When he finished, he crushed the parchment in his fist and turned away from me, staring out the window.

He knew. He knew what I was here to tell him.

I hesitantly took a step toward him, then stopped, my heart beating so hard beneath my ribs it actually hurt.

"You promised." His voice was low, as taut as the air in the moments before a storm breaks.

"I know." Could he hear the tears I was trying to hold back in my voice? "But we can't just let Rafe kill him. *I* can't let that happen."

"And if I send any of my men after him, he'll die. I know. I read it."

Suddenly, he slammed his fist against the windowpane, making it rattle and threaten to shatter. I flinched, the tears I was trying to hold back spilling onto my cheeks.

"Damn them. *Damn* them *all*." He hit his window again, but with less force this time. "They are determined to take you from me." When Damian turned to me, his face was empty, his piercing eyes dulled by hopelessness. "And there is nothing I can do to make you stay . . . is there?"

"I'm sorry," I whispered.

We stood motionless in the darkness for long moments that bled into minutes of strained silence. Finally, he made a noise that was somewhere between a gasp and a sob, and then he strode toward me, grabbing me in his arms and crushing me to him.

Damian bent his head down, so that his face was pressed against my neck. His hand stroked over my hair, again and again. My body trembled with my own terrified sobs.

"This isn't good-bye — not permanently," I said fiercely.

"You can't keep cheating death forever." He lifted his head to look down into my face.

"I came back to you once, and I will come back again. I'm *not* going out there to die."

Damian shook his head. "And what if there's nothing to return to? I don't know what my uncle is preparing to do, but we don't have the strength to survive an attack from Dansii *and* Blevon."

"There is no threat from Blevon. Dansii is behind all of it, I know it. You must contact King Osgand, tell him something has happened to General Tinso, and ask for help from the *Rén Zhûsas*."

"How do you —"

"Eljin told me about them. He told me everything."

"*I* don't even know everything," Damian admitted. "Only what little my mother told me before she died. I couldn't travel to the temple to find out about my heritage properly when I had to make sure no one could find out that I was a sorcerer. She was going to tell me everything when I got older. She never had the chance."

"Well, now you don't have to travel there to find out." I quickly related everything Eljin had told me. Damian's eyes grew wider and wider, and his arms tightened around me.

"That must be what Armando is after. He wants more power, and he thinks he can get it from that fountain. But he has to go through Antion to get to it." Damian let go of me to turn away, reaching up to thread his hands through his hair and squeeze his temples with his palms as though trying to push away a headache — or the truth of the situation. "Together, Antion and Blevon have a chance of stopping him, and he knows it. But if he can get us to keep fighting . . . then . . ."

"Then he can march his armies and black sorcerers through the chaos and straight to the temple."

"Is that why he's done all of this? Is that why he's determined to ensure the war between Blevon and Antion keeps going — why he's trying to restart it? He and my father must have planned this all along. To weaken our two countries enough so that he could march through and claim his prize."

I thought of my parents lying on the ground, killed by a black sorcerer, all those years ago. . . . "He's the one who's sending the black sorcerers. It's always been him. He wanted to make sure the people of Antion hated Blevon." I paused, the devastating truth nearly choking me. "My parents were killed by Dansii. Not Blevon."

Damian's shoulders slumped slightly, and he shook his head. "I'm so sorry, Alexa. I'm sorry that you had to lose your family because of my family's greed."

"I'm not the only one who has lost their loved ones."

Damian didn't respond. Instead, he walked over to his desk and picked up the object he'd been holding earlier. I recognized it now as the locket he'd shown me in General Tinso's castle in Blevon. It was the one with the portrait of his mother inside. His hand closed around it, and then he looked up, meeting my gaze. "If you go after Rafe, you will be walking directly into his trap. He'll find a way to control you — to kill you."

He already does control me. The words were on the tip of my tongue, but I couldn't do it. I couldn't admit it to him. "He won't kill me. They want me alive for some reason."

"Then why did that man try to kill you today?"

I shook my head. "I don't know. He said something strange before he died — something about us giving him no choice, and it being better to bring the king my blood than nothing at all."

Damian's eyebrows pulled together in alarm. "He must have heard that he was to be beheaded tonight."

"So he decided to attack and try to take my blood back to his king, since Vera and Rafe failed to do it," I finished for him. "Rather than be killed and leave Armando empty-handed. He was just biding his time, waiting to use his power to get what he wanted, but the loss of Vera and the threat of death made him reckless."

Damian's hand was clenched so tightly around the locket that his knuckles were white. "Why do they want you? Why would Armando want your blood?"

Something deep inside of my belly clenched, sending a rolling wave of nausea through me. "I don't know."

Damian stared down at his fist. "Please don't do this. Please don't go. If you do . . . they'll take you from me. Forever this time." He closed his eyes. "I can feel it. If you go, I will lose you."

I crossed to where he stood and put my hand over his. When he looked into my face, his expression was bleak. "Together we can do anything, remember?"

"But we aren't doing this together. You're going alone."

With my free hand, I reached up to cup his face and gently

pulled his mouth toward mine, until our lips met. He trembled beneath my touch, threatening to break apart. He'd let me past the careful wall he had built around himself for so many years, giving me the power to hurt him more deeply than I could probably imagine, and that knowledge made me want to scream and cry and never let him go. His arms came around me, his hands clutching at my tunic as he pressed my body against his. The desperation we battled seeped into our kiss, evidenced by the bitter taste of salt on my tongue from tears. I wanted to lose myself in the heat of his touch, in the need that pounded through my blood, coalescing in my limbs and belly.

But I couldn't do that to him. I couldn't love him completely and then leave him alone.

With a gasp, I tore myself away, and he let me go.

We stood motionless, breathing heavily, and then I said, "I'll come back. I promise."

He just stared at me, silent and resigned.

Summoning every ounce of strength I had, I turned and strode away toward the curtain that hid the door to the passageway. Just when I lifted the fabric to pull it back, Damian spoke.

"I love you, Alexa."

I didn't dare turn around and look at him, afraid it would be my undoing. "I love you, too." And then I stepped out of his sight and into the darkness.

⇥ NINE ⇤

A FTER A RESTLESS few hours of trying — and failing — to sleep, I finally strapped my sword on and prepared to leave. I'd decided to start at the campsite where I had last seen Rafe, but then I'd have to track him north, hopefully catching him before he made it to Dansii. I'd never been to the northern reaches of Antion, and I'd certainly never been to Dansii. I barely knew anything about Armando's kingdom, and I had no idea what to expect, or how to prepare for what lay ahead.

Outside my window, the black sky was barely melting into gray. The indistinct shade of nothing, when it was no longer night, but not quite morning yet, either. The jungle was a hulking, seething monster, waiting to envelope me in its feral embrace, rising beyond the palace walls. I stood irresolute for a long moment, thinking of Damian in the next room. He was only a few feet away from me now, but soon he would be a day's walk away. And then an entire kingdom would be between us. I'd promised him I'd come back, but I could tell that this time, he didn't believe me.

He'd said good-bye to me last night, thinking it was for forever.

Fear clutched my chest, but I took deep breaths and turned to my door. I'd lived with varying degrees of fear as my constant companion for so long, I couldn't let it beat me now. I would go; I would find some way to save Rylan and get us back to Damian. And maybe I could find a way to get Rafe killed, releasing us from his control. If I was really lucky, maybe I could even find out what Armando was planning — and how we could possibly stop him.

I wondered how long he'd been planning this. When had he found out about the fountain and decided he wanted to drink from it? If Damian's suspicions were right, and he'd sent his black sorcerers with men pretending to be part of the Blevonese army to attack the smaller Antionese villages like mine — when my parents had been killed — to keep fueling the anger against Blevon, ensuring the continuation of Hector's war, then he'd been planning it for a long, long time. Almost my entire life.

As I opened my door and stepped out, I was so lost in thought I almost tripped over a package lying on the ground right outside my bedroom. I glanced around, but the hallway was empty. No one was there guarding Damian's door, which meant the king was not in his bedroom after all. For some inexplicable reason, my heart sank to realize he wasn't even as close to me as I'd thought. I looked down to see a strange oblong shape wrapped in fabric, with a note attached, lying at my feet. The parchment was sealed shut with red wax, and for a moment, panic seized me. But when I bent down to look closer, I realized it wasn't the same as the one from last night — instead, it was the Royal Crest of Antion, a jaguar crouched and ready to pounce.

It was a message from the king.

Hands trembling, I tore open the missive.

Alexa,

I noticed that you've been without your own bow or arrows for some time now. I want you to have every advantage when you face whatever lies ahead of you. I believe in you — in your strength and your courage. This isn't the end for us, and I apologize if I let my fears get the better of me last night. I don't want you to leave believing me to be afraid. I will do all I can to protect my people, my kingdom, and myself so that when you return, we will be ready to welcome back our queen.

With all of my love,
Damian

Blinking away tears, I untied the string to reveal a beautiful, hand-carved bow and a quiver full of arrows, tipped with the midnight black of sharpened obsidian blades. A rare and valuable gift. I folded the note and carefully placed it in the pack on my hip that I usually used to carry a small amount of food. Then I strapped the quiver to my back and slung the bow over my chest.

I grabbed the fabric he'd wrapped it in, tossed it into my room, and shut the door. When I turned around, Eljin stood before me. I jumped back with a gasp of surprise.

"Where did you come from?"

"Better not let anyone else sneak up on you like that if you want to come back here in one piece." Eljin smirked at me. His mask was still gone, and he was armed similarly to me. After the coldness of his dismissal last night, I was grateful that he seemed back to his usual self this morning. And that he was up and about. Lisbet must have worked on him some more during the night.

"Right. Thanks for the advice." I turned to walk away, but he followed me. I stopped and turned to face him. "Do you need something?"

"Look, let me spell this out for you, since you're a bit slow this morning."

"Excuse me?"

"I'm coming with you, Alexa."

"You're coming with me?" I lifted my eyebrows in surprise.

"Damian doesn't want you going alone, and since he can't go with you, he's sending me." Eljin looked at me steadily, the teasing glint gone from his eyes, replaced by deadly seriousness.

"Damian sent you?"

"Are you going to repeat everything I say? Yes, Damian sent me. He's been up pretty much all night doing everything in his power to help you, since he can't go himself."

I swallowed once, hard, afraid I would break down in tears at any moment if I let myself think of him up all night, finding me the bow and arrow, somehow getting Eljin completely healed and convincing him to come with me, and who knew what else. . . . "What about your father?" I asked, trying to rein in my emotions.

A dark look crossed Eljin's face. "Whatever has happened to my father can't be undone. Damian is sending scouts to his castle to try and find out where he is and what's happened. Damian's promised me that he will do everything in his power to find him, and if he's still . . ." He trailed off, looking away from me. "The true danger lies in Dansii, and if we don't put a stop to this, both

64

of our kingdoms will end up massacred. My father" — his voice grew strained, almost choked — "is just one man."

He didn't have to say anything else. I reached out to touch his arm, but he flinched away.

After a pause, I said, "Well, I suppose we had better get started." I turned and headed toward the staircase that would take me down to the main floor, giving Eljin a moment to compose himself.

I was only halfway down the first flight of stairs when Eljin caught up to me. We finished descending in silence, but when we reached the bottom, I asked if he wanted to stop by the kitchen before leaving, to stock up on food and water, and he agreed.

We were halfway there when I heard the sound of heels clicking on the stone floor, heading toward us. Sure enough, within moments, a young woman rounded the corner of a side hall, and when she saw us her eyes widened. I recognized her immediately as well — it was Miss Durand, the young woman who had been so rude to me a few days prior, and who had been in the hallway with Jerrod when Damian and I had come out of his quarters holding hands after the fight with Vera. I expected her to sneer, or make some snide comment, but instead she froze, staring at both of us.

I could only imagine what she thought, seeing two armed, scarred guards striding down the hallway together, especially since I'd heard her less-than-savory opinion of me . . . and particularly now that she knew there was something between me and Damian. I was certain she'd had her sights set on the king of Antion for herself, so I expected more vitriol from her. Instead, she actually ducked her head in a small semblance of a bow as we passed. I

65

didn't turn to look over my shoulder at her, even though I was tempted to.

If Damian's fears were correct, and I didn't return, how long would it take before he began to look elsewhere for a queen? If he survived what lay ahead, he *had* to marry and ensure the continuation of the royal family. Would he look to her? With her smooth, dark complexion, her wide eyes and ebony hair, she was definitely beautiful.

I shook myself, refusing to let those thoughts take root. Eljin remained silent at my side, not commenting on the girl's strange reaction to us, or the uncertainty that might have been plain on my face if he looked over at me.

When we got to the kitchen, there were already two packs of food waiting for us, and flagons of cool water. Something deep inside my chest constricted as I put the food into the bag strapped to my side, next to Damian's note. I turned away from Eljin as I hooked the flagon onto my belt, hoping he wouldn't notice the emotions I was trying to suppress. After two slow breaths, I was able to push them back down, deep inside where I could try to ignore them.

"Are you ready?" I asked, facing him once more.

Eljin didn't say a word about the sheen in my eyes, but I noted the way his face softened when he nodded. "Let's go."

We took a servants' door out of the palace, skirting the tent city of women and babies to reach the palace wall.

"Did you tell Tanoori you were leaving?" I asked quietly as the mewling cry of a baby broke the stillness of the morning.

Eljin wouldn't meet my questioning gaze. "She was still asleep from the herbs my aunt gave her to help calm her down. I didn't have the heart to wake her up."

I saw the way a muscle among the scars on his jaw twitched as he told me this, and guilt burrowed through me. "I'm so sorry, Eljin. I'm sorry that you got dragged into this."

He was silent for a moment as we neared the door that would let us out into the jungle. Just before we were within earshot of the perimeter guards who were watching our approach, he stopped and faced me. His dark eyes were lit with an unexpected fire. "I am deeply indebted to you after what happened with Vera. If helping you rescue Rylan and returning you to the king safely can in some way repay that debt, then I will accompany you and do what I can."

"You aren't *indebted* to me. I nearly killed —"

"No." Eljin cut me off. "*I* would have killed *you*. You were only defending yourself, and you stopped me without killing me. It's more than most would have done. And as I said, the true fight lies in Dansii. I was not coerced into accompanying you."

Without another word, he turned and walked away.

I followed behind a bit more slowly, some sense of dread making my steps sluggish. Just before I reached the gate, I had the strongest urge to turn back. I glanced over my shoulder and noticed the curtains pulled open in one of the large windows on the main floor of the palace. A tall, dark shadow of a man stood silhouetted in the window. Something inside of me lurched when I realized it was the library that had once been the former queen's — Damian's mother. He stood there, watching me leave, as everyone he had ever loved had left him one by one. But none of them by choice — except for me.

I stopped and turned to fully face him. I saw him straighten, and though I couldn't see the details of his face from this distance,

I imagined the brightness of his eyes, the curve of his lips, and the light of the morning sun on his dark hair. Lifting my hand up to my mouth, I kissed my fingers and then pressed my hand to my chest, above my heart, hoping he'd understand my message.

I love you. I'll come back to you.

My eyes burned when he lifted his hand to his own lips and then pressed it to his heart. I stood frozen for a moment, every instinct in me screaming to turn back, to run to him. But I couldn't leave Rylan to die. I just couldn't. Swiping at my cheek, I forced myself to turn away and rush after Eljin, through the gate and out into the sweltering heat of the jungle.

⇥ TEN ⇤

"HEY'RE GONE," ELJIN announced unnecessarily when we reached the campsite I had escaped what seemed like mere hours ago, even though I knew it had been much longer. There was a pile of ash where the fire had been, and trampled ground cover and bushes, but no men. No tents. No Rafe — or Rylan.

He'd told me they were heading to Dansii, but some small part of me had hoped it was another ploy, and that they'd be waiting for me here.

Instead, Eljin and I sat down in the empty clearing to eat a tiny portion of our food and rest for a moment before continuing on.

Sweat beaded along my hairline. My tunic stuck to my skin underneath the straps of my quiver of arrows as I bit into one of the rolls I'd brought.

"What do you know of Dansii?" I asked to fill the strained silence.

Eljin finished chewing his cheese before answering. "I've never been there, but I've heard it's very different from anything you've seen before. King Alonz, Armando and Hector's father, had a massive wall built across the entire border of Antion and Dansii, guarded day and night by his soldiers."

"To keep the people of Antion out or his people in?"

Eljin shrugged. "No one really knows. Probably so he could control both." After taking another bite he continued, "I've heard that the land in Dansii has rolling hills, and is very hot and sandy, with strange bushes and trees and very few streams or sources of water. In times of drought they have been known to attack border villages in Antion to gain access to their water."

I thought of our lush jungle — of the abundance of rivers and streams that ran through our land — and the small gold mines in the southern tip of the kingdom that helped support us, and a new thought occurred to me. "Do you think that Armando might be after our water and our mines, now that Damian is king and not his brother? We've always traded goods with them, but maybe he wants to take it all for himself. Maybe those are his goals — and not the temple."

"That might be a by-product of what he hopes to accomplish, but if that were all he was after, he would just attack Antion. Damian's army is depleted, he has very few sorcerers to help him defend his people or his throne, and Dansii has apparently not only been creating black sorcerers, but also experimenting to create an entirely new breed of dark sorcery." From somewhere in the depths of the greenery that surrounded us on all sides, an animal keened. A high-pitched sound that turned into a screech; it sounded like it was dying. Eljin stood up abruptly, brushing off his lap and taking a quick swig from his water flagon. "We should keep moving."

Spooked, I followed his lead, putting my half-eaten roll back in my pack and taking a drink of the water that was now lukewarm from the constant, oppressive heat of the jungle. Above us, through the canopy of leaves, the clear morning was working its way into an afternoon storm. The sky churned with gray-black clouds, increasingly blocking out the pieces of azure sky that broke through the treetops and the light of the sun.

We looked to the ground for signs of which way Rafe had gone. It was easy to pick out his party's path; they hadn't even tried to conceal their tracks this time. Eljin and I were silent as we trekked through the dense foliage. I, for one, hoped that whatever predator had made a meal out of the poor animal we'd heard was full for now. But just to be safe, I slid my sword out of its sheath and kept it partially lifted in front of me as we pressed forward, heading north.

"Are you anticipating an ambush?" Eljin smirked as he glanced down at my white-knuckled grip on the sword.

"I've already been attacked by a jaguar *and* a snake in the last couple of months. I'd rather be prepared for any possibility," I retorted.

He just shrugged and kept moving forward. Rather than going for stealth like they had before, Rafe's men had literally cut through the rain forest this time, leaving a fairly wide path of destruction — hacked-off branches and trampled foliage and a very easy-to-follow trail. How far behind them were we? When I saw a broken branch lying on the ground, its leaves stained red, I froze, thinking it might be Rylan's blood. But when I walked closer, I realized it was just some crushed berries.

Eljin glanced at me when I exhaled sharply, but didn't comment this time.

I couldn't let myself think about Rylan — injured and possibly dying. I couldn't let myself remember the last time I'd hiked

71

through the jungle with Eljin, when I'd believed him to be my captor; when I'd started to discover the truth about Damian and realized how alike we truly were. When I'd started to fall in love with him. I couldn't let myself think of the pain and fear in his eyes when I'd gone to him last night to tell him of Rafe's threat, or everything he'd done to try and support my decision to leave, despite his fear that it was to my death.

Instead, I kept my mind carefully walled in to the present. My gaze roamed above us, to watch for threats overhead, and in front and to the side of us, straining to hear the faintest sound of anything that might be stalking us. But there was nothing to hear besides the squelch of our boots in the moist earth, and the occasional call of a bird, or the screech of a monkey. We crossed through streams and climbed hills, only to have to descend and then climb again. For hours and hours, we pressed on. Eventually, the storm broke, a steady drizzle of rain that quickly soaked us, but still we continued forward. The boot prints from Rafe and his men began to grow indistinct as the soil turned to mud beneath our feet, but it was still easy enough to pick out their trail of chopped tree branches, vines, and trampled bushes.

Finally, when darkness began to slip over the jungle, like a blanket slowly being pulled across the sky until all light was extinguished, we were forced to stop and make camp. Rather than bothering with a tent, we had only brought light sleeping rolls. I found a large tree that offered some protection from the ongoing storm, and after a cold dinner of soggy rolls, cheese, and some bruised papaya that we'd found in our packs, Eljin and I unrolled our "beds" next to each other and lay down to try and go to sleep. Even though the night air was thick with the humidity of the storm, I still felt chilled. Maybe because I was still half-soaked, as was my sleeping roll. I pulled my knees into my belly and wrapped my arm around my quiver of arrows, holding it to my chest. No jungle creature would want to steal my weapons, I knew, but for some reason I wanted them as close to me as possible.

"Goodnight, Alexa," Eljin said from behind me. We'd hardly spoken the whole day, lost in our own thoughts. I wondered if he was fighting his own fears and worries, like I was. He had to be. He still didn't know what had happened to his father. He'd had to leave Tanoori without saying good-bye — right after she'd been through such a traumatizing ordeal. His kingdom had technically declared war on us again. There was plenty for him to be worried about.

"Goodnight," I finally responded quietly.

It took me some time, but I finally drifted off into an uneasy sleep. My dreams were plagued with blood and death and all my worst fears chasing me through the darkness. I jerked awake at one point, shaking from the terror of my nightmares. Sometime during the night, Eljin had rolled closer to me. I could feel his back against mine through my sleeping roll. The warmth and solidness of his body was surprisingly soothing to the frantic racing of my mind. He could be taciturn at times, but I knew he was also my ally and my friend. Suddenly, I was intensely grateful to Damian for convincing Eljin to accompany me. With the comforting pressure of his body against mine, I was finally able to relax enough to drift off again.

Though we woke up before dawn and moved as quickly as we could through the dense vegetation, we never caught up to Rafe, and as the day wore on, I was beginning to worry that we wouldn't find them before they reached Dansii.

"He must be setting a grueling pace to be able to stay this far ahead of us," I commented in frustration as the day began to wane toward evening. "There's only two of us and a whole group of them."

"True, but didn't you reduce their numbers significantly before your escape?" Eljin pointed out, reminding me of all the men I'd been forced to hew down with my sword recently. Men who were intent on hurting — or killing — me as well. But it didn't assuage the guilt that rose like poison, burning through me. Somewhere in Dansii, those men had families. Mothers. Wives. Children.

I didn't respond, and we lapsed into silence again. We'd skirted two villages that afternoon; the path Rafe had taken had kept him away from the people of Antion so far. Until an hour later, when we realized their trail headed *toward* the village that lay ahead of us in the oncoming twilight, not around it.

Dread quickened my steps as we rushed toward the medium-sized settlement carved out of the jungle's threatening embrace. Smoke curled up from the chimneys of the homes that dotted the fairly large clearing. A rutted road cut down the center of the row of homes and buildings, heading toward the largest building. This was larger than the village I had grown up in — but if it was anything like mine, that building was where the people bartered for goods. It was a market and a school and whatever else it needed to be. The jungle was too hard to keep at bay, so the people of Antion had learned to only use as much space as was absolutely necessary. Hector had outlawed all festivals and celebrations of any sort when he became king, except for weddings and funerals. But I wondered what it had been like before he came to Antion and stamped out the old ways; if once, perhaps, this building had been used for other means as well.

As my gaze traveled over the little town, I noticed that they had two extra buildings that ours hadn't had. One of them was two stories tall and had a sign out front, with the symbols of a horseshoe and a bowl with a spoon in it painted on the wooden surface. Behind the two-story structure was a building that appeared to be a small stable.

"Is that an inn?" I whispered.

Eljin nodded. "And a place where travelers can exchange horses for a nice fee. We must be closer to the main road than I realized." Horses were a rare commodity in the jungle and generally were only kept and used by those closest to the largest roads. The animals were an ineffective mode of travel on the smaller paths through the dense foliage of the jungle between most of the villages.

We crouched in the protection of the forest as darkness swiftly fell, blotting out the details of the village.

"Let's do a sweep before we investigate any further. Keep an eye out for Rafe and his men," Eljin murmured to me, gesturing that I head to the left and that he would cut right. "Meet me behind there if you don't find anything." He pointed at the largest building, close to the inn and stable. Small, tightly constructed homes lined the rutted, weedy road that led out of the village and deeper into the jungle. I nodded and slunk forward, slipping between shadows and trees to conceal myself. The light of fire and candles created a warm glow in the windows of the homes I skirted. In my village, we'd had wooden shutters that we latched at night, but some of these villagers were wealthy enough for glass. The laughter of children was a quiet, almost dreamlike sound on the apathetic breeze that did little more than stir the hot, humid night air. I paused, peering through the darkness, wondering if Rafe and his men were here somewhere. Would they have stopped at the inn for the night? Could we be this close to Rylan?

My mind churned and my heart ricocheted against my lungs as I hurried forward, straining for any sign of Rafe, or of a struggle of some sort. But by the time I made it to the back of the largest building to wait for Eljin, I'd seen no sign of them. Only families gathered in their homes, safe from the threats Antion brandished at night, behind their closed doors and secured windows.

I waited as the minutes dragged by with no sign of Eljin. Had something happened to him? What if he'd run into Rafe? Sinking into a low crouch, I silently unsheathed my sword and crept forward, my back to the dark, silent building. The buzz of insects was the only sound besides the hammering of my pulse until the snap of a twig on the other side of the wall I hid behind made me flinch. Someone was heading right for me. I lifted my sword, preparing myself.

A man rounded the corner, and I jumped forward and then froze, with a gasp lodged in my throat. It was Eljin.

"What took you so long?" I hissed, lowering my sword.

Eljin had stiffened when he saw me jump forward with my blade raised, but now he just lifted one eyebrow. "There was a sign of struggle near the stables. I was trying to find out if Rafe and his men were still there."

"And . . . are they there?"

"I don't think so. You need to come look at this."

Warily, I followed Eljin through the darkness toward the stable. The air was so thick with humidity, it coated my skin, slicking it with sweat. I kept my sword out, just in case.

When we neared the stable, there was no sound of neighing or any other noises a barn full of large animals would make. Eljin led me around the side of the building and pointed at the stable door, where it hung off its hinges, broken. The ground was stained with blood, and when I peered into the black interior of the barn, it was to find the stalls empty.

I turned back to face Eljin, my stomach sinking. "They stole the horses."

Eljin's expression was grim. "It appears that way."

"We'll never catch them now if they're on horseback."

I was tempted to punch the door but knew that would just bruise my hand and do nothing to ease the frustration and anger that churned in me.

"Perhaps we should turn back —"

"No." I cut him off furiously. "We have to keep going. I can't just abandon him."

"Forgive me for asking . . ." Eljin started hesitantly. "But you've accepted Damian's proposal of marriage, correct?"

I nodded, still trying to subdue my emotions and figure out what we should do now.

"So you love him."

I nodded again.

"Then why are you risking yourself like this for Rylan? I understand that he is your friend, and a fellow guard, but *you* are going to be the queen of Antion. Damian needs you. His kingdom is under attack from all sides, and his best guard — and fiancée — isn't at his side." Eljin held up a hand when I tried to cut in again. "Just let me finish. Chances of saving Rylan were slim to begin with, but now that they have horses, there is no way we'll intercept them before they reach Dansii. *If* he survives the journey, I have no idea how we'll find him. And *if* we find him, how do you propose we rescue him? It'll be us against a kingdom known to use black sorcerers. And after what happened at the palace yesterday, I'm quite concerned about what other dark sorcery they've managed to come up with. Is it truly worth all this risk to continue?"

"Rylan is more than just my friend or a fellow guard. He . . . he was almost like another brother to me. It's my fault he's hurt. I can't leave him to his fate or I'd never be able to live with myself." A myriad of emotions twisted through me, tightening my stomach into knots.

Eljin's gaze was unwavering, searching for some answer that I wasn't sure I had. "Is that all?"

Was that the only reason? Because I'd hurt him, and I didn't want to live with the guilt if he died? I thought of his wide, easy smile, of the way he looked at me, the gold flecks in his brown eyes making them practically glow with warmth. I thought of the hundreds, if not thousands, of times we'd sparred, of the countless times we'd fought together and protected each other. We had both lost our entire families to a war that had never been necessary to begin with. It was technically *my* fault Rylan's brother, Jude, had died. He'd sacrificed himself to help me stop Iker. But Rylan had never held it against me.

"I can't let him die because . . . because I love him, too," I finally admitted quietly.

I loved Damian with my whole being, my very soul. He was my fiancé and would hopefully be my husband one day. But I *did* love Rylan as well. Although it wasn't the same kind of love, I realized that didn't make it any less important. The thought of his death was unbearable.

Eljin's face was a mask, betraying nothing of his feelings upon hearing my admission. He and Damian were very close. . . . Would he think of it as a betrayal to the king of Antion?

"Then we'd better keep going," was all he said.

"Hey! What are you doing back there?" A shout startled us both, and we turned in unison to see a man striding toward us, brandishing a lantern in one hand and a sword in the other.

⊰ ELEVEN ⊱

𝒯HE MEAGER LIGHT the lantern offered flickered over the man's dark skin and even darker eyes.

Eljin lifted his empty hands. "You have nothing to fear from us," he called out as the man drew closer, his features twisted with a mixture of anger and dread.

"Then why is he" — the man squinted at me in the darkness and then amended his statement — "I mean, *she*, holding a sword?"

I quickly resheathed it and lifted my hands as well. "I am Alexa Hollen, guard to King Damian, and this is Eljin, one of his most trusted friends and advisors. We are tracking a group of men from Dansii. They are holding one of King Damian's guards captive, and we're trying to rescue him. Did they come through here today?"

The man stopped a few feet away from us, the anger gone, replaced by exhaustion and a hint of wariness when he lifted the lantern up higher to get a better look at us. After being alone with Eljin for such a long time, I'd forgotten about my scarred face — or his. I just saw *him*, not the horrifying scars he'd earned trying to protect his mother as a child. But the man's eyes widened when he looked at my face and then Eljin's, reminding me of our disfigurements. "I think I know the men you're talking about. They asked for some rooms, and claimed they were going to pay me to rent a few of my horses and then have them returned in a few days. I showed them my stable, and the next thing I knew, one of them hit me in the back of the head and knocked me clean out. When I woke up, my stable boy was dead on the ground behind me, the horses were gone, and so were they."

Eljin grimaced, the combination of anger and sadness on his face echoing my own tumultuous emotions. "I'm very sorry."

I squeezed my eyes shut, trying to think my way through this. Our only option was to continue on foot, move as quickly as possible, somehow sneak into Dansii, and then figure out where Rafe went. Even though neither of us spoke Dansiian. And there was no way we'd be able to blend in, with our Blevonese coloring, our accents, and our clothing.

"Rafe's taking him to the king. That's what his letter said." I pinched the bridge of my nose but opened my eyes to look at Eljin. "We're going to have to 'get caught' and hope they take us to Armando. He wants me alive for some reason. If his men find us, they have to take us to the king."

"And then what?" Eljin's lips pursed into a thin line.

"What's this guard they're holding captive worth to the king?" the owner of the inn cut in. "If I were able to find you some horses . . . would he be willing to recompense me for my losses?"

"Yes," I answered without hesitation. "If you could do that, I would personally see to it that King Damian remunerated you for your losses."

"My brother runs an inn and stable two hour's walk from here. I can send my son right away and he could return by morning with a horse for each of you."

I didn't want to waste another minute waiting, but getting horses of our own was our only hope of catching Rafe before he crossed into Dansii. On foot we'd be days, maybe even weeks, behind them.

"How far is the border from here?" Eljin asked the man, as if he'd heard my thoughts.

"Five or six days of hard riding. Three times that or more if you walk it."

"We'll take the horses. And a room for the night, if you have any available. If you keep your word, I promise you will be well compensated by the king." Eljin glanced at me, and I nodded. It was our best option.

The man's eyes narrowed, sizing us up. Weighing Eljin's offer. "This way," he finally said, turning and gesturing for us to follow him back across the small distance between the now-empty stable and the inn.

I woke long before dawn, the echo of a scream still on my lips. The nightmares were even more unbearable with the uncertainty of the future looming before me. Sweat slicked my skin, and the darkness writhed around me, a living, oppressive thing, breathing down my neck with the heat and relentlessness of nighttime in the jungles of Antion. Through the open window I heard the far-off sound of a group of monkeys chittering back and forth. Thunder rumbled ominously in the distance, warning of the storm to come.

I sat up in bed, looking down to make sure Eljin still lay on the floor beside me. The innkeeper had offered us two rooms, but we'd elected to stay together. I was grateful to have Eljin close by, but I missed the comfort of actually sleeping beside him. If I closed my eyes and shut my mind off long enough, I could almost convince myself that he was Marcel. With everything that had happened in the last couple of months, I'd barely had any time to let myself mourn my brother's death, and suddenly, sitting there in the darkness, with the soft pattering of rain beginning to slap at the roof, his loss nearly overwhelmed me. How had I gotten here? Almost completely alone, save for a Blevonese sorcerer, rushing through the jungle that I hated and feared, leaving my fiancé behind to go after my friend in hopes of rescuing him from the biggest, most powerful kingdom known to me.

Marcel, are you still near me? Do you still try to watch over me as you did when you were alive? Are you with Mama and Papa? Are they proud of the person I've become — do they watch over me, too? My heart was raw, flayed by loss and grief and fear for what was still to come.

Throwing off the thin blanket I'd slept beneath, I stood and crossed to the window. My fingers curled around the windowsill, my nails biting into the hard wood as I squeezed my eyes shut and lifted my face to the soft, damp breeze. It carried the scent of rain and flowers, of moist soil and green things sucking the water in and growing ever larger, ever stronger. The jungle was resilient; it never stopped trying to press forward, to expand and thrive. As much as I hated the dangers it held, I couldn't help but admire the beauty it possessed — and the tenacity it represented.

Opening my eyes, I stared out into the night sky spreading like thick, choking smoke over the canopy of the rain forest. Heavy clouds of black and gray pulsed with occasional lightning, and the sprinkling rain was slowly growing more insistent. Bending out to grab the handle, I pulled the window shut, securing it before the rainstorm began in earnest.

When I turned around, Eljin was sitting up watching me. I jumped back with a swallowed scream, my hand instinctively dropping to my sword, but finding only empty air. I'd unstrapped my scabbard and slept next to it, feeling safe enough not to sleep with my sword in my hand.

"You scared me," I said shakily.

"I apologize. You seemed upset; I didn't want to disturb you." Eljin rose to his feet with the natural grace of a fighter.

I moved back over to the bed, sitting down heavily and staring at the floor. "I was thinking of my brother."

There was silence for a moment, and then he said, "I wish I'd had the pleasure of knowing him. I've heard nothing but praise for the kind of person he was."

I nodded, my eyes burning again, not daring to speak for fear the grief I'd had to bury would come pouring out. We didn't have time for me to dissolve into a complete breakdown. Maybe one day, if we ever succeeded in stopping Armando . . . if there was ever true peace . . . maybe then I'd have the luxury of allowing myself to truly mourn.

But for now I swiped at my cheeks, took a deep breath, and stood, picking up my bow and quiver of arrows off the ground and strapping them on. "We'd better head out. We've already lost a whole night that they might have continued on through."

"I'll go see if the horses are here yet." Eljin quietly moved to the door and slipped out of the room, leaving me alone to compose myself.

I couldn't bear to lose anyone else I loved. I wasn't sure I would be able to survive it. And that was why I couldn't turn back and leave Rylan to his fate. But as I strapped on my scabbard and sword and walked over to the bucket of water the innkeeper had brought us to quickly wash my face, I had to acknowledge the other fear that pulsed deep within me, which I'd been successful in ignoring until now.

As Eljin had pointed out, Antion was besieged from all sides. Threats against the king were rampant. I was Damian's best guard, and Eljin was the only other sorcerer in Antion to help Damian protect his palace. And now we were both gone, chasing Rafe back to Dansii.

What if I succeeded in saving Rylan but in the process lost Damian?

⇥ TWELVE ⇤

AFTER A RUSHED breakfast of papaya, mango, and some sort of bread made with an assortment of herbs, which the innkeeper's wife called *m'katae*, we followed the man and his son out into the lifting gloom to get our horses. Rain still fell, but it was more of a soft, gentle moisture in the air, misty and surprisingly cool on my skin. Our packs were refilled with new provisions, again thanks to the innkeeper's wife.

The son tightened the girths on the horses and led a bay mare over to me. He was tall and lanky in the way that boys who have grown into the height of a man but not quite the stature yet can be. "Her name is Mira," he said quietly as he handed me the reins.

Mira wasn't as tall as the dappled gelding Eljin had already mounted, but I still had to quell a rush of nervousness as I gripped the leather in my hands and looked up into her intelligent brown eyes. "You're a nice girl, right? Yes, you are. You're going to be nice to me." I continued to murmur to her as I put my foot in the stirrup and pulled myself up into the saddle with all the grace of a sack of flour being flung over the horse's back.

Because there were very few horses in Antion, I'd had very limited contact with them. Towns along the main roads like this one usually had a few, and those who traveled by cart to sell their wares often had one. But no one had owned any in my village growing up. The commanding officer who had drafted us into the army had an enormous roan stallion, but the rest of us had marched behind the horse as we went from town to town, heading toward Tubatse and the palace. That was before Marcel and I distinguished ourselves through our fighting in the test given at Tubatse, allowing us to move to the palace to train and eventually earning our spots on the prince's guard. Damian also had a horse, and before our "abduction" to Blevon, he'd ridden it quite often, but since being crowned king, he'd had little chance to ride anymore. I wondered if he missed it as I sat awkwardly upon the huge animal, staring down at the ground that was now much too far away from my feet for comfort.

"Ready?" Eljin sat tall on his gelding, obviously at ease, while I clutched the reins with a death grip that drained the blood from my knuckles. Perhaps I'd finally found something that scared me even more than snakes.

"Um . . ."

"My name is Farid Utsel. You will make sure your king knows?" the innkeeper cut in, looking up at me.

"Yes, Farid. As soon as we return to the palace, we will make sure King Damian knows of your help and sends recompense for your losses," I assured him.

He nodded, his eyes flicking to his son and then up to the heavy gray dawn. The rain had finally stopped, but the air was still thick with a lingering dampness. It swelled up from the dank soil and pressed in from the jungle that surrounded us, the ever-present green fortress.

"You'd better go. This storm isn't done yet," Farid warned us, slapping my mare on the rump.

Mira jumped forward, and I cried out in alarm, instinctively gripping her as tightly as possible with my legs so that I wouldn't be thrown off.

"Shorten your reins!" I heard Eljin shout from behind me. I looked down at the leather straps that were slapping uselessly against Mira's neck. The ground rushed past us as she bounced forward out of the inn yard and onto the weedy road. I heard the sound of hooves approaching, and suddenly Eljin was there, alongside me. He reached over and grabbed my reins in one hand and pulled back. Mira immediately slowed to a walk and then stopped, flinging me forward. I dropped the reins completely to grab onto her mane, desperately clinging to her neck so I wouldn't fall off. I was barely able to breathe past the wild thudding of my heart.

"So, you've never ridden a horse before," Eljin commented with his eyebrows lifted.

"Why would you assume that?" I groused as I pushed myself back into the saddle, keeping my grip on Mira's mane. That seemed a better place to hold on to than the reins if she was going to take off again.

Eljin just laughed. "She was only trotting. We're going to have to go a lot faster than that if we want to catch up to Rafe in time."

"She can go faster than that?" I could have sworn we were practically flying, the ground had been moving so quickly beneath Mira's feet. Horses hadn't seemed quite so terrifying when I'd watched other people ride them. In fact, it had almost looked fun. I knew better now.

"All right, let's start with the basics. Sit deeper in to the saddle, and drop your heels down in the stirrups, so you can sit tall. Like this."

I tried to imitate the way Eljin sat, with his heels lower than the stirrups, his back tall and his thighs and calves gripping his horse's flanks.

"Now the reins. You need to hold them shorter, like this, so you can feel her mouth. That way you can guide her and slow her down if needed." He talked me through the basics of riding, from pulling on the bit with one hand or the other to tell her to go right or left, to squeezing my legs for more speed, or sitting deeper and pulling back on the reins to slow her down.

"We don't really have time to practice or take this slow. You're going to have to just do the best you can. If all else fails, just don't let go."

He clucked to his horse, squeezed his legs, and took off, leaving me to follow.

"Remember our little talk?" I said as I shortened my reins the way Eljin had instructed me to and pressed my heels down in the stirrups. "Be nice to me. I'm kind of important to the king, and I think he'd get pretty upset if I got killed by a horse after everything else we've been through."

Mira huffed, tossing her head. Eljin was already quite a way down the rutted road, and she was obviously eager to follow.

"All right." I took a deep breath. "I can do this."

I squeezed my legs and imitated the noise Eljin had made at Mira. She leaped forward again, but this time I was more prepared and was able to keep my seat. She was trotting again, as Eljin had called it, jarring my bones with each impact. Whatever Eljin's horse was doing, it looked much nicer — and faster — so I squeezed again, and Mira's gait changed into a rocking motion that finally started closing the distance between us and Eljin. The jarring stopped, and I found I was able to hold on much easier at this speed, even though it was faster than trotting.

When Mira pulled up alongside Eljin, he glanced over and gave me an approving nod. Ahead, I could see the main road, a wide, rutted path through the jungle. There was a group of men paid to travel the road and keep it free from weeds, but the jungle was tenacious, and it was impossible to keep it completely clear. As I followed Eljin's lead, pulling on the left rein to direct Mira north onto the hard-packed dirt that was quickly turning to mud from the morning's rain, I remembered Felton, Lady Vera's man, telling Damian that the roads were *in tolerable condition — especially for a jungle kingdom.* He'd been so condescending, but he wasn't completely inaccurate. Thick green bushes and weeds choked the edges of the jungle on either side of us and inched forward into the dirt beneath our horses' pounding hooves. We'd only been riding for a few minutes when Farid's prediction came true. The clouds opened above us. Sheets of water obscured our vision and turned the road to slop. But we pressed on, rushing toward Dansii and Rylan.

For days, we rode from sunrise until well after dark, only stopping to water our horses and allow them to graze and then tying them to the trees we slept under. We took turns sitting up and stoking the fire, hoping the flames would frighten off any predators that thought to make us — or our transportation — dinner.

Exhaustion wore me down, and on the fifth day, I could feel Mira struggling to maintain her pace as well.

"We're running them into the ground." We'd stopped to eat a hurried lunch of the mangoes Eljin had spotted just off the road. There was also a stream where the horses were greedily drinking, and where we'd refilled our water flagons. Our food supplies were long since gone, and we'd had to resort to living on whatever we could find in our rushed flight to Dansii. Hunger clawed at my belly constantly. Certain muscles itched from nonuse and fatigue, while other new ones I'd never used before ached from all the riding. I'd never gone so long without training — except when Eljin had kidnapped us and taken us to his father's castle in Blevon.

The horses' mouths and necks were flecked with white, and their bellies were soaked with sweat beneath the girths I'd learned to put on and take off each morning and night.

"They can't keep up this pace anymore," I continued as I took my last bite of mango and tossed the pit away, far from satiated.

"I know." Eljin stared at his hands, where he held his own half-eaten mango. We'd put a few more in our packs just in case we couldn't find anything to eat later. I longed for the time to catch some fish from the stream and broil them over a fire. The thought of warm, flaky fish made my mouth water.

"What are we going to do?" I pressed, forcing away the thoughts of any food besides fruit.

"We keep going. We're going to have to let up on our pace, at least for some of the time, so the horses don't get hurt or worse. And we hope they're having the same trouble." Eljin took another bite of his mango, but instead of swallowing it, he spat it back out and stood up, walking over to his gelding — whose name was Gusto, I'd found out — and held his hand out. Gusto lifted his head and lipped the mango into his mouth. Mira lifted her head as well, and Eljin repeated the process for her, making me feel bad that I'd eaten my entire mango myself.

"Let's get moving. Looks like another storm is coming." Eljin took Gusto's reins and swung himself up onto the saddle.

I stood up and hurried over to Mira, following suit, leaving the stream and the dream of fish behind us.

The next afternoon, the foliage began to thin out around us. The sun was hot and oppressive as the trees, vines, and bushes became more and more sparse, until suddenly, the jungle ended. The world opened up around us, stealing my breath with its majesty — and with the fact that we were suddenly very exposed. To the east and west of us, I could see the curve of the jungle, stretching on and on out of sight. At the edge of the horizon to the west, a massive mountain range split the sky with jagged, snowcapped peaks.

"Striking, aren't they?" Eljin said from beside me, following my gaze to the mountains. "Those are the Naswais Mountains I told you about. You're lucky to see the tops of them — they are so tall, they're usually encased in clouds. No man has ever made it over them alive."

I stared at the mountains in awe, unable to imagine even *trying* to travel over them. The highest peak was so far up in the sky, it almost seemed as though it would touch the sun.

Finally, I looked forward to see the road wind down into a fairly large city sprawling across the gently rolling grasslands. And just beyond the city was a massive gray wall with spikes along the top of it. It stretched as far as I could see to the right or left, all the way to the mountains to the west and whatever lay to the east. Papa had told us once of a "wasteland" — with miles and miles of black rock, a mountain that breathed fire, and that beyond that stretch of lifelessness was water. Endless water. I wondered if the wall reached all the way to the water or if they'd quit building it when they'd reached the rivers of fire.

"And that" — Eljin cut into my thoughts — "is the wall I told you about."

"So that means . . ."

"Yes."

I stared at the wall, and the tiny figures of men walking back and forth across the spiked top. They almost looked like toys from here. Harmless. But I knew better.

"We didn't catch them in time." Deflated, I forced myself to look away from the wall before I started to cry. I was beyond exhausted and practically starving. I'd left Damian behind to make this wild dash through the jungle in hopes of saving Rylan before he was taken out of our reach, and I'd failed.

"What now?" Eljin asked, his voice surprisingly gentle.

I stared at the Naswais Mountains, willing myself to regain control. I breathed in deeply through my nose and out through my mouth, pushing my trembling hands into Mira's mane. She craned her neck to look back at me with one wise eye, and then gave a little toss of her head, whinnying softly. Almost as if she knew what I was feeling and was trying to make me feel better. I rubbed one fist along her neck, shocked to realize how connected to each other we had become. My fear of riding was definitely gone, replaced by a surprisingly strong attachment to Mira. Despite the horrible circumstances, riding her had become a comfort to me. My fingers tangled in her mane, and I lifted my head to the surprisingly fresh breeze that drifted in from the northeast, and I closed my eyes.

"Alexa?"

Finally, I turned to Eljin.

"I'm going after him. I'm going to Dansii."

⊰ THIRTEEN ⊱

*I*T WAS AFTERNOON when we'd emerged from the jungle, but we waited until the sun had set, dropping below the edge of the horizon where the massive mountains and the jungle met and then faded away into the darkness. The night was stifling as we drew closer to the city that butted up against the Dansiian wall. It was called Bikoro, according to the weather-ravaged carved sign I'd spotted near the road just before we guided our horses off the well-worn path and out into the brush of the plains leading to the wall. The earlier breeze had disappeared. Nothing moved the air, so that the heat swelled, a fetid, oppressive weight as we urged Mira and Gusto forward slowly. Their hooves squelched on the moist soil beneath us, still damp from the earlier storms.

We'd debated for a short time about whether we should try to sneak through the city undetected or make our presence as King Damian's personal guard and advisor known. Finally, we'd agreed to wait until the cover of night and skirt the city, heading straight for the wall. Surely, everyone in Antion had heard the story of Damian's scarred *female* guard defeating Iker and helping place him on the throne by now. If anyone did recognize me, and tried to help — or stop — us, it could end badly for them. Especially if things didn't go well once we made it to Dansii. Better to leave the people of this city alone and hurry on our way.

I looked toward Bikoro. It was even bigger than Tubatse, the capital city that had been carved out from the bowels of the jungle in the small valley below where the palace stood, surrounded by its protective walls. In Tubatse the houses and buildings were crammed together, using every available inch of space stolen from the forest. Vines and the creeping, relentless tentacles of the jungle were constantly pressing forward, reaching up the edges of the structures, choking the roads and paths if those responsible for maintaining them got behind on their work by even a few days. People struggled just to keep their existence out of the jungle's grasp.

In comparison, Bikoro's buildings were taller, and built from stone and wood. The homes closest to us were bigger than any I'd seen in my own village or in Tubatse. Large, overflowing gardens stretched out into the fields surrounding the city. The flickering glow of firelight warmed the windows of nearly every structure. We were too far away for me to spot any of the people, but I wondered about them. About their lives. Were they all Antionese? Or had this once been a Dansiian city that Antion had claimed?

It was frustrating to know so little of my own kingdom's history, but other than teaching us the basics of how to read and write, Papa hadn't made our education a priority. Our ability to defend our lives had been much more vital.

And there'd certainly been no time for a member of Prince Damian's guard to dally in the library — even if Hector had given us access to it, which he'd refused to do.

As we continued our slow, silent trek around Bikoro, the shadow of the wall loomed larger and larger before us, and I let my mind wander. I let myself dream. Perhaps . . . if I made it back alive, if we somehow managed to survive this, and I was able to return to my king . . . once I was married to Damian and made queen, and once we'd somehow ensured peace for our people, maybe *then* I'd be able to indulge in reading and learning more of the history of our world.

Until that time, I supposed, it would be up to me to make history, not learn it.

I turned away from the city, forcing my thoughts to what lay ahead. Letting myself dream of being back with Damian was dangerous ground. It shook my resolve, shredding me inside as I thought of him alone at the palace, fearing the worst. I *was* doing the right thing, wasn't I? As the massive wall loomed closer and closer, I wasn't so sure. It was *my* fault Rylan was injured — my fault his life was in danger. But now it was also my fault that Damian was alone. Abandoned by the one person who truly loved him. Again.

"Alexa." Eljin's sudden urgent whisper shook me from my tortured thoughts.

I turned to see him staring behind us instead of looking at me. I craned my neck to look over my shoulder.

"Looks like we have visitors."

I squinted through the darkness. There appeared to be a small group of men on horseback. Were they coming toward us? It was difficult to tell. The cloud cover that encased the night in darkness not only helped conceal us, it obscured our ability to see the men behind us.

They were still quite a distance back. If they were pursuing us, we could make a run for it and get to the wall long before they reached us. But then it would definitely appear as though we were doing something suspicious. My hands tightened on the reins, some instinct warning me that we needed to make it to the wall before those men made it to us.

"Let's see if it's us they're after." I urged Mira forward, squeezing my thighs and calves until she broke into a trot. Eljin had explained the different gaits to me during our trek through the jungle, and had taught me how to sit each of them. Apparently he'd grown up riding, much like Damian.

Gusto quickly caught up, trotting next to us. Eljin glanced over his shoulder every few seconds as we posted — what Eljin called rising and sitting in the saddle to match the uneven gait.

"They've sped up. They're definitely pursuing us."

Our eyes met, and I could see my own concern reflected in the dark depths of his gaze.

"What do we do?"

He glanced back one more time, and when he looked at me again, his expression was hard. "We can't involve more people. We make a run for it."

He tightened his reins and dug his heels into Gusto's side. The gelding leaped forward into a gallop. I did the same to Mira, and soon the wind whipped past my face, tangling in my hair and stealing the moisture from my eyes as we pounded toward the wall. There was only one entrance that I could see, a massive iron gate, guarded by multiple men on both sides.

"What are we going to do?" I shouted at Eljin.

We were close now, only about a hundred feet away from the wall, and another fifty feet to the west of the gate, where the men on guard had turned toward us, lifting bows and arrows to take aim.

"Am I to shoot them?" I yelled, transferring the reins to one hand and reaching for the bow strapped over my chest.

"No!" Eljin suddenly sawed on the reins, leaning back and pressing his heels down. Gusto responded to his signal and slammed to a halt, kicking up clods of dirt and weeds from his hooves digging into the ground.

Shocked by his sudden stop, Mira and I went flying past them. I had to yank on Mira's mouth, turning her back to Eljin and Gusto and then signaling her to stop as well. Eljin had already dismounted and stood near Gusto's head, rubbing the gelding's large jaw as the horse huffed from the sudden mad dash through the darkness. I dismounted from Mira as well.

"Who goes there?" one of the guards shouted at us in Antionese.

"What are you doing?" I whisper-shouted at Eljin angrily.

"We have to let them go." He looked up at his horse mournfully. "From here on, we go by foot."

"*What?*" I clutched Mira's reins protectively. It was inconceivable that I'd gone from being afraid of her to devastated at the thought of leaving her behind so quickly.

"Hurry, there's no time." Eljin let go of Gusto's reins and moved back to slap him on the rump. The horse tossed his head and trotted forward hesitantly, glancing back at Eljin as if in confusion.

"I don't understand," I argued, still not letting go of Mira.

"The men might think we've stolen the horses, since we avoided the city. If we let them go and make a run for the wall, they'll let us go. My guess is no one from Antion cares about who goes *in* to Dansii. Only who comes out. As long as we don't take their horses with us." He walked over to where I stood, one hand on Mira's hot flank. I could feel the rise and fall of her breathing, the warmth of her body. It had been foolish of me to let myself grow attached to her. Stupid to let myself care for an animal. I should have known it would come to this.

"Hurry, Alex."

"Reveal yourself at once or we will open fire!" another guard shouted.

I looked up to see him advancing on us, an arrow drawn tightly in his bow. Another glance revealed the men on horseback rapidly approaching. With a choked cry, I stepped back and followed Eljin's lead, slapping Mira on the rump. But she only sidestepped a bit, her head swiveling around to pin me with her big brown eyes.

"Go, you stupid animal! Go away!" I flung my arms in the air, spooking her enough to make her trot away a few steps, but then she stopped again. Tears stung my eyes as I shouted at her. "Go, Mira!"

Eljin shouted at her as well, making a motion as though he'd thrown a rock at her. Although he held nothing in his hand, that finally startled Mira enough that she turned and trotted off after Gusto, who was headed toward Bikoro and the other men.

Wiping angrily at my cheeks, I turned away.

"I'm sorry," Eljin said quietly next to me, but I just shook my head.

"Now what?" I forced my voice to come out hard and steady. I'd pretended not to care for years; I could do it again. She was just a horse.

"Duck!" Eljin shouted as he suddenly leaped toward me. We both tumbled to the ground as an arrow whizzed past to embed itself in the soft earth beyond where I'd been standing.

I reached for my own bow and arrow, but Eljin stopped me. "They're Antionese. Just tell them who you are."

Another arrow flew past us, barely missing Eljin's shoulder.

"Antionese with terrible aim," I agreed.

As one, we both rolled away and then jumped to our feet. I lifted my hands in the air, making a show of not reaching for my bow. The guard stood only twenty feet from us, another arrow notched and ready to fly.

"Don't shoot!" I yelled. "We're Antionese! Don't shoot us!"

The guard wavered. Behind us, I heard a whinny. Unable to resist, I glanced back to see Gusto and Mira galloping away toward the jungle, the men on horseback in pursuit. Eljin had been right; they'd only cared about the horses.

"You have to do the talking," Eljin muttered beside me. "He'll question my accent."

I faced forward again, to see the guard lowering his bow.

"What is your business here?" the guard yelled.

"We need to get into Dansii." I started to walk toward him, and Eljin followed. When we got closer, the guard's eyes widened, traveling back and forth between our faces. Our scars.

"What business do you have that would take you to that forsaken place?"

"It's the king's business," I said.

His eyes dropped to the royal insignia on my vest as I came to a stop directly in front of him, and he immediately stiffened, having gone pale, probably realizing he'd almost shot one of Damian's guards.

"I — if the king orders it, then . . ." he stuttered, glancing over his shoulder. "But you still have to convince them to let you in." He jerked a thumb toward the gate. The other Antionese soldiers were watching our exchange with a mixture of bafflement and wariness. But on the other side of the gate stood three men in dark cloaks, the hoods pulled up over their heads. A cold finger of dread scraped down my spine when all three hoods turned toward us.

"Who are they?" I asked the guard.

Gone was his bluster, and if anything he went even more pale. "I don't know. Never seen them before. They showed up this morning, after the group of Dansiians went back through the gate."

My stomach clenched at his words. "How many men?" I asked urgently.

"What?"

"How many Dansiian men went through the gate? Was anyone hurt? Did it look like they had any prisoners?"

"Yes. There was a prisoner. . . ." He trailed off suddenly, his eyes losing focus, going blank in that horrible, soulless way that made my blood turn to ice. "Are you seeking him? Is that who you have come for — the prisoner?"

There was no chance I was going to answer him. Rafe had been here, and I wasn't about to wait to see what he'd commanded this man to do to us.

"Run!" I shouted at Eljin, grabbing my bow and an arrow. Yanking it over my head, I notched the arrow as I dashed toward the gate, with Eljin on my heels. I felt the draw of magic beside me as he lifted his hands. There was a thud behind us, but I didn't turn back to see what he'd done. The two Antionese men guarding the gate lifted their weapons in alarm — one held a sword and the other another bow. I let my first arrow fly without breaking stride before the other man could even take aim. It went through his shooting arm, rendering him unable to fight, but it was not a life-threatening injury.

"Move out of the way," I shouted, waving my free hand at both of them. "Don't make me shoot again!"

"Halt!" The other guard shouted, but his voice wavered.

Eljin and I stopped, my bow pulled tight with another arrow. The three men wearing hoods stood still behind the gate, watching us approach. I felt the pull of magic again as Eljin lifted his hands once more. The uninjured guard dropped his sword to suddenly grasp at his neck, clawing at unseen fingers that choked the air out of him. The moment his eyes rolled up into his head, Eljin dropped his hand and the man fell to the side, unconscious but not dead. At least, I sincerely hoped not.

"What are they?" I murmured to Eljin, a spike of adrenaline and fear driving into my arms, legs, and belly.

"I think we're about to find out."

The gate began to grind open.

⇥ FOURTEEN ⇤

*E*LJIN LIFTED HIS hands once more as the three men in robes moved forward, past the gate toward us. I heard movement behind us, and I glanced over my shoulder to see the first guard — the one whose eyes had gone blank — recovering from whatever Eljin had done to him and climbing to his feet.

A sudden sinking sense of desperation assailed me. And then Eljin grabbed me with one hand, pulling me in to his side, and the ground surrounding him began to shake violently. My arrow slipped when Eljin grabbed my arm, but I immediately renotched it. Quickly taking aim at the robed man on the left, I let it fly. But before the arrow reached its target, he lifted his hand and it disintegrated into ash.

Cold dread lodged in my chest when I saw that he wore the same strange glove made of metal and jewels that Iker had worn when I'd fought him.

He was a black sorcerer.

A ball of fire suddenly ignited above his upturned palm. We had no chance of surviving this. Before I could second-guess myself, I tore free of Eljin's grip, lurching forward and throwing my arms out to keep from being flung to the ground by his earthquake.

"Alex!" Eljin shouted, but I ignored him, tossing my bow to the dirt. The ground suddenly grew still.

"Stop!" I yelled. "If you don't hurt us, I will turn myself in to you."

The man wielding the fire paused. I could see a hint of his face in the glow of the unearthly flames — a narrow nose and deep-set, dark eyes. "And who might you be?" His voice was cold and heavily accented. Though he didn't yell, it carried to where I stood as clearly as if he were only a few feet away.

"Don't do this!" Eljin's hand closed over my bicep, trying to pull me back, but I ignored him.

"I'm Alexa Hollen, guard to King Damian."

"No!" Eljin shouted, pushing me behind him. But it was too late; I'd already seen the gleam of teeth beneath the shadow of the hood.

"Your offer is accepted." The man closed his fist and the fire disappeared. A shiver of terror sliced through me as he strode toward us.

Eljin turned to me, his eyes wide and frantic. "How could you do this?"

"We would have both died. Go to Damian. Help him win this war." It was all I was able to say before the man reached us and snaked a hand out to snatch my arm; his grip was iron tight. The edges of the metal glove bit into my skin.

"You will come willingly or he dies."

Fear pounding through me, I looked up into the man's face. "What will you do with me?"

Without answering, he yanked me to stand in front of him, just in time to see the other two men close the distance between us and roughly grab Eljin as well — each man taking one of his arms.

"What are they doing? Let him go — it's me you want!" I struggled to turn back, to see what they were doing to Eljin, but to no avail. The black sorcerer's grip tightened on my arm as he shoved me forward, toward the gate and Dansii.

"He comes," the black sorcerer growled, "to ensure your cooperation."

Dread coalesced in my limbs, making my feet leaden as the man shoved his fist — the one encased in a glove made of sharp metal and hard jewels — into my spine, forcing me forward, away from Eljin and the other two hooded men. I arched my back away from the pain, trying to twist out of his grip, but he was ruthless, only holding on tighter. I could have pulled out my sword with my free hand, but I didn't dare risk it. Not with Eljin very likely being held by two more black sorcerers.

The black sorcerer marched me through the gate, with the others right behind us. In the darkness I could see the outline of buildings; another city.

Once we were all through, the hinges on the grate screeched, and then, with a resounding clang, it ground shut.

I glanced over my shoulder to see Eljin standing between the other two sorcerers, his face devoid of emotion.

We were trapped in Dansii, surrounded by black sorcerers.

Every minute my chances of returning to Damian were growing more improbable. My only hope now was to somehow find Rylan, to negotiate for his life in return for mine.

The sorcerers quickly removed our weapons, tossing them on the ground behind us. I had to bite down my teeth as hard as I could to force the tears back when I saw the beautiful bow and arrows Damian had given me lying on the dirt.

"This way," the black sorcerer growled, jerking me toward a darkened alley between two homes, leaving our weapons behind. We walked for a few minutes, and then he turned us toward a smaller, sand-colored building. The windows were dark, but two more men dressed similarly to him stood guard in front of the door, though their hoods were pulled down to reveal their faces.

Their heads lifted simultaneously as we approached. One man was as pale as Asher, but he had dark brown hair and a full beard; the other was sunburned, his cheeks even redder than his hair. The redhead's eyes widened when he saw me.

He asked something in Dansiian as the black sorcerer pushed me toward the door.

The black sorcerer snapped back at him, and the redhead's gaze immediately dropped to the ground as he turned and shoved a key into the lock. The door swung open silently.

"After you," the sorcerer whispered near my ear. I forced my chin up, suppressing a shiver of fear, and marched forward to whatever fate awaited me.

❧ FIFTEEN ❧

THE SORCERER YANKED me toward a dimly lit hallway, two small gas lamps offering a meager glow to illuminate the barren interior of the building. There was no furniture, no decoration of any kind. We passed room after empty, windowless room. My skin began to crawl the farther in we went, a strange foreboding rushing over me.

At the end of the hallway was a staircase that plunged steeply down into a pit of impenetrable darkness. The man's fingers tightened cruelly on my bicep as he shoved me forward, into the unknown. Down, down, down; the stairs seemed endless. The darkness grew thicker and thicker the farther we went, until I was afraid I was going to suffocate. There was only the sound of my harsh breathing and our boots slapping the stones. The dank smell of earth filled my nose.

When the stairs finally levelled out, I stumbled forward, unable to see the ground in the unending blackness. The sorcerer pulled me to a stop and we waited for a moment, until the sounds of more feet tromping down the stairs behind us grew closer and closer.

He said something in Dansiian, and another voice responded. I could barely make out the outline of their bodies as my eyes sought for any hint of light by which to see.

"Alexa?" Eljin's voice came from only a few feet away, but before I could respond there was a dull thud and he grunted.

"No talking," one of the other sorcerers snapped in his thick Dansiian accent.

A sudden flare of light made me jump back. The sorcerer who still gripped my arm held his other hand out in front of him — the one in the jeweled glove — and had conjured a small flame.

"Go," the sorcerer said, releasing my arm and pushing me toward the darkness that pulsated outside the scant circle of light from the flames he wielded.

I clenched my hands into fists. My skin was slick with sweat as I forced myself to step forward. Perhaps, I could take him by surprise and kill him. But then Eljin would die. That was why they'd brought him — to threaten me if I changed my mind about turning myself in. And though Eljin, too, was a sorcerer, he was no match for the two black sorcerers who still stood on either side of him. I had no choice but to continue to place one foot in front of the other.

We walked silently through the tunnel for what felt like hours. We passed staircases multiple times, but our captors didn't stop. The air was damp, chilling me to the bone as we trudged forward. The dirt walls seemed to press in on us, closer and closer, as the time went on without any sign of a break.

"Are you taking us to the king?" I finally asked when I couldn't stand it any longer.

The sorcerer grabbed my arm, yanking me toward him, his fingernails clawing into my bicep. "No talking," he repeated through gritted teeth. His eyes flashed in the light of the flame he still wielded, and I nodded, forcing down the urge to attack him, burying it beneath the careful facade of pliancy I was trying to convey.

One of the other sorcerers said something to him in their language, and he nodded.

Eljin's gaze met mine, and the bleakness of his expression spoke more than anything he could have said to me. He didn't think we were going to make it out of this alive.

He was probably right.

When the sorcerers finally let us stop, across from yet another staircase, my legs burned and my breathing was harsh from the panic I struggled to keep at bay. Every hour the tunnel seemed smaller and narrower. The earth and ever-present blackness pressed in on me, filling my mind with visions of being buried alive.

"You will sleep here." The sorcerer led us to a door across from the staircase and opened it to reveal a tiny room of sorts, nothing more than a square carved out of the earth, barely big enough for both Eljin and me to lie down side by side.

He suddenly shoved me in the spine, sending me sprawling to the ground. Eljin was next, yanked forward and then pushed past the sorcerers. Though he stumbled, he managed to stay on his feet. The door shut behind him, enclosing us in complete darkness. We both heard the click of the lock.

"You'd better take advantage of the chance to rest. It will be your last for a long time." The sorcerer's voice was muffled by the door. And then there was nothing.

I curled into a ball, my eyes squeezed shut, telling myself I was all right, that I was lying on my bed, that I was in a big, spacious room with windows and moonlight. But no matter how hard I tried, my breathing wouldn't slow and my hands grew clammy.

"Alexa?" Eljin's whisper startled me. I'd almost forgotten he was there.

I heard him move, and then his hand brushed against my shoulder.

"Just breathe. In and out. Focus on your breath." He stretched out beside me on the ground, his hand still on my shoulder, connecting me to him — to something other than my absurd fear. "I've seen others with this same problem. It helps to turn inward." His voice was low, soothing. "Visualize somewhere calming and just breathe."

I did as he suggested, picturing myself standing in the courtyard of the palace, Damian by my side, the open sky above us. I inhaled slowly and exhaled. *Inhale. Exhale. In. Out.* Eljin pulled his hand away, and my eyes flew open at the loss of his touch; I immediately tensed and completely lost the image of Damian.

"Just breathe," he reminded me, but I couldn't. My lungs rose and fell sharply as the panic surged back in. "Here, does this help?" he asked, reaching for my hand and holding it in his. I curled my fingers around his, clutching him tightly.

"Yes," I whispered, ashamed at my irrational weakness.

We were silent for a long moment as I struggled to calm my breathing again. I rolled onto my back, so that we lay side by side in the darkness.

"It's all right to be afraid," he said quietly. "It doesn't mean you're weak."

I shook my head, angry at myself for getting us into this position — for being afraid of this dark, small place deep beneath the earth. Neither of us voiced the bigger fears: Where were they taking us? And what would happen when we got there?

"Did I ever tell you about the time my father taught me how to ride a horse?"

"No."

"As a child, I was actually quite terrified of them."

"Of *horses*?" I asked in surprise. He'd seemed so confident and comfortable when the innkeeper's son had brought Mira and Gusto for us. A pang of guilt and worry sprang up at the thought of our horses — I wondered what had happened to them.

"Yes." He chuckled softly. "I always had an excuse or pretended to be sick when he'd tell me it was time to learn to ride. Finally, one day when I was eight, he grabbed me by the arm and practically dragged me to the stable. He already had a horse saddled and waiting for me, a small black gelding."

As he spoke about getting bucked off and his father forcing him to climb back on and try again, his words slid past the knot of tension that coiled through my chest, gradually loosening it, until I was able to breathe slowly once more. My fingers relaxed in his as he told me about the rolling hills near his home and how he eventually worked through his fear and actually grew to love riding. As he described the freedom he'd felt as he'd galloped through the wild lands of Blevon, I pictured myself on Mira's back again, the wind in my hair as she flew across the ground. Nothing but the sky above us. I hadn't even realized my fear had slipped away entirely until my exhaustion overtook me, and I slowly drifted to sleep to the cadence of Eljin's stories.

⤙ SIXTEEN ⤚

WHEN THE DOOR opened, jerking us both awake, I jumped to my feet, even though my body begged for more rest. How long had it been since I'd had a full night's rest? I couldn't even remember any longer.

"Come," the sorcerer said, but his voice sounded different. It was hard to tell with the dark robes and the hoods pulled up over their heads, but I was fairly certain he was not the same sorcerer who had brought us to this room.

I walked out into the dank tunnel first and was surprised to see five men standing there instead of three, two of them holding lit torches.

"You will do exactly as we tell you, and your friend will live."

I nodded as Eljin followed me out into the tunnel, his eyes widening slightly at the number of men waiting for us.

"Walk," the Dansiian sorcerer said, pointing down the tunnel.

"Of course," I muttered, realizing that my hope of being led up the stairs and into the light had been in vain. I glanced ruefully at the stone steps that would take us away from the darkness as we filed past them.

One of the men with the torches marched in front of me this time, which was a slight improvement, as I could at least see a little bit farther ahead of us, instead of being forced to step continuously in the blackness.

We walked in silence for hours, only stopping once at another small room where there was a pot we all had to use to relieve ourselves. Eljin and I had to wait and go last. The smell nearly gagged me when it was my turn. My stomach heaved, threatening to make me vomit, as I did my best to crouch over the pot. But because my belly was completely empty, there was nothing to come up anyway.

The sorcerers replaced their torches with new ones that were piled inside the small room, and then we continued on.

"Faster," the one behind me barked after we'd walked for at least another hour. My legs ached, and my stomach burned with hunger. Weakness wormed through my body, driven by starvation, thirst, and lack of sleep.

"We need food, or at least something to drink." Eljin spoke up for the first time.

"If you want to eat, walk faster," the sorcerer repeated sharply.

I pushed myself to move as quickly as I could, but I knew I was getting slower and slower as they continued to march us through the never-ending tunnel. I despised feeling so weak, but without food or water, my body wouldn't allow me to move any more quickly. I didn't understand why they were forcing us through this underground pathway, why they weren't feeding us or giving us water, when I knew the king wanted me alive for some reason. Where were they taking us — and why did we have to go this way?

Finally, after yet another hour or two, the man who seemed to be in charge let us stop. He again put us in a small room, but this time he said, "Sit here to rest for a moment. But do not sleep."

The door shut, leaving us in the darkness once more. I slid down the wall, until I sat on the floor, my feet straight out in front of me, my head leaning back to rest against the dirt.

"Why are they doing this? Why are they forcing us to go through this tunnel?" I asked after a long moment of strained silence. I couldn't see Eljin; I couldn't see anything. Not even my own hands or legs.

"I don't know." Eljin's voice came from my left side, and I turned my head toward him, even though it didn't make a difference.

We were silent for another minute, and then I quietly said, "I'm sorry."

He didn't respond right away, and I could picture the anger and frustration that was probably on his face. When he finally spoke, the kindness and pity in his voice took me by surprise. "It was the only way we would have made it into Dansii alive. You did what you had to do."

Before I could respond, the door opened and the torchlight outside the room revealed one of the hooded men walking toward us, holding a flagon in one hand and a small bag in the other.

"You must share." He tossed the bags at us and then turned and walked out again. Just before the door shut, I scrambled forward to grab the items.

I fumbled to open the bag in the darkness.

"What is it?" Eljin asked.

I finally got it open and reached in to pull out what felt like a single hard roll and a small chunk of something softer. When I lifted it to my nose, the aroma made my stomach cramp. "It's a roll and a little bit of cheese."

"That's all?"

I didn't respond, my fingers clutched around the food. Even if I was able to eat the whole amount, it wasn't nearly enough.

"You eat it," Eljin said quietly.

"All of it?" I asked incredulously. "You can't mean that."

"It's hardly anything. You have to stay alive — you have to save Rylan and get back to Damian. If I die, they won't be able to use me to control you any longer. I'm not nearly as important —"

"Stop it," I broke in. "Here's your half. I'm not going to let you starve."

I'd already torn the roll apart, and I stretched my hand out in the darkness, hoping he'd come forward and take it from me. There was nothing but silence for a long moment, but then I heard him moving across the small space toward me. When his fingers brushed mine, I pressed the piece of roll into his hand. Then I broke the cheese apart and gave him part of it as well.

"Thank you," he muttered.

"You have to get back to Tanoori. And we still have to rescue your father. You have just as many reasons to live as I do."

We fell quiet after that, hurrying to eat our paltry meal. Before we'd had a chance to finish and drink the water, the door opened.

"Stand up. It's time to leave," the hooded man commanded.

I grabbed the flagon as I stood up, unstopping it and swallowing the last bit of cheese whole, then took a large gulp of the water and tossed it to Eljin, who did the same.

The man stepped toward us and yanked the flagon out of Eljin's hand.

"That's enough. Go." He shoved Eljin in the back, sending him stumbling toward me.

They marched us through the darkness until our legs practically gave out and then shut us in a room to rest for a couple of hours once more. The same cycle repeated for what felt like days, until I couldn't stop the continuous trembling in my hands, from hunger and unrelenting panic. I began to believe I'd never see the sun or sky again. The only change was the hooded men who guarded us. Every so often, they would switch. I couldn't believe they were *all* black sorcerers. If they were, Damian's fears that we would never survive an attack from Dansii were even more accurate than we'd believed.

Finally, when I was certain I was going to lose my mind completely or collapse on the ground and die from starvation and exhaustion, we stopped by yet another winding set of stairs.

"Up," the sorcerer next to me said, grabbing my arm and yanking me toward the stone steps.

"Up?" I repeated in disbelief.

He didn't respond except to jerk me forward, making my shoulder pop. I didn't ask again, hurrying up the stairs as quickly as I could. My heart thumped harder and harder against my lungs the higher we got, as the smell of earth and the constant, oppressive darkness began to lift. When we reached the top stair, a massive wooden door blocked our exit. The sorcerer beside me pulled a ring of keys out of his robes and pushed one into the lock. With a click, it released and the door swung open.

Two more men in dark robes, their hoods pulled up, stood past the door, blocking the way. The sorcerer next to me said something in Dansiian, and the two guards stepped aside to let us through. Eljin and the other men were right behind me as we moved forward into a hallway lined with doors.

There were no windows, but torches were propped in brackets in evenly spaced intervals. Even though I knew whatever lay ahead couldn't be good, my legs went weak with relief — I could see more than a body's length ahead of myself. I was no longer surrounded by damp earth.

Another sorcerer came up on my other side, and then each of them grabbed one of my arms, as if they were afraid I was going to fight back now, after remaining so compliant the entire time. Their fingers dug into my muscle and bone as they dragged me down the hallway. I heard people behind the doors; the muffled sound of someone sobbing in one, and a strange scratching noise in another. Almost as if the occupant was scraping stone on stone. Who were they? And where were we?

My momentary relief was extinguished when we turned a corner to a smaller, darker hallway with only two doors, rather than continuing forward to the staircase at the end of the bigger corridor. The doors were guarded by two massive men who held curved swords in their hands.

The larger of the two, who had to be at least a head and a half taller than me, barked something at us in Dansiian, but the sorcerer responded calmly. Whatever he said was effective, because both of the guards straightened and quickly moved toward the door on the right, one of them unlocking it and pulling it open.

"Who is it?" someone inside asked in Antionese — a voice I'd begun to worry I'd never hear again.

My heart constricted as I strained forward against the men who still held my arms, desperate to see in.

"You will wait here until the king decides what he wants to do with you," the sorcerer on my left told me, and then he shoved me toward the cell. I stumbled through the doorway, then slammed to a halt when I saw him lying on a cot below a tiny barred window, his injured leg wrapped in dirt-encrusted, bloody bandages, thinner than I'd ever seen him, a beard darkening his jaw.

"*Alexa?*" He stared up at me, his familiar brown eyes darker than normal in the dim light provided by a small lantern that was the only illumination in the cell.

"Rylan," I choked out.

I rushed to his side just as the door behind me slammed shut.

ᚱ SEVENTEEN ᚱ

"W HAT ARE YOU *doing* here?" he marveled as he forced himself to sit up so he was able to wrap his arms around me.

I couldn't respond past the tears that choked me. "You're alive," I finally managed to say. "You're *alive*."

Rylan had always been so strong, it made me cry even harder to feel how much weight he'd lost during his weeks of captivity, as I sat beside him and slipped my arms around his back, pressing my head to his shoulder. His arms tightened around me.

"More or less," he finally responded. "But why are you here? I told him you'd never come — that he was wasting his time."

I pulled back to look into his eyes. "Rafe sent me a note telling me he would kill you if I didn't come alone. I couldn't let him do that."

Rylan reached up hesitantly to wipe the wetness from my cheeks. "So you followed us to Dansii? By yourself?"

With a jolt, I realized, in my shock at hearing Rylan's voice, I'd forgotten about Eljin. I jumped to my feet and rushed to the door, banging my fist on it. "Where is he? What did you do with Eljin?" I shouted through the wood, but no one responded.

"*Eljin* is here, too?" Rylan asked behind me, his voice heavy with disbelief.

"Where is he?" I pounded against the wood until my knuckles felt raw, but if the guards were still out there, they ignored me.

The cot creaked, and I turned around to see Rylan trying to stand up. He half hopped, half limped toward me, hardly able to put any weight on his leg — the one I'd sliced with my sword before leaving him behind with Rafe. He noticed me staring at the bloody bandages and halted, his gaze dropping to the ground.

"Why would Eljin come with you?" he asked, not lifting his eyes.

"Damian convinced him to." I leaned back against the door, my head aching. My body felt heavy, weighted down by all the mistakes I'd made. Eljin had risked himself to come on this ill-fated rescue attempt, and now he was gone. He'd told me that his father was just one man, that it was not worth leaving Damian to go after him. But that's exactly what I'd done. I'd left my king and my kingdom to go after one man, dragging Eljin with me, and now we were all captured. "He didn't want me to go, but Damian knew I wouldn't let Rafe kill you. So he asked Eljin to come with me, to help me rescue you."

"You shouldn't have come." Rylan finally looked up at me, and I was surprised to see anger in his eyes. "Damian needed you — *Antion* needed you. And you left him weakened in order to come save me. *One* person."

His harsh words made me flinch. "It's *my* fault you're hurt. I would never have been able to live with myself if I left you to die without even trying —"

"You should have!" he burst out.

I blinked in shock, his words hitting as though he'd physically punched me.

"You should have stayed with the king. If you had any idea what they're planning — what they're going to do —"

Before I could ask him what he meant, a key scraped in the lock behind me. I hurried to straighten and turn, just as the door swung open.

"Well, what a lovely surprise."

Fury coiled in my belly and I leaped forward, lifting my fist to attack the man who stood in the doorway, but the moment I did, my anger drained away, leaving me confused as my hand dropped to my side again.

He barked out a laugh, a horrible, burning sound that I'd hoped never to hear again.

"It's so good to see you again as well, Alexa." Rafe grinned at me.

⊰ EIGHTEEN ⊱

RAFE WALKED INTO the cell, and the door shut behind him once more. "Did you enjoy your reunion?" He glanced at Rylan, who sat down on the cot again, one hand on his injured leg, gripping it.

"You promised to heal him," I bit out.

"He's not dead, so you should be thanking me for that." Rafe turned on me, his unnaturally green eyes narrowing. I quickly looked away, refusing to give him the chance to give me any more commands that I would have no choice but to obey. "He didn't think you'd come. But I knew better. I'd already learned just how far you were willing to go to protect someone you cared about — someone you *loved*." He sneered on the last word.

"She doesn't love me," Rylan muttered.

"I beg to differ," Rafe said. "She's here, isn't she? She risked her king to come for *you*."

I glanced over to see Rafe reach up and stroke his chin.

"What a difficult decision that must have been. Stay and protect the king who you managed to rescue from my sister's control or come after the man you nearly killed in your effort to escape me."

Despite my best intentions, my gaze snapped to his at his words. He knew about what had happened to Vera — he knew that she was —

Before I could even finish my thought, he'd lunged at me, grabbed my arm, and yanked me toward him. I struggled, twisting to free my arm so I could throw him to the ground — he wasn't much bigger than me, and not nearly as well trained in hand-to-hand combat — but a confused haze settled over my mind, and I went still.

"This is for my sister," he hissed into my ear, and then fire exploded in my side. An involuntary scream wrenched through my lips as I staggered back. He clutched a bloodied dagger in his hands, his eyes flashing in the dimness.

"Alexa!" I heard Rylan's shout through a strange roar in my ears as I lifted one hand to my side and it came away coated in blood. *My* blood. Warmth coated my hip, running down my leg. Pain pulsed through my body with each throbbing beat of my heart. A terrible spreading weakness stole my ability to stand, and I dropped to my knees on the ground.

Dimly, I heard the door open and Rafe's voice again. "Get that healer down here. Tell him to do only enough to keep her alive."

And then Rylan was there, kneeling next to me, catching me just as I swayed and crumpled the rest of the way to the ground.

"Alexa," he whispered, his hands on my face, stroking my hair back. I could feel how they trembled, I could hear the panic in his voice. "Don't you dare die. Hold on, Alex. Hold on."

He pushed something against the open wound where Rafe had stabbed me, trying to stanch the blood. My eyelids fluttered shut, and though I tried to open them again, the agony in my side took hold of me and dragged me under.

When I woke again, I was lying on a cot, staring up at an unfamiliar ceiling. I turned my head, but it was too dark to make out many details other than the fact that I was alone in a barren room. My body ached, and the place where Rafe had stabbed me still throbbed with pain. I tried to sit up, but my head swam and my stomach lurched sickeningly, threatening to make me vomit. I lay still for a few long minutes, waiting for the nausea to pass. My head felt heavy, my mind sluggish and fuzzy. Had they drugged me?

Afraid to move too much, I hesitantly lifted my hand to my belly. I found the tear in my tunic where Rafe's dagger had penetrated, but when I pushed my fingers through it, rather than my own skin, I felt the rough fabric of a bandage across the wound. His parting words came back to me then — "only enough to keep her alive" — and I wondered what exactly that had meant.

Tears threatened to surface, but I clenched my teeth and forced them back down. I refused to give them the satisfaction of coming in and finding me crying — whoever it was who would be sure to check on me sometime soon. I had to *think*. There had to be some way to get out of this. I was unable to hurt Rafe, and Rylan was also under his control . . . but Eljin wasn't. If I could somehow find him, or get a message to him. He could cause an earthquake, and then conceal himself and come get me —

The door opened, and I turned to see an unfamiliar man walk in. He wore clothing similar to what Vera's men had been dressed in when she'd come to Damian's palace — a long tunic with loose pants beneath it, in a light, airy fabric, with a sash across his chest. His sash was a deep, rich blue, and the fabric he wore was white. But when my gaze traveled to his face, I had to suck in a gasp of surprise. He had olive skin, and dark eyes with the slight tilt at the corner. He was Blevonese.

"Here," he said in my language, but his voice held a strange combination of a Blevonese and Dansiian accent. "Drink this."

He came over to help me sit up. My head swam again, and my stomach rebelled once more at the movement. My body convulsed as I tried to hold back the urge to vomit, but the man pressed the cup to my lips anyway.

"Force yourself to drink this; it will help. I promise."

I was barely able to do as he asked, but the moment I swallowed the liquid that tasted faintly of herbs and lemon and it hit my mutinous belly, it was as he promised — the nausea abated slightly. I took another sip and then asked, "Who are you?" My voice was scratchy from disuse, and my throat felt strangely raw.

His dark eyes met mine, but he didn't answer right away. Instead, he helped me finish the drink and then had me lay back down. He couldn't have been that much older than me, I realized, now that I got a good look at him. Maybe closer to Damian's age, in his mid-twenties. "I'm a servant in the king's household — his head healer."

"Is that where I am?" I asked.

Again, he didn't answer me right away. Instead, he raised my tunic and examined the bandage on my stomach, lifting one corner to glance at my wound.

"You are to go before him tomorrow, and it is my job to make sure you are able to do that." He pushed the bandage back down again, sending a surge of pain through my abdomen.

"Why don't you heal me completely, then?" He had to be a sorcerer, I realized, like Lisbet. But why would a sorcerer from

Blevon be working for King Armando — and have a bit of a Dansiian accent?

"I was instructed to only heal you enough so that you could stand on your own two feet before the king. Nothing more." He stood up and turned to leave.

"Wait!" I cried out, desperate to find out more, to not be left alone. "What's your name?"

He paused by the door. "Akio," he said quietly.

Then he left.

I lay there for what felt like hours, drifting in and out of sleep, trying not to let my mind wander. I couldn't afford to wonder about Rylan, or Eljin, or what the king would do to me when I was brought before him. And I especially couldn't afford to think about Damian. To wonder what he was doing — if he was safe. Had Armando begun to openly fight against Antion yet? Or was he still letting Blevon and Antion fight each other for now?

Twice, I tried to get up, to try and figure out some way to escape, but both times, my head spun, and I nearly lost consciousness. Apparently, whatever Akio had given me was just enough to hold the nausea back, but not enough to give me the strength to stand. Not yet. Not until they needed me to.

Helplessness assailed me — a feeling I was unused to and immediately hated. Unable to do anything except stare at the ceiling wondering what fate awaited me, I plotted instead, imagining ways that I could somehow get to King Armando when they brought me before him, and kill him. Rafe had commanded me to protect him; he'd made it so I could never harm him. But he'd given me no such command for the king. If I even got within twenty feet of him, somehow, I'd find a way to make sure Armando was as good as dead.

127

⇥ NINETEEN ⇤

THERE WERE NO windows in my cell, but I assumed it was
morning when the door opened again and Akio walked back
in, followed this time by two armed guards wearing all black
beneath their blue sashes, curved swords hanging at their sides.
The one man's biceps were bigger than my legs — put together.
Perhaps King Armando believed brute size and force would intim-
idate me.

He was wrong. He didn't realize I'd trained for years with
Deron, a man just as big as the guard who came over and grabbed
my arm, yanking me up in bed. And not only had I trained with
Deron, I'd beaten him.

But in my current state, I was no match for even someone
my own size. As the guard dragged me to my feet and the room
began to spin, my legs threatened to give out on me. The other
guard came over and roughly pulled my arms behind my back,
tying my hands together. I flexed my wrists, hoping to keep the
bindings from going too tight, but then my stomach lurched,
and I lost focus on my hands as I fought to keep from vomiting
again.

Akio stepped forward, lifting another cup to my lips. "Drink,"
was all he said.

I obeyed, hoping it would settle my stomach and perhaps control the dizziness that assailed me as I swayed on my feet before the sorcerer.

"Better?" he asked when I'd swallowed the last drop of liquid.

"Yes." I nodded, and it was true. The room had finally settled into one place and I was able to stand without leaning on the guard's arm. But the pain in my side was worse now, pulsing with each beat of my heart. I didn't think it was bleeding, but I could tell if I moved too quickly, it would tear wide open. My hands were secured behind my back without even an inch of wiggle room in the bindings.

"Good. Let's go." Akio turned and led the way out of the cell. We were in a different hallway than the one we'd originally come through with the black sorcerers. My hopes of seeing or even hearing Rylan or Eljin on my way to the king died as quickly as they'd risen.

Akio said something to the guards in Dansiian, and they each grabbed one of my arms and began to pull me forward.

"Why did they bring me here through those tunnels?" I asked as we marched down the hallway, past a few other doors, and then turned to our right, heading for a staircase.

Akio ignored me as we began to climb the stairs. The pain grew worse, but I forced myself to ignore it, to stand tall and walk as quickly as possible next to the guards' long strides.

"Tell me why they forced us through the dark for days. Why not just bring us to your king directly — why not stay above the ground?" I pressed, hoping to annoy an answer or a response of any sort out of Akio.

When we came to the top of the stairs, I had to keep my jaw

from falling open as we stepped into an opulent hallway lined with windows. Sunlight streamed in through the stained glass, creating a tapestry of color and light that nearly blinded me after so long in the dark. I couldn't contain a shiver of dread for whatever awaited me in this lavish place — where the sand-colored stone floor was covered by thick, hand-cut carpets, and the side tables were adorned with priceless sculptures and vases. The palace in Antion was beautiful, but this palace made Damian's seem like it was nothing more than a home in my tiny village at the edge of the jungle.

"To keep you alive." Akio finally spoke, pulling me out of my shock, finally answering my question about the tunnels.

I couldn't keep myself from laughing. "You expect me to believe I was dragged through an underground prison for days, and practically starved, to keep me *alive*?"

Akio stopped, and the guards beside me halted as well. He spun to face me, his dark eyes unreadable. "Yes. It was to protect you. When word spread that you had been captured and were being taken to the king, there would have been any number of threats that could have meant your death on the journey to King Armando's palace if you'd been out in the open. The tunnels are only known and traveled by his most trusted sorcerers and guardians. It was to keep you safe."

I stared at him unflinchingly, sure he could read the hatred on my face. "I find that I don't really care for the Dansiian definition of *safe*," I said evenly.

A muscle in his jaw ticked, but he turned without another word and marched forward again, leading us through lavish hallway after lavish hallway. We went out an ornate iron door into a courtyard where I got a brief glimpse of the exterior of the palace — an immense, three-story monstrosity that was all glass and pale stone, with towers that jutted into the heavens. The sun hung in the cloudless expanse of sky, a massive, relentless orb of light, beating down on the dry, plantless ground. I was pretty sure the guards purposely slowed down to make sure my bare feet got burned by the hot sand as long as possible before we went back into the palace again through another door.

I was surprised that they let me walk across the plush carpets and pristinely cleaned floor with my dirty feet as they pulled me down another hallway, toward two massive, ornately carved wooden doors. I took extra care to make sure and grind the dirt into the carpet as I walked.

Outside the doors stood four men, two on each side. They all wore the same dark cloaks with the hoods pulled up as the black sorcerers by the gate between Antion and Dansii. Fear crawled over my skin as we got closer and their heads all lifted simultaneously to stare at us. I could barely see their faces, their shadowy features obscured by the dark confines of the hoods they wore.

Akio stopped a few feet away from the doors, and the guards on either side of me halted as well, jerking me to a stop.

"I, Akio, high healer for the kingdom of Dansii, seek audience with the king, as commanded by His Royal Majesty, to bring the prisoner Alexa Hollen before his throne." Akio knelt down on the ground, bending his head, and the guards each grabbed one of my shoulders and shoved me to the ground as well. But I refused to lower my head, keeping my chin lifted instead, glaring forward at the black sorcerers. They could injure me, weaken me with drugs, make me kneel — but they couldn't force my will to bend to theirs.

"You may enter, sorcerer," one of the robed men intoned, his voice a low hiss.

Akio quickly stood as two of the robed men turned and opened the doors, which gave a low groan. My guards yanked me back to my feet, pulling at my wound. A sharp blast of pain lanced through me, but I forced my face to remain impassive. I refused to let them see that they had hurt me.

We walked past the huge doors and the black sorcerers into the largest room I'd ever seen. The entire wall across from us was made of floor-to-ceiling windows, soaring at least three stories above us. The floor was pure white marble that glistened with flecks of gold in the sunlight.

"So, this is the girl who is causing me all this trouble?" A deep voice came from my right, speaking in Antionese.

My guards spun me to see a man stepping down from a massive golden throne and striding toward us. The sunlight glinted off the golden crown nestled in his graying hair. "She seems rather . . . pathetic."

My breath caught in my throat and ice filled my veins. I struggled against my bindings; every instinct inside of me screamed to shoot an arrow through this man's heart or embed a sword through his gut. I knew exactly who he was, because he looked just like his brother, only taller and stronger, his eyes the same blue as Hector's, the same blue as his nephew's. But there was nothing I could do. My hands were tied; I was surrounded by sorcerers.

"Your Majesty," Akio murmured, lowering his head. He and my guards all dropped to their knees, yanking me down with them. But again, I kept my chin lifted, hatred burning through me as Armando, the king of Dansii, approached us.

❧ TWENTY ❧

K ING ARMANDO STOPPED a few feet away from me, his eyes
narrowing when his gaze moved over my scars. His scrutiny
sent a chill scraping down my spine. There was something about
the coldness of his eyes that made my muscles quiver with the need
to turn and run away. He was dressed completely in black, except
for a blood-red sash, trimmed with the same blue the rest of his
men wore, across his chest. He had a perfectly groomed beard that
he reached up to stroke as his gaze flickered down my body, then
back up again.

"Rise," he said curtly, and Akio hurriedly jumped up. My
guards pulled me to my feet, and though I tried to hide it, I was
unable to keep from wincing at the pain that shot through me yet
again.

King Armando's expression darkened. "Why is she injured?"
he asked, continuing to speak in Antionese. Though his voice was
calm, my guards flinched, their heads dropping lower. "You."
King Armando pulled the sword that hung at his side out and
pointed it at one of the guards next to me — the smaller one,
though he was still a good head taller than me. "Answer me
immediately."

He responded in Dansiian, but King Armando shook his head.

133

"In her language." He glanced at me again, his eyes flashing. "All of my sorcerers and guards have been taught Antionese and Blevonese, so that when we rule over all three kingdoms, my men will be able to communicate with even the lowest heathen in our command." He turned back to the guard and snarled, "So you will speak in Antionese right now because I want her to understand *everything* that happens this day."

"We were instructed to bring her to you exactly as she came to us," the man repeated in Antionese this time, his accent so heavy I could barely understand his response. "I don't know why she is injured."

"I ordered her to remain alive. I need her to be *healthy.*" The king's face remained completely placid, but in one swift movement, he swiped the blade he held up and across the man's throat. With a horrible gurgling cry, his hand released from my arm, and he collapsed to the ground. His body convulsed as the blood pooled around him, staining the beautiful marble and turning the sunlight on the floor to crimson.

The king turned to Akio and lifted the sword until it rested below his chin. Akio trembled as Armando leaned toward him.

"Perhaps *you* might be willing to explain to me why she is injured?"

Akio stood stiffly, the point of the sword pressing into his skin. "Rafe is the one who stabbed her, Your Majesty. I was ordered to heal her just enough so that she could stand before you, but no more."

King Armando stared at him silently for a long moment as if considering. Then finally, he let the sword drop to his side. "I see." He snapped his fingers, and three servants rushed forward from where they'd been standing against the wall to my right, unnoticed until now.

King Armando tossed his sword at one, who barely managed to catch it before it struck the floor. "Have that cleaned. And you two, deal with this mess." He gestured to the now-dead man on the ground.

"Yes, Your Majesty," the three servants responded, keeping their gazes trained on the floor and rushing forward to do his bidding.

"Fear," King Armando said, his eyes on me again. "It's a marvelous thing, isn't it?" He smiled, a terrifying upturn of his lips that reminded me so much of his brother, King Hector, that my stomach tightened with anxiety. "My father taught me from a very young age just how powerful it truly was."

He turned and began to walk toward his throne. Akio glanced back at my remaining guard, and then they hurried to pull me forward, following the king, leaving the servants and the body behind us.

"Do you know what my first lesson as a child destined for the throne of Dansii was?" King Armando continued to speak as we crossed the grand hall to stand below the throne of which he spoke, where he turned and sat down, his cold eyes trained on mine once more. He was silent, waiting for me to respond.

My guard dug a sharp elbow into my ribs, and I gasped, "No," through the sudden piercing pain.

"I was six, and Hector was four. You remember my brother, Hector? The man you and my nephew murdered?" King Armando watched me intently as he spoke, his eyes on my scars again, his expression indecipherable.

I was completely in his power. Weaponless, defenseless. But I refused to let him scare me. Part of me was glad my hands were tied behind my back — he couldn't see how they shook when I said, "I will gladly take responsibility for killing that snake you sent into our midst. But I'm not the one who drove the sword through your brother's heart."

The king lifted one eyebrow.

"I only wish it *would* have been me," I finished.

His eyes narrowed, and he burst out, "I spent my lifetime protecting him!" Sudden rage darkened his face. "My father ruled over us all with blood and horror, and I hated him for it. But in the end, we learned what he intended for us to know — we learned what it means to be a true leader. We learned that threats are only as powerful as your ability to follow through on them."

Akio squeezed my arm once, twice. A warning of some sort?

"Eventually, I grew strong enough to make good on *my* threats to *him*. In the end, *I* was the stronger king." King Armando took a deep breath and the anger slid away, replaced by the mask of emotionless disinterest he'd worn before I incited his outburst. His rapid mood changes were more frightening than King Hector's consistent derision and cruelty. This man was truly mad.

I wondered what his words meant — his threats against his father? All I'd ever heard was that King Alonz had died of old age shortly after his sons invaded Antion, leaving the throne of Dansii to Armando, who then crowned his brother, Hector, king of Antion. Was there more to the previous king's death than mere age?

"But let us speak of the future, not the past." King Armando leaned forward. "After all this time, I finally have you here before me. The key to my success."

I shook my head. "I don't know what you're talking about."

"Of course you don't. You're a mere pawn in a game you've never truly understood. But now you are *my* pawn."

"I will never be anyone's pawn."

Akio squeezed my arm again, even harder this time, but Armando took us all by surprise by throwing his head back and laughing. "You have spirit. I like that." He stood up and walked down the stairs to stand directly in front of me. He was only a few inches taller than me, so our eyes were almost on the same level. I stiffened when he lifted one hand to grab my chin and jerked my face toward his; he stroked one finger along my striated skin as if relishing my disfigurement. His hot breath blew into my face when he said, "I will show you why you *are* my pawn. And before I'm done, you will willingly offer yourself as a sacrifice to my purpose."

"Never," I said, my voice low and furious, even though his nails still dug into my jaw.

Before he could respond, the doors opened again, and he looked beyond me. His hand dropped from my face, and he strode past me toward whoever had entered the room.

"Your Majesty," a voice that sent a flash of loathing through me began, "I was told that she merely needed to be alive. I would have never —"

"*Silence!*" King Armando roared, and Rafe cut himself off. "You serve me, not the other way around."

I craned my neck to look over my shoulder and saw Rafe cowering before the king, on one knee, near the bloodstain that a servant still knelt beside, scrubbing vigorously. I'd seen this act before, in the kitchens at Damian's palace, when he'd pretended to

137

be a terrified taster. But I also knew the monster that hid beneath the unassuming exterior now.

"Of course, Sire. I will never forget my place again."

"No, you will not," King Armando agreed. He snapped his fingers, and again, servants rushed forward. "See to it that this man is chained and taken to The Summoner's chambers. He is to have one of his eyes removed."

"Sire, no —" Rafe burst out, but the king continued ruthlessly.

"Cross me again, and I will remove the other. You will be as powerless as a baby and just as helpless." King Armando turned on his heel and strode back toward us. Rafe knelt there, his mouth hanging open in shocked horror as the servants bowed to him and then pulled his arms behind his back, securing them in place and lifting him to his feet, all carefully avoiding his eyes.

I couldn't believe he was submitting to his punishment so easily. *Would his ability work as well with only one eye?* I wondered. Surely he would fight back, or try to convince the servants to let him go. Perhaps after they left the room. I only wished the penalty had been worse. If the king had slit Rafe's throat, I would have been free of his terrible command.

"Akio, I need her in perfect condition before we begin. I've had a room prepared. Make sure she is completely healed before I see her again. An unhealthy, unwilling solution to a problem this immense will only lead to a failed attempt at success." The king resumed his seat on his throne, spreading his arms to place his hands atop the armrests on either side of his body. He wore two massive rings, one on each hand. I suddenly wondered if he was married — if he'd ever had any children. I'd never heard anything about Damian having cousins in Dansii.

138

Akio nodded and bowed to his king, keeping one hand on my arm. "Yes, Sire. As you command."

"She will remain in chains until we are assured of her cooperation," Armando added. "But see to it that she is bathed and given clean clothes. I don't want her brought to me looking like this ever again."

"Of course, Your Majesty," Akio agreed.

"That is all. Take her away." King Armando dismissed us.

My last glimpse of King Armando showed a smile spreading across his face as he stared down at the bloodstain on his marble floor.

⫷ TWENTY-ONE ⫸

THE ROOM AKIO brought me to was more luxurious than any I'd ever slept in before, except Damian's. The bed wasn't as big as his, but the sheets were silken, sliding over my body like water when I climbed into it that night after a servant had washed my hair and helped me bathe, before dressing me in light, soft clothes that were similar to the ones I'd seen other servants wearing — a long tunic over loose pants that gathered in tightly at the ankles. If it weren't for the iron shackles on my wrists, I almost could have believed I was an esteemed guest, instead of King Armando's prisoner. For two days, Akio worked on the wound I'd been given, healing it completely. He wasn't as fast as Lisbet, but he was thorough. When he finally finished, the silver scar was so thin, I could barely see it.

I was given strange but flavorful food to eat. Flat breads that tasted of garlic, roasted poultry of some sort, a dish of thin, crisp green vegetables mixed with a tomato sauce and beef served over rice that the servant told me was called *fasolia khadra*, and even the occasional sweet roll drizzled with honey and rolled in small dried fruits. Sometimes, the spices on the meat, breads, and rice were too strong, irritating my tongue and throat. But I was too hungry to push it away. I didn't know what lay ahead, but I knew

140

I'd need my strength. Armando wanted me for some reason, though for what I couldn't imagine. If I had any hope of surviving this — of somehow finding a way to escape — I needed to be strong, not half-starved.

When I asked about my friends, about Rylan and Eljin, I was met with stony silence, making me fear the worst. Would King Armando have had them killed? My only hope was that he wished to keep them alive, at least for now, to use them against me if needed.

Though the shackles prevented me from some of my routine training, I tried to do what I could, using the weight of the iron bands to keep my arms strong as I pretended to parry unseen blows and jab an invisible sword through the hot, dry air. My room had a window, but there were bars over it. I found myself staring out of it for hours at a time, over the strange, barren landscape beyond the palace, dreaming of a different palace — a different king. The land here rolled in gentle, sandy hills in all directions. A river ran through the center of the landscape I could see; its banks were lined with verdant bushes and trees, but everywhere else was devoid of plant life. Strange animals with gangly, long legs and humps on their backs carried men in and out of the palace walls, alongside small, quick horses with flowing manes and tails.

I was told there was a city outside of the palace walls when I asked, but that it was on the other side of the building, which was why I couldn't see it from my room. I wondered what their buildings looked like, how their people lived. Did they fall asleep at night fearing death? Or did they love the ruthless man they called king — did they appreciate the violence with which he reigned over his kingdom?

Akio was a mystery to me. I asked him about his life, how he came to be here in Dansii, why he served King Armando when he was clearly Blevonese, but he refused to answer my questions, changing the subject or ignoring me altogether.

On the third morning after I was brought to the cell-in-disguise, Akio entered the room with a woman on his heels. "She is to ready you to see the king," he said before I could ask. "He has commanded you to be brought to *El Evocon* so that he might begin preparing you for your glorious purpose." His voice was toneless, but I thought I saw a flicker of something — perhaps pity — flash in his dark eyes before he gestured for the woman to come forward.

He said something to her in Dansiian, and she nodded.

"What are you going to do?" I asked, but she merely shrugged at me as she stepped forward, setting a basket of supplies down on the bed next to me.

"She doesn't speak your language," Akio said.

"Oh."

She gestured for me to turn, and I did as she asked, though I wanted nothing more than to knock her basket aside and rush out of the room. Considering my chains were connected to an anchor in the middle of the floor, it was an impossible wish.

"Who is *El Evocon*?" I asked Akio as the woman began to brush through my hair, which had grown even longer in the last few weeks, coming past my shoulders and nearly falling to my shoulder blades now.

"It means 'The Summoner' in your language," was all Akio said.

After a few minutes of pulling and twisting and jabbing, the woman decided she was done arranging my hair and came around to sit in front of me. When she started to pull some jars and smaller brushes out of her basket, I shook my head.

"No," I said, turning my face away from her. Fixing my hair was one thing; this was another. I refused to let her paint me up like some strumpet going willingly to her master.

She said something to me in rapid Dansiian, her irritation translating easily, though her words did not. Apparently, the king's command that his sorcerers and guards be taught the languages of both Antion and Blevon hadn't extended to his other servants.

"You must submit to her, or the king will have her punished," Akio warned me.

The image of Armando slitting the guard's throat without even blinking hit me in the gut, and I forced myself to face her and let her begin to apply the cosmetics. I didn't know who this woman was, but I couldn't bear it if she was harmed because I'd refused to let her line my eyes with kohl or stain my lips a darker red.

She worked quickly and soon put her supplies back in the basket and stood again.

"Come, Alexa. It's time to go." Akio bent down to the floor, using a key from a ring he'd had hidden in the folds of his tunic to unlock my chains from the floor. I dashed forward, using the momentary distraction as leverage to yank my chains free from his hands, but before I made it to the door, two men in dark robes moved to block my exit. One lifted his hand, the jewel-encrusted glove visible beneath the sleeve of his robe, and I ground to a halt.

"Please, don't make this harder on yourself than it has to be," Akio said, moving toward me, holding the end of my chains once more. "I convinced the king to only shackle your wrists. If you try to escape, he will force us to do your feet as well."

I glanced between him and the black sorcerers, and then dropped my gaze to the ground. I didn't miss the way Akio's eyes flickered over my hair, the way his cheeks grew slightly pink when he looked into my face — not the way a man looked at me in disgust because of my scars, but the way a man did when he thought someone was attractive. Could that even be possible, despite my ruined skin — that perhaps he could come to care for me a tiny bit? If so, it might be possible to use that to my advantage somehow.

"Thank you," I said quietly.

"Excuse me?" he asked in surprise.

"For convincing the king to chain only my hands. That was kind of you. And for healing me. I never told you thank you."

When I glanced up, he was eyeing me suspiciously. I couldn't play my part too heavily, or it would backfire and make him grow more wary, not less. "Are you taking me to the king now, or do I need to take myself? I'd hate for him to kill you, too, for being late."

Akio shook himself, as if realizing that very well could be his fate, and rushed toward the other sorcerers. They parted to let him through. The chain pulled out until it was taut and then yanked me forward. The two robed sorcerers flanked me on either side as we walked through the palace, down the steps into a lower level below the ground, but not toward the dungeons, which I remembered were in the other part of the palace, across the courtyard I'd been led through to meet the king the first time.

The dry heat of Dansii crept through every crevice of the palace, even this early in the morning. At night, it grew alarmingly cold. But the moment the sun rose each morning, the heat did, too, scorching the earth and sucking the moisture from the air. When I glanced down at my hands, I could see the toll the dryness was taking on my skin.

But as we descended lower into the palace, it grew cooler once more. The walls were lined with lit torches, sending firelight flickering over the back of Akio's dark head in front of me. When he finally stopped in front of a massive black door, a shiver of fear snaked down my spine. What on earth could they possibly be doing down here that would require my presence? I wondered about this man — The Summoner — trying to figure out what his name could possibly mean. I was about to find out.

Akio knocked on the door, one short rap and then three longer ones.

It cracked open, and he whispered something in Dansiian to the person on the other side.

"The king bids you enter," the person said in Antionese, and the door swung wide open.

Akio went in first, pulling my chain to force me forward. Not wanting to feel any more like an animal on a leash than necessary, I quickened my pace so that there was slack in the chain, closing the gap between me and the Blevonese sorcerer.

But the moment I walked through the doorway and saw what lay beyond it, I froze, horror clawing at my chest.

❧ TWENTY-TWO ❧

"WELCOME, ALEXA," KING Armando said, stepping forward to greet me, his mouth turning up into a pleased smile when he took in my altered appearance, his eyes raking down my body, then back up again, only pausing for a moment on my scars. "You are surprisingly stunning, I must admit. I personally find the marks of battle only enhance the beauty of the rest of your face. They are a visible testament to your strength." He stopped a mere foot away and took my hand in his, lifting it to his mouth to press a kiss to my knuckles. His touch made my skin crawl, but I forced myself to stand still, all too aware of his tendency toward violence if provoked. And even when he wasn't. "It is shocking that you passed yourself off as a boy for so long."

When I still didn't respond to his baiting, he continued.

"Tell me, what do you think?" He stepped back and spread his arms wide.

I stared at him in disbelief. Did he expect me to *praise* him? I glanced around the cavernous room, hardly able to believe what I was seeing was real. A terrible, cloying smell — like burned flesh — assailed my nose. Cots stood in rows along one wall of the room, where dozens of people lay, moaning, seemingly only half-conscious. Most of them were younger, close to my age, but a few of the women were older, with swollen bellies. Some of their heads tossed and turned, but the servants who attended to them had tied them to their beds, so that no other parts of their bodies could move. On the opposite wall of the room, tables were set up with bowls on top. Flames licked at the air above the rims of the bowls. Men in robes stood over them, holding knives to their hands, cutting themselves — or small animals — and letting the blood drip onto the fires, which explained the smell. It reminded me of the night we'd been commanded to go to Iker's room and had interrupted him in the middle of doing exactly what these sorcerers seemed to be doing — sacrificing his blood to call upon the demons who fueled his dark power, for greater strength.

And directly across from me were tables with strange instruments I'd never seen before. One robed man stood by them, but I couldn't see what he was doing, as his back was turned to us.

"This is the future, Alexa," King Armando said, taking the chain hooked to the shackles on my wrist from Akio. I had a brief, fleeting thought of leaping forward and throwing my arms over his head and choking him to death, but the sorcerers on either side of me stepped closer, grabbing my arms, as if they could hear my thoughts. "I want you to understand what I'm doing — what I'm accomplishing — so that you will willingly give yourself to me. To the *world*."

I began to protest, but Akio happened to meet my eyes just then, and he shook his head infinitesimally. Confused, I snapped my mouth shut, choosing to stay silent instead of responding.

King Armando took my silence as interest, because he continued, "Those subjects are an integral piece in my experiments — even though not all of them came willingly. Those who did offer

147

themselves up, giving themselves to me for my experiments or allowing their bodies to be conduits, so that they might give birth to an entirely new breed of sorcerers, will be rewarded richly. The others . . ." He trailed off and shrugged. "But soon, none of this will be needed any longer. Because of *you*."

"Excuse me?" My shock forced the words out.

"Your blood is the key. Your blood will assure my victory."

"My blood," I repeated in disbelief. Manu's words were beginning to make more sense — his wild outburst that it was better to take his king a vial of my blood rather than nothing at all. But *why*? What could they possibly want with it?

A tall man who wore the same black robes with the white overvest that Manu had worn walked toward us. When his gaze met mine, the strange chill I'd felt in Manu's cell enveloped me, and terror seized my body. He had the same silver eyes with abnormally large pupils that Manu had possessed, reminding me of the horrors Manu had brought to Antion. I battled to force my fear down. I couldn't think clearly if I let it take hold completely.

"This is the girl," he said in Antionese, a sickening look of hunger crossing his narrow face.

"Yes," King Armando agreed. "I will not fail, now that she is in our possession."

"I have made many advances for you, Sire. But with her, I will be able to conquer *all*." The man in the robes smiled, a terrible, chilling upturn of his lips.

Despite my best intentions, terror ran through my blood, making my hands tremble. What could they possibly be talking about?

"Tell me. Where is my brother?" the man in the robes directed his question to me, but I stayed silent. This had to be *El Evocon* that Akio had told me I was being taken to — The Summoner.

"Answer him!" King Armando roared, jerking on my chains, and I flinched.

"He's dead." Though I hadn't realized they were brothers, I knew he had to be asking about the man who had called himself *Manu de Reich os Deos.* "I killed him."

"It cannot be," the man in front of me breathed, his already-pale skin losing all color completely. The temperature dropped even more, making me shiver. "He was gifted with power nearly comparable to mine. He could not possibly have been bested by you."

"It is the fulfillment of my father's prediction," the king said, his voice tight. "She is the one no sorcerer will be able to stop. But now she is ours. She will never kill again."

Cold anger flared in the man's unnatural silver eyes. "If you will chain her over there, I will get to work immediately." He gestured to the tables where the strange instruments lay. Bottles were attached to long, thin metal tubes of some sort with sharp points. Like miniature daggers that had hollow centers. The sorcerer who had been standing next to one of the cots was now sitting on it, with one of the tubes *in* his arm. His blood ran into the bottle next to him through the instrument. Had he pushed it *into* his own vein?

And then it hit me. My blood. They wanted it for some reason. They were going to take it from my body *while I was still living.*

"No." King Armando's response took me by surprise. I tore my glance away from the sorcerer, who had reached up to pull the instrument — the strange, hollow dagger — out of his arm, to stare at the king. "She will sacrifice herself willingly. It would lessen the power of her blood if we take it forcibly."

The man in the robes glared at me greedily, his jaw clenched. But to the king he said, "Of course, Your Majesty. As you command. But if she bested my brother, who is to say that she won't be able to escape from these chains? That she won't kill everyone? Even I — the greatest of us all?" The man's eyes sent a shiver of terror creeping down my spine to lodge deep in my gut. "And don't forget, time *is* running short, my king."

"I am well aware, *Evocon*," King Armando snapped. "She won't be able to hurt any of us. She is in *my* power now. Do not forget your place — *I* am the greatest of us all. You are mine, and therefore beneath me."

"Of course, Sire," The Summoner murmured, but I didn't miss the loathing that burned in his eyes for a brief moment, making the air flare hot around us, before smoothing into a look of placid agreement once more.

The king turned to face me. "Alexa, do you understand what is happening here?"

"No," I answered, hating the way my hands still shook. I clenched them together in front of me, hoping to hide my fear. Armando thrived on it, and I couldn't let him have the satisfaction of knowing he'd succeeded in frightening me.

"I have created sorcery such as the world has never seen before. The Gods that strengthen my sorcerers have given us many gifts already — gifts that the Blevonese weren't brave enough, or strong enough, to deserve. You've already seen evidence of our blessings: Rafe and Vera, two of our successful creations."

"Your gifts come from demons, not the Gods. And Vera is dead," I said coldly. "So not very successful after all, perhaps."

"Silence," King Armando shouted, slapping me against the mouth so hard my head snapped to the side and my lip split open. I lunged forward, but the sorcerers at my side yanked me back. "You might have stopped her, you might have even stopped Iker and The Summoner's brother, but now that you are in my control, you *will* see the beauty of my power. You will sacrifice yourself to me so that I might take what is rightfully mine!" His declaration ended in a shout.

I longed to yell back at him, but my mouth still throbbed from his strike. The bitter tang of blood encouraged me to swallow my angry retort. "What is it that you want?" I asked instead.

"Everything." His voice dropped to a whisper, his eyes burning with the fire of insatiable greed. "And now that you are here, you can't take it from me. Not anymore."

"How could *I* take it from you — why do you think I am so important?"

"You are the one!" King Armando cried, grabbing my jaw, yanking my face toward him again, as he'd done the first time I'd met him. The sorcerers pulled my arms back, keeping my shackled hands pressed against my belly, not allowing me any slack with which to attack their king. "My father told me you would come. But I have made myself stronger than he ever could have dreamed possible. I have created sorcerers the likes of which this world has never witnessed. *You* won't stop me — no one can!"

The flash of madness in his blazing blue eyes frightened me more than anything else I'd seen to that point. "Your father never knew me," I said quietly, and his fingers turned into claws, digging his nails into my skin. "I'm not the one you think I am."

"Yes, you are! You *are* the one — the warrior no sorcerer can stop. He claimed you would come, that you would stop my plans. But now we will bleed out your invincibility and take it for ourselves. We will claim every ounce of your power for Dansii — for *me*." He leaned forward until his mouth was only inches from mine. I stiffened, my heart thrumming a panicked triple beat beneath my ribs. "You are mine now." He remained there, staring into my eyes, his hot breath blowing over my bloody lips for a long moment. But then, suddenly, he let me go and turned back to the room. My chest rose and fell rapidly as I tried to contain my emotions. My entire body trembled, despite my best intentions to not let him see that he'd frightened me.

"I killed him, you know," King Armando said without facing me. "He told me that I would never be a good king. He predicted that you would come — that you would stop me — so I poisoned him. Just as I *will* eventually kill you. But it will be a worthy sacrifice, Alexa. You will die to serve a greater purpose."

I knew without asking that he meant his father. He'd killed his own father. Not out of necessity, as Damian had been forced to do, but out of anger. Out of spite.

Out of greed.

And I was next — once they were done with me.

As I watched, the robed man took the bottle partially filled with crimson liquid over to one of the girls, who looked a few years younger than me. He had wrapped his arm in a cloth that was stained with his own blood. I stared at that stain as he lifted her head with one hand and pressed the bottle to the barely conscious girl's lips with the other, making her drink. Acid boiled through my stomach, threatening to rise up into my throat, as I watched her swallow his blood with her eyes only half-open, some of it dribbling out to drip down her chin. Was this how Armando had created Rafe and Vera? How Manu and the man who still watched me from across the room with the same silver eyes had been created? Or did he have other, even more terrible secrets?

"I will never submit to you," I said quietly, my voice mutinous.

Rather than yell or hit me again, as I was afraid he might do, Armando only turned and smiled. "You say that now, but then again, that's what they all say, at first," the king said. "You'll find that I am a patient man. And I have a knack for persuading people. I have spent decades creating my sorcerers, building my army. Putting events into motion that cannot be stopped. I can wait a few more days to finish what I started."

And with that, he turned his back to me again and waved his hand toward Akio. "Take her away. And only give her water for the next day and night. No food. Perhaps that will help her start to see reason."

"Of course, Your Majesty."

So much for having me in perfect health, I thought as Akio took my chain from the king and dragged me out of the horrifying room, back to my opulent prison.

⊰ TWENTY-THREE ⊱

HUNGER GNAWED AT my belly by sundown the next day, but I refused to ask for food. Instead, I stared out my window, wondering what had become of Eljin and Rylan. They had to be alive. After making it this far, I couldn't have lost them. I convinced myself that King Armando would have kept them alive to manipulate me if necessary. I couldn't bear to think of Rylan somewhere in the depths of the dungeon, his leg growing infected, his blood turning to poison in his veins, slowly killing him.

Finally, shortly after the sun dropped below the horizon, the door opened. I spun around but then quickly shrank back against my bed.

"I'm to be your escort tonight," Rafe said, striding over to where the chain was anchored to the middle of the floor, then he unlocked it and jerked me to my feet. He wore a white patch over his eye with a strip of fabric tied around it to keep it on his face. A small stain of russet was beginning to seep through the material. His empty socket must have still been weeping blood. Apparently, the king hadn't allowed Akio to heal it for him.

"What are you staring at?" he barked at me. He yanked on the chain viciously, forcing me to lunge forward after him as he dragged me out into the hallway. The ever-present hooded guards immediately flanked me, discouraging any attempt at attacking Rafe, even though every instinct in me screamed to do something. It had taken every bit of training and ability I had to defeat Iker; there was no chance of my success and survival if I tried to take on two black sorcerers and Rafe, while shackled.

And of course, there was the small matter that he'd made it so that I was unable to hurt him. I dreamed of bludgeoning him in the head with the iron bars around my wrist, but when I let the image get too solidified in my mind, a haze of confusion came over me, erasing the desire to hurt him. With a sigh I looked away from him as we rushed through the halls of the palace in the quickly dimming light of sunset. I caught a glimpse of the last dying rays of light through one of the windows we passed, a myriad of oranges and yellows that dripped into the unending expanse of pale sand on the horizon.

"Hurry up," Rafe ordered, yanking me forward once more.

"I can't believe he actually had your eye removed," I retorted. "Considering how much effort he put into creating you, it seems a waste to destroy your one power so needlessly." My wrists were raw beneath the iron shackles, and every time he jerked me forward, the shackles bit harder into my skin, threatening to tear it open.

"I still have my power." Rafe stopped and spun to face me, his expression livid. I'd never seen him so angry. "And he didn't create me. *Manu de Reich os Deos* did. He and *El Evocon*."

"It's unfortunate, then, that I killed Manu," I baited him.

He lifted a fist as if to strike me, but I didn't so much as let myself flinch, staring straight forward. "You should learn to shut your mouth. If the king hadn't ordered you to remain unharmed,

I would have already exacted my revenge on you for what you've done."

"For killing Manu? Or for helping Damian kill your sister?"

Rafe lunged toward me, but one of the men at my side snapped something in Dansiian at him and he stopped himself. "Don't push me," he warned, his voice low and furious. "Order or no order, if you dare speak of my sister again, I *will* hurt you. Slowly. And with great pleasure." Then he turned to look at the man in the hood. "Why don't you pull your hood back and face me? Look me in the eye next time you tell me what to do."

The black sorcerer merely remained silent.

"Maybe he doesn't like being threatened in Antionese," I observed.

Without another word, Rafe spun away and jerked me forward again.

We only walked a little farther, past the great hall where I'd met King Armando the first time, and turned down a hallway across from it. Rafe knocked on the door, one hard rap then two short, quieter ones. Did they each have unique knocks to alert the king to who it was he should expect on the other side?

The door opened, and a man I hadn't seen before ushered us in. He was only an inch or two taller than me and very thin, with mostly gray hair that looked like it might have once been red. But his green eyes were sharp, bright with a keen intelligence.

When he saw Rafe, his gaze flickered to the patch and then away again. "Come in. The king is waiting for you, Son."

Son? So this was his father. A duke of some sort, if I remembered what Vera had told Damian correctly. And supposedly the king's right-hand man.

"I do not like being kept waiting." King Armando's voice came from deeper in the room. Rafe led me in to stand in the center. The walls were covered in shelves. Some of them held books, but others had strange devices on them — one looked like a glove made of metal, with spikes on the knuckles. Another was a whip with barbs on the end, encased in glass. A gruesome library of torture devices and books. There was a chair in the center of the room, next to where I stood. When I looked ahead, the king stood behind a massive desk.

"Please, sit," he invited, as though I were a guest and not his prisoner.

I stubbornly remained standing. He expected me to continue to resist.

"I said, *sit*," the king repeated, this time nodding at Rafe. He yanked on the chains, making me stumble forward and hit my shins on the legs of the chair. Then he shoved my shoulders down, forcing me to sit.

"Good. That's better."

For some reason my gaze was drawn to the whip yet again. It appeared to have been used plenty; the barbs were stained a deep mahogany. The color of dried blood.

King Armando noticed me looking and gave me a tight-lipped smile. "Curious, are you? A strange item to put on display, you might think."

The duke, Rafe's father, had moved to stand beside the king, just a little bit behind him. He watched me as well. I wondered if he could control people with his eyes and words, or if only his children had that ability.

"I personally wouldn't choose to decorate with old, dirty weapons, but to each their own," I said.

"I see you noticed the blood that is still dried on it." King Armando walked over to the shelf where the whip was encased. "Hector's, to be exact. And a little of mine, as well." He put his hand on the glass, staring down at the weapon. "If you can make someone fear you, you will make that person your subject. A favorite lesson of my father's — even for his own sons. But he didn't make me fear him by hurting me; he was more cunning than that."

He paused, glancing over at me as if waiting for me to ask.

"What did he do?" I forced out, though I wasn't sure I wanted to know. I didn't want to pity this man, or Damian's father.

"If I disappointed him in some way, if I didn't meet his expectations, he didn't beat me. He made me watch while he beat Hector, *because* of me." King Armando's eyes flashed with fury. "People are often willing to suffer quite a bit themselves for their failures. But it's another thing entirely to watch someone else suffer — someone innocent — because you made a mistake."

I struggled to swallow past the lump of disgust that had lodged just above my stomach.

"It was a brutal lesson. Brutal but effective. I feared my father. He controlled my life because of that fear."

"But not forever. Eventually your fear grew into something stronger — and you exacted your revenge," I pointed out.

"Which is why I am even more ruthless with *my* subjects than he was with me. He made me fear him enough to control me when I was young. But he didn't break me. Eventually, my fear made me strong." When he looked at the whip again, it was no longer anger on his face but a chilling twist of delight and triumph. "Beating my brother kept me in his control only until I grew strong enough to do something about it. Until I grew powerful enough to invade

158

Antion and take it for Hector, and then return home to kill my father and take his throne for myself.

"So instead of beating those who disobey me," he continued, "I kill them. Or their loved ones. I take their women and use them to breed my sorcerers. I claim their children for my experiments. My people don't just fear me — they are *terrified* of me. I have broken them so that they will never have the strength to turn their fear into revenge."

I stared at him. The tiny fluttering of pity I'd felt turned to pure, sickening horror. A sudden ghastly understanding of Hector and what he'd done in Antion wrapped around my heart like the barbs on that whip. The boys being forced into the army, the murder of all sorcerers when he came into power, the breeding house — all of it was to control his people. It was to terrify us into submission. He'd killed his own wife to control his sons. It was his attempt to emulate his older brother's methods and, perhaps, even try to surpass them. To prove to Armando that he, too, could be strong — which to them, meant being utterly ruthless.

"But that is enough of that," Armando said, turning away from the shelf and striding back to his desk. "I brought you here tonight so that we might dine together and discuss my vision of the future. I also invited one of the men who has been at my side, helping me, for decades." Armando sat down with a flourish, tossing the cape he wore so that it billowed out behind him.

"This is the Duke of Montklief, Alexa." He gestured to Rafe's father. The smaller man still standing at the king's side glared at me, not even attempting to conceal his loathing. "He came to me twenty years ago and offered his twin son and daughter to be experimented upon. I didn't have to take them from him; he freely *gave* me his children to demonstrate his loyalty to me. That is powerful, my dear girl. Wouldn't you agree?"

I didn't respond, too nauseated and angry to dare speak. What of his wife — their mother? Had she no say in the matter? I couldn't imagine giving my children to this mad king for any reason. I would have rather died protecting them.

The duke glared at me, abhorrence easily visible in his eyes. He'd obviously been told about his daughter's death. King Armando glanced up at him, then over at me, his own gaze calculating.

"You'll have to forgive his lack of manners. He holds some ill will toward you for killing his daughter."

"She tried to kill me first," I retorted. "And I didn't kill her, though I wish I had. Damian did that."

King Armando's eyes widened slightly, revealing a bit of emotion in his surprise. "Well, then perhaps I'm glad you got rid of her. Her power went to her head if she had the audacity to disobey my direct orders."

The duke's lips tightened into a thin white line, but when King Armando added, "Wouldn't you agree?" and looked over at the other man once more, Vera's father nodded immediately, his expression wiped free of the fury that had so clearly burned only a moment before.

There was a knock at the door, four quick raps breaking through the sudden tension, and the king made a welcoming motion with his hand. "Ah, that would be the food now."

A servant I hadn't noticed until then hurried to open the door, and then more servants came in, carrying trays that held multiple plates of food. The trays were set down on the table in front of

King Armando. Too far away for me to eat, but certainly close enough for the enticing smell to fill the room and make my stomach grumble, despite my disgust at the topic he'd been discussing prior to the food's arrival.

"Very good. You may go," the king pronounced, and the servants rushed out of the room. Once the door was shut, Armando gestured to the table where the feast was laid out. "Hungry, Alexa?"

I stayed completely motionless and silent.

"Of course you are. But I have to warn you, I'm not actually going to let you eat yet. Not until you agree to something for me."

King Armando lifted a fork and took a bite of the food in front of him. It looked like some sort of dish made with vegetables and chicken in an unfamiliar, heavy sauce. The smell of the exotic spices they used in Dansii wafted toward me. My stomach clenched.

"So." He finished chewing. "If you'd like to eat, here is what I need from you. I need you to agree to let us take a sample of your blood. Willingly. It won't be much. Not yet. Just a small amount. If you promise to let me do that, I will let you eat this dinner."

"And if not?"

His eyes narrowed. "Then I will have you taken back to your room, and I will find a better way to convince you."

I didn't miss the threat in his voice. "I don't want your food," I made myself say, even though my stomach rumbled again, belying my words. Before the anger on his face could coalesce into action, I hurried on. "But I *will* do as you ask if . . ."

He slowly set his fork down, his eyes never leaving my face. "If what?" He took my bait, his voice cold.

"If you will command one of your men to take me to the dungeons so that I might see for myself that my friends are healed and unharmed. If you will make sure *they* are in perfect health, and let me verify it myself, then I will give my blood to you. Willingly."

King Armando leaned back in his chair, stroking his beard thoughtfully. "You wish for your friends to be in perfect health," he finally repeated. "And you wish to see them."

I nodded.

"Sire, I do not think —"

He lifted one hand, silencing Rafe's protest.

"You may keep me in shackles. And have my friends here accompany us as well, of course." I gestured to the robed men on either side of me. I'd begun to suspect that Armando had all his highest guards wear the robes, concealing their faces and hands, so that I never knew if I was being guarded by a black sorcerer or not — and neither did anyone else who came to the palace. It wasn't possible that he had this many sorcerers — let alone black sorcerers. But what better way to keep your people and prisoners guessing than to have them all dress alike, so that they couldn't ever be sure?

After a long, strained moment of silence, King Armando sat up tall in his chair again. "I will think about it and give you my answer in the morning." He waved his hand toward us, his eyes already dropping to his food. "Take her away."

The sorcerers on either side of me grabbed my arms and yanked me to my feet, then Rafe pulled on my chain, forcing me toward the door, away from the food.

"You promise to give your blood to me willingly?" Armando suddenly called out.

My guards paused so I could glance over my shoulder at the king and the Duke of Montklief. "You will eventually force me to do as you wish. You will make me suffer to bend me to your will. If you will let me see that my friends are alive — and healthy — then yes, I promise to give you my blood willingly."

King Armando's sharp blue eyes, the same penetrating blue as Damian's, never left mine. But where Damian's eyes held a wealth of emotions, this man's held only malice. "Do not try to cross me, Alexa. If you do not submit to me, exactly as I expect — if you break your word — not only will I resort to taking your blood by force, but I will kill your friends myself. While you watch."

My blood pounded through my body, a drumbeat of desperation, as I nodded.

"That is all."

Rafe pulled me out the door, leaving the king and his threats behind.

⊰ TWENTY-FOUR ⊱

*T*HAT NIGHT, I couldn't sleep. Not only because I was starving, despite my flippant response to the king's dinner earlier, but because my mind was running in a million different directions. If he refused my request, it would all be for nothing. But if he granted it . . .

I stared at the dark window, where a sliver of the moon was barely visible, hanging low in the sky. I still hadn't grown accustomed to the biting chill of nighttime in Dansii, and even though I was huddled beneath the one blanket they'd given me to sleep with, I still shivered.

Long after Rafe had rechained me to the floor and locked the door behind him, the scrape of a key in the lock sounded again. I froze in my bed, closing my eyes to feign sleep. The door made a barely audible squeak as it was pushed open. Quiet footfalls sounded across my floor, coming toward where I lay on the bed. I tensed, preparing for an attack of some sort. My mattress dipped slightly, and I lunged up in bed, swinging my arms forward, the heavy iron bands my only available weapons.

Akio smothered a cry of shock, leaping back from the bed, his eyes wide in the shadowy moonlight. Something clattered to the floor, and I glanced over the edge of my mattress to see a plate facedown on the stones.

When my gaze flew to his again, guilt colored the skin of his neck red.

"You were bringing me food?" I whispered.

He shrugged, clearly embarrassed — and concerned. He glanced over his shoulder toward the door, then back to me.

"I'm sorry," I whispered, throwing off my covers and climbing out of bed to kneel on the cold ground. When I lifted the plate, the smell of what he'd brought made my stomach lurch with hunger. Some sort of spiced meat and rice and a couple of slices of an unfamiliar fruit. I began to scoop the rice back onto the plate, but only after I picked up the meat and tore a piece of it off with my teeth and quickly chewed it. I didn't even care that it was so spicy it made sweat break out on my forehead. It was *food*.

Akio knelt down beside me and helped me pick up the remaining grains of rice. His hands trembled slightly as he worked. Was he nervous about being this close to me without the black sorcerers to keep me from attacking him — or was he scared of what might happen if he was discovered helping me in any way? When he glanced over his shoulder toward the slightly ajar door again, I guessed it was the latter. If I'd wanted to attack, I would have done it by now.

"Thank you," I murmured when the food was all cleaned up and I'd taken another bite of meat.

He watched me for a moment, a strange sadness lurking in his dark eyes. "I'm sorry, too," he said at last, his voice quiet. And then he stood and silently crossed the room, pulling the door softly shut behind him. The lock clicked again, leaving me with his offering and a hundred questions burning in my mind.

No one came back until long after the sun had risen and the heat had once again billowed back into the air. When I looked out my window, gusts of sand blew on the horizon, whipped up by the winds that howled outside the palace. It looked like smoke from an unseen fire, undulating back and forth, lifting up into the sky, only to be thrust back down to the ground.

When the door opened once more, I fleetingly thought of the plate I'd hidden under the bed, shoved up in the frame, beneath the straw mattress. I hoped no one would discover it and tell the king.

But when Akio walked back into the room, his mouth set in a grim line, my fears about the plate vanished, my mind going to the demand I'd made last night instead.

"You will follow me." Akio bent down and unlocked my chain, and then led me from the room. The robed guards fell in to their usual place, each holding one of my arms. The carpet beneath my bare feet was unbelievably soft and thick. As we marched down the hallway to the stairs, and then in the opposite direction of the great hall, we passed sculptures of intertwined figures made of a beautiful, shining black stone, and gold statues of men in armor, wielding curved swords. Paintings bigger than me hung from the walls; landscapes and animals and more.

So much luxury, so much opulence. But the wealth was built on a pyre of blood and suffering. It made me sick.

When Akio opened a door and led me out into the courtyard we'd crossed days ago, sudden hope sprang into my chest. Could he possibly be fulfilling my request — was I being taken to see Rylan and Eljin?

The sand beneath my feet hadn't grown hot yet. The surface was warming to the sun, but my toes sank past the top layer with each step to the cold that still hid below. The wind whipped the fine grains of grit into our eyes, but when I lifted my hand to block it, the sorcerer at my side jerked my arm back down. I had to squint instead, trying to blink the sand out.

We walked back through the same door we'd exited when I'd been brought to see the king the first time, and within a few minutes, we were descending into the darkness of the dungeons. Desperation pulsed through me as we stepped into the hallway lined with locked doors. At the end, the door we'd come through from the tunnels below faced us, still guarded by two robed men. But rather than heading toward them, we turned down another hallway and then stopped in front of a door that looked like the rest of the doors we'd already passed.

"You are allowed to look in from here and ascertain the health of both men. You will be given one minute to do so with each. Then we will go directly back to The Summoner to begin your sacrifice," Akio instructed me. "I am to warn you that any attempt at escape or any other indication that you are breaking your word will end in their demise."

I swallowed past the knot of fear in my throat. "I understand."

He nodded at the guard who stood next to the door.

Akio said something in Dansiian, and the guard reached for a ring that hung from his waistband and flipped to the correct key, then inserted it into the door.

When it swung open, I stepped forward, my lungs tightening so that I could barely breathe.

"Alexa?" Eljin stood up from the single cot in the room, his

167

scarred mouth twisting into something between a smile and a grimace. "What are you doing here?" He looked me over, his eyes lingering on the shackles on my wrists.

"Are you completely well?" I asked, widening my eyes slightly, conscious that my time was ticking down.

He gave me a piercing look. "I'm not as healthy as I'd like to be, which is to be expected when they slip bloodroot into a sorcerer's food. But other than that, I am fine, I suppose."

Bloodroot. They were poisoning him — taking away his ability to use his sorcery. Everything inside of me sank, as though I'd swallowed a stone.

"As you can see, he is in perfect health," Akio said.

"Not perfect," I disagreed. "He's being poisoned."

"He has no need to use his abilities any longer. In all aspects that matter, he is healthy," Akio argued, motioning for the guard to pull the door shut. "Your time is up."

Be ready, I mouthed to him, and Eljin nodded infinitesimally, his eyes flashing with confusion and alarm.

The door shut, and when the lock clicked again, it was as if a fist had pushed below my ribs to squeeze my heart. Eljin was physically healthy, but powerless. I wasn't expecting that.

My guards turned me to face the door across from Eljin's. I took a deep breath as I stepped toward it — toward Rylan. Would his leg be healed? If it wasn't . . .

Akio nodded at the guard, who reached for his key ring again.

My hands grew slick with sweat as he shoved the key into the lock and turned it. When he pushed the door open, I haltingly stepped forward.

Rylan jumped up from the bed, his dark eyes widening when he saw me. *"Alexa?"*

My eyes flew to his leg — the bandages were gone; he was standing on his feet with equal weight. When he stepped toward me, he did have a slight limp, just as I'd feared. But he was as healthy as possible at this point.

"Is this your doing — are you the one who convinced them to heal me? I've been so worried about you —"

"Yes." I cut him off, resolve settling in me, familiar and powerful. "I needed you to be healthy so you could help me."

Rylan's eyes widened as Akio stiffened next to me.

Before he could react, I spun and brought my arms up so fast my guards couldn't pull me back. Akio didn't have time to do more than gasp before I slammed the iron shackles against his temple. He crumpled to the ground as Rylan lunged forward, leaping to tackle the guard next to me. They tumbled to the floor, but the other hooded man at my side pulled out his sword, and I leaped back just before he almost impaled me.

"Your king might be less than happy if you kill me and waste all my precious blood," I taunted as I spun away, out of his reach. I couldn't go too far; Akio had been holding my chain and his hand was still gripping it beneath the weight of his unconscious body.

I spared a glance to see Rylan manage to get a good punch in on the guard he'd attacked, but then his body went flying and slammed into the wall. He hit the ground hard.

A sorcerer, then. But was he a black sorcerer?

The one I was fighting obviously wasn't. I barely twisted out of the way of another jab from his sword as the other guard climbed back to his feet. Desperation burned through me as the third guard — the one who had the keys to the doors — grabbed me from behind.

The sorcerer lifted his hand, letting the robe fall back to reveal the jeweled glove he wore — identical to Iker's. Fire burst above his open palm as I kicked back as hard as I could, hitting the man behind me in the shin while simultaneously elbowing him sharply in his side, near his unprotected internal organs. He grunted, his grip loosening a tiny bit, just enough for me to suddenly let myself drop. Using his own weight against him when he got pulled forward to keep his arms around me, I managed to twist out of his grasp and spin around him, so that his body blocked me just as the black sorcerer threw his fireball, hitting the guard instead. His body jerked, and then he collapsed, leaving me exposed once more; the stomach-turning stench of burned flesh filled my nose.

In my peripheral vision, I could see Rylan fighting the other guard, blood dripping down his face, dodging the robed man's sword and trying to get hits in with his bare fists. The black sorcerer had already called more fire into his hand, and I had to throw myself to the ground when he hurtled it at me, rolling as fast as I could to avoid his next blow, tangling myself in my chain. It exploded against the wall right above my head with a dull boom. I could only hope we were far enough away from the other guards — and that the thick stone walls that divided the cells would be enough to keep the sounds of our fight from alerting them to what was happening.

As I scrambled to untangle myself from my chains, the black sorcerer stalked forward, more fire already rising in his palm.

"You can't kill me," I reminded him as I fought with my chains.

"But I *can* maim you," he retorted in heavily accented Antionese, pulling his hand back to throw the fire at me.

There was a dull thud next to me, the sound of a body hitting the ground, and the sorcerer spun to see Rylan lunging toward him, holding the other guard's sword, the blade coated in blood. The sorcerer threw the fire at him instead of me, but rather than ducking out of the way, Rylan kept rushing forward, dodging to the side. The edge of the fireball exploded against his non-sword arm. With a bellow of rage and agony, Rylan leaped toward the sorcerer, slashing his blade through the air with so much speed the black sorcerer couldn't spin out of the way fast enough, and the sword cut through his bicep, deep into the elbow, almost taking his arm clean off.

"Rylan!" I screamed, finally untangling myself enough to jump to my feet and charge forward toward the black sorcerer, who had begun to summon a dark cloud around himself and Rylan. He stumbled back, yanking his sword out of the man's arm and lifting it once more just as the blackness enveloped them both.

I plunged into the darkness and hit the black sorcerer square in the chest, knocking him to the ground with the force of my inertia. With a sound that was barely even human, he pressed his gloved hand to my chest, right above my breasts, digging his clawed fingernails into my skin. I was immediately unable to move. My entire body felt like it was burning up, as if he'd somehow injected the fire he wielded directly into my blood through his hand on my chest.

And then a sword pierced the darkness, swiping down across the black sorcerer's throat. His fingers spasmed against my skin, and then his arm dropped to his side on the ground. I threw myself backward, off his body, as the darkness dissipated.

Rylan stood next to us, breathing hard, gripping his sword with both hands.

≼ TWENTY·FIVE ≽

WE BOTH STARED down at the black sorcerer, hardly able to believe he was dead. I clambered to my feet and hurried to Rylan's side. All three guards were dead, and Akio still lay unconscious. But would more be coming? I didn't know if we could survive another fight. And Rylan was injured. His left arm was a mess of bloody, charred skin, with small pieces of his shirt still visible where it hadn't burned away. And I was still shackled.

"Are you all right?" he asked, letting the sword in his right hand fall to his side.

"Your arm." I lifted my hands toward him, but he shrugged me off.

"There's no time. What's the rest of your plan? How are we going to get those off of you?"

I stared at his ruined flesh, my heart pounding incessantly beneath my ribs. Then my gaze turned to the guards lying on the ground. "We take their robes and disguise ourselves. We'll have to fight the other two black sorcerers guarding the door at the end of the hallway, and then take our chances in the tunnel." I gestured to Akio. "I'm hoping he has the key that will release the irons, since he has the one that unhooked the chain from the floor."

Rylan stared at me for a long moment, probably hoping for a better plan. Then he clenched his jaw and nodded. He dropped to the ground next to Akio and rolled his body over to search for the keys. He found them hooked to his belt and quickly began trying them on the shackles that still bit into my wrists. Finally, on the third try, the lock popped and the irons opened, releasing me.

As soon as they were gone, I flexed my hands and began to rub my raw wrists. Rylan's eyes widened at the sight of my abused skin, but I quickly turned away and knelt next to the sorcerer closest to him and began to remove the robe from the sorcerer's body. He did the same to the others, including the black sorcerer we'd barely managed to defeat together. Eljin would need a robe, too. Once we both wore them, and I had the keys from the guard who had been standing in front of the cell doors in one hand and a curved sword in the other, Rylan turned to Akio once more.

He'd begun to stir, his eyes fluttering, but he hadn't woken yet.

Rylan stepped toward him, lifting his sword to finish the job, but the memory of Akio bringing me food last night, of the sadness in his eyes when he'd told me he was sorry, surged up, and I jumped forward to put my hand on his arm, stopping him.

"What are you doing?" he whispered angrily.

"He's helped me. I can't be the one to kill him — or to watch him be killed."

Rylan stared at me. "He is one of King Armando's top sorcerers. He's the enemy, Alex."

But something inside warned me to leave him be. He didn't deserve to die — at least not by our hands. "I'm not sure what he is. But I'm not killing him."

Rylan shook his head in frustration. "Fine." He knelt down and hit Akio on the head with the hilt of his sword, making sure he stayed unconscious for a while yet.

"Let's go," I whispered as I stepped toward the door, leaving behind the destroyed cell. The wall still smoked where the sorcerer's fire had hit, and bodies littered the ground. I shut the door and turned to face Eljin's cell. There were multiple keys on the ring, and Rylan kept watch while I tried one after another, until finally one slid in and the lock turned.

When I swung the door open, Eljin was standing there waiting. When he saw the robes, he stiffened, until I hurried to pull the hood back so he could see my face.

"Alex," he breathed, with wide eyes. "What happened? What have you done?"

"There's no time to explain. Put this on and be prepared to fight."

Eljin did as I asked, his eyes flitting to Rylan, who held his injured arm awkwardly at his side. I couldn't imagine how he was able to handle the pain he was in right now. I knew the agony of a black sorcerer's fire. Had I made the worst mistake yet, in trying to attempt this escape? We were so close, though. So close to freedom. At least, from King Armando's palace. If we didn't try, it would have meant a sure death. At least we had a chance of living this way. Even if it was slim.

"What now?" Eljin asked once his robe was on.

"Now we go back into that tunnel." I hated the thought of willingly descending back into that dark, terrifying place. But my fear of staying here in Armando's palace and letting him take my blood was stronger.

Eljin's dark eyes widened. "There are two black sorcerers guarding the door. And even if we make it past them, it took days to get here from the wall dividing the two kingdoms. We barely survived with those guards, and we won't have food or water this time. And even if we did survive, and didn't run into any more black sorcerers down there, how would we get back through the wall again, into Antion, without being discovered and killed?"

"Do you have any better ideas?"

He was quiet for a moment, and then: "No."

I glanced around the cell, at the dirt and stones that made up the dungeon of King Armando. The mad king who wanted to rule the entire world with blood and terror in his left fist and ultimate power in his right. "If we stay here, we'll *all* die. They're going to take my blood. The king thinks it will make his sorcerers invincible for some reason. He's done all sorts of terrible experiments with his black sorcerers. And he wants to use me now."

"I've heard the guards through the door," Rylan added. "Armando's gathered a huge army. Vera and some other powerful sorcerers' deaths have got him spooked, according to the rumors I overheard them talking about. He's convinced that Antion and Blevon are going to war again, and that now's the time to make his move before he loses anyone else. He's going to invade Antion very soon, and once he defeats us, he's going to continue on to Blevon."

Images of Damian trying to fight his uncle's massive army, led by black sorcerers and a deranged king, with his own diminished forces, without me or Rylan or Eljin by his side, threatened to tear apart the little courage I'd managed to dredge up to attempt this ill-fated escape.

"If *any* of us has a chance to make it — even if it means leaving the other two behind — you go." I made my voice firm, refusing to let them hear the fear that I struggled to subdue. "No matter what," I continued, when Rylan tried to protest. "Damian has to be warned. He needs to take our people and retreat to Blevon. If they band together, perhaps there *will* be a small chance of winning this battle. He has no idea what is coming. He has to be warned," I repeated emphatically, my voice rising despite my best efforts to stay calm.

Eljin reached out and touched my arm, and Rylan nodded. "It's all right, Alexa," Eljin said. "We'll make it. We'll all make it so we can warn him."

I glanced at each of them in turn. "And if we get separated — if one or two of us aren't going to make it?"

"Then whoever can escape will. But only if you promise to do the same, Alexa." Rylan sounded angry, but I was glad. Anger was good. Anger made him faster, more dangerous.

"I promise," I agreed. "We better go before the king grows suspicious about what is taking so long and sends more men down here."

Eljin and Rylan exchanged a glance. But then Eljin lifted his sword and quietly said, "For Damian."

Something inside of me constricted, something deep in my chest, near my heart. "For General Tinso and Tanoori and Jax," I added, lifting my sword to cross his.

"For *all* of us — even those we have already lost." Rylan's eyes were bright with unshed tears when he lifted his sword to meet ours.

An image of my brother grinning at me, teasing me with a cup of water after sword practice, flashed through my mind. "We can do this." My hand tightened on the hilt of my sword.

Eljin nodded.

"Let's go," Rylan said.

With a deep breath, I let my sword drop to my side. I met Rylan's eyes one last time, wishing I had the chance to say so much more, but then he lifted the hood back over his head, turned, and opened the door, stepping out into the hallway. Eljin and I did the same, leaving the cells behind and striding forward to the fight awaiting us by the door to the tunnels.

⇥ TWENTY-SIX ⇤

RYLAN REACHED UP and plucked a lit torch from the wall, just before we turned the corner into the hallway where the black sorcerers stood, guarding the entrance to the tunnel. Would they both be black sorcerers this time? Or just one? Or neither of them? It was impossible to know. But with Rylan injured and Eljin powerless, my plan wasn't going exactly as I'd hoped.

When we stepped out into the hallway — three robed figures holding swords at our sides — the two men at the end of the hallway straightened from their slightly relaxed positions, leading me to believe they hadn't heard the sounds of our fight. But they were certainly on alert now, as we moved toward them silently. If only one of us spoke Dansiian, we could have pulled off our disguises better.

As we drew closer, one of the robed guards said something in Dansiian. Taking a risk, I nodded my head.

It was apparently the wrong response, because the guard reached for his own sword and shouted something else at us in Dansiian. I felt Rylan and Eljin stiffen on either side of me, preparing for the fight to come.

When he shouted for a third time and we still didn't respond, he lifted his sword and sank into a fighting stance. The other guard lifted his hand, revealing the telltale glove.

"For Antion!" Rylan suddenly shouted, lifting his sword and running forward. Eljin and I exchanged a shocked glance, and then we both lifted our swords and rushed after him.

The black sorcerer had already summoned his fire, and he threw it at Rylan. But this time, Rylan flung himself to the ground, rolling forward, jumping back onto his feet, and continuing toward the guards. The fire exploded against the wall in between two doorways, shaking the dungeon. Dirt sprinkled down on our heads as we continued to run.

Rylan got there first, and the clang of his sword hitting the other guard's echoed through the hallway. I heard voices behind the closed doors calling out in alarm, but I ignored them, focusing on the black sorcerer, who held a sword in his other hand and leaped forward to jab at Eljin, just as he hurtled another fireball, this time at me. I threw myself on the ground, but it grazed my shoulder. Pain exploded down my arm, and my vision tunneled to black for a moment. I rolled onto my back, trying to breathe through the agony, flexing and unflexing my hand to make sure it still worked. I heard someone cry out, and I forced myself to ignore the pain and dragged myself to my knees, gripping my sword with one hand.

The black sorcerer and Eljin were fighting, while Rylan engaged the other guard. Both of the Dansiians were well trained, but Rylan, at least, should have been able to defeat the guard more quickly than this — his injury was slowing him down.

As I forced myself to my feet, Eljin battled furiously with the black sorcerer, swiping his sword at him again and again, trying to keep him from being able to summon more fire or any other abominable tricks, but I knew from my sparring with him that

Eljin wasn't nearly as talented at sword fighting as I was — not without his sorcery to aid him. He relied on using his power too much, and now that it was gone . . .

The black sorcerer parried his blow with his sword in one hand, while summoning his fire again in the other. They spun around, so that Eljin's back was to the door. He had nowhere to go.

With a scream building in my throat, I hurtled toward them, lifting my sword. But I wasn't fast enough. Eljin's eyes met mine just as I leaped forward. My blade impaled the sorcerer from behind an instant too late, right as he released the fire at Eljin. My friend was trapped. Time seemed to halt for a split second as Eljin's eyes filled with sadness, and then the fireball exploded against him and the door with a blinding flash and a reverberating boom.

The black sorcerer collapsed forward onto the ground, and I landed on top of him, my sword through his chest.

"Eljin!" I screamed, scrambling to my feet, my shoulder throbbing. I yanked my sword out and rushed toward the burning, gaping hole where Eljin and the door had stood only moments before. "ELJIN!"

I ground to a halt on the top stair, all the air suddenly stolen from my lungs. He lay sprawled halfway down the stairs, his face and body burned, his neck at a horrible angle, his eyes open and unseeing.

⊰ TWENTY-SEVEN ⊱

N*o!"* My howl of agony tore through my body. There was a thud behind me and I spun, terrified I'd see Rylan lying dead behind me, too. But he stood there staring at me, his chest heaving, the guard sprawled at his feet, unmoving.

When his eyes met mine, I just shook my head, tears suddenly blurring my vision.

There was a shout from the staircase down the hallway from us — more Dansiians were coming.

We both hurried to the smoking doorway, and I rushed down the stairs to kneel beside Eljin's body as the tears spilled out onto my cheeks.

"I'm so sorry. I'm so sorry," I whispered over and over as I gently closed his eyes. I let my head drop toward him. It was my fault he'd come here — my fault he was dead. I couldn't let myself think of Tanoori, back at the palace. So hurt already, and now this. Now, because of me, the only man she'd ever let herself love was gone.

"We have to go, Alexa," Rylan said next to me. *"Now!"*

The echo of boots on the stones above us forced me into action, even though my entire body was shaking, and I could barely see through the tears. Rylan hurried down the rest of the stairs, and I made myself follow him, leaving Eljin behind. Rylan hit the bottom first and turned down the tunnel, back the way Eljin and I had come. Everything inside me hurt, echoing the pain of my wounded shoulder as I reached the bottom and let myself glance up the stairs at Eljin one last time.

Men in robes stood in the doorway, holding torches and swords. They shouted something in Dansiian, and terror seized me.

I spun to face Rylan, who had paused, waiting for me. "Run!" I shouted.

We took off blindly down the tunnel. In the fight, he'd lost his torch. Rylan had longer legs, and even though he had that slight limp, he started to outdistance me. When he noticed, he slowed his pace slightly.

"No!" I yelled. "Go! Just go!"

I could hear the Dansiians behind me, swarming into the tunnel. Rylan picked up his pace again. I pushed myself as hard as I could, but the one meager meal Akio had brought me last night was all I'd eaten in days, and I'd already been weakened before that by all our mistreatment over the course of our captivity. I was too slow, and I knew it.

A sudden blinding flash of light was the only warning I had to throw myself to the ground, just as a fireball rushed past my head and exploded past me in the tunnel. Why were they all trying to kill me? Had Armando decided he could drain the blood from my corpse if I tried to escape?

"Rylan!" I screamed, scrambling back to my feet and forcing myself to stumble forward into the choking smoke and debris.

"I'm here!" His answering shout was somewhere ahead of me. "I'm all right!"

I nearly collapsed with relief, but instead I made myself start running again. I could hear the men behind me. Close. Too close.

"It's a cave-in!" he shouted again, his voice tight with desperation.

His words didn't compute until I'd made it a few more feet and run into a blockade — a wall of dirt and debris, with a few tiny flames licking at the darkness.

I was trapped.

"Alexa!" His frantic yell came from the other side of the rubble. I was just barely able to make out his face, staring at me, in a small gap. "Start digging, you can make it. Hurry!"

I shook my head. "*Run*, Rylan. *Go*. You promised!"

"No. I'm not leaving you here! You'll die!"

"Go, Rylan — warn Damian! You have to keep your promise!"

"*You'll die*," he repeated, an agonized shout.

"I'm just one person, Ry! You have to stop this — it'll be a massacre. You can't let *all* our people die to try and save me!"

He shook his head, but then more dirt fell from above us, piling on top of the already massive mound of rubble.

"Tell Damian I love him — tell him I didn't want to die!" I cried over the rising sounds of the Dansiians getting closer. I glanced over my shoulder. They were running toward me. The black sorcerer had his hand raised, more fire waiting to be thrown at me.

"Stop! I surrender! I surrender," I repeated, my voice breaking on a sob as I dropped my sword. It clattered to the ground as I lifted my hands.

"Alexa!" Rylan howled my name. He sounded like he was crying.

"I love you, too, Ry," I shouted, just as the first Dansiians reached me and grabbed my arms, pulling me back from the cave-in. "Now *go!*"

A whole swarm of hooded men rushed toward me, but they parted as Rafe walked through their midst, his one eye trained on me with pure, undefiled hatred burning in its green depths. I quickly looked away.

He strode up to me until he was close enough to grab my jaw and yank my head forward. I squeezed my eyes shut. "You will pay for this. And I look forward to it eagerly."

And then he hit me in the head with the hilt of his sword, just as Rylan had done to Akio. The darkness swooped up to claim me, and I fell forward into my enemy's waiting arms.

⇥ TWENTY-EIGHT ⇤

W HEN I WOKE, my head pounded and my arms ached. I
slowly realized I was sitting on a hard surface with my arms
stretched out to either side of me, chained to a wall at my wrists.
My legs were bound as well. Only my head was free to move. Part
of me didn't want to wake, didn't want to face the reality that Eljin
was gone. That Rylan had escaped but was severely injured and
probably had very little chance of surviving, let alone making it
back to warn Damian in time. But it wasn't in me to quit, to give
up. Instead, I lifted my chin, blinking away the grasping darkness
and the terrible, pulsing pain behind my eyes.

But what I saw made me long for the oblivion of the darkness
once more.

I was in The Summoner's lair again.

To my right was the row of cots, just like the one I was chained
to, that held the other subjects, moaning and thrashing on their
beds. To my left were the sacrificial altars the black sorcerers used.
The smell of burned flesh and blood mixed with vomit was nearly
overwhelming. I breathed slowly through my mouth — to calm
my heart and my heaving stomach.

"Ah, she awakens."

185

I looked up to see The Summoner walking toward me, his silver eyes unwavering on mine until I looked down at my legs, all too aware of what his brother, Manu, had been able to do to me in the dungeons when I'd interrogated him. I didn't know if they had the same abilities, but I wasn't keen on finding out.

Because I was looking down I was unprepared for him to stab me in the arm.

My body jerked, but I swallowed my scream of pain, refusing to give him the satisfaction. He'd shoved one of the sharp, narrow devices into the bend of my elbow, into the thick blue vein that pulsed beneath the thin layer of my skin. My blood began to run into a bottle that he held beneath the strange metal dagger. The sight of my life flowing out of my arm, into that glass jar, made my head swim. Instinct urged me to yank my arm away, to force him to stop, but I couldn't do anything except struggle against the manacles that held me to the wall.

"The king ordered me to wait until you were conscious before taking the first sample. He wanted you to watch us using your blood to strengthen my creations."

"They're not your creations," I mumbled, my mouth horribly dry. My tongue felt engorged, as though it had swelled to twice its normal size, filling my whole mouth. Had I been drugged? Or was I just severely dehydrated?

"They were *nothing* before me. Sorcerers — nothing more. Armando didn't do anything. *I* did. I am the one who summoned the power necessary to create all of this."

That explained his name, then. I wondered if he'd given it to himself.

When the bottle was halfway full and spots had begun to dance in front of my eyes, he ripped the blade out of my arm, letting my blood run freely for a moment. I'd seen blood many times before — I'd been the cause of death more times than I cared to count. But this was something entirely different. To take blood from subjects willfully, to use it in horrific and disgusting ways . . . If there had been anything in my stomach I probably would have vomited all over him, adding to the smell in the room. Finally, he took a scrap of fabric and pressed it to the wound, stanching the flow.

"Do you know what *Manu de Reich os Deos* means?" he asked me suddenly, his voice soft but threatening, like silk sliding over the sharp edge of a blade.

I shook my head, turning my face away from him and the arm he'd tied a strip of fabric around to stop the bleeding.

"In your language it means 'The Right Hand of God.' That's what he was. I gave him his name because he was at my right side, helping me create sorcerers strong enough to take what is rightfully ours. I am as the Gods, turning their creations into something even greater, making them stronger and better than they could ever have been alone."

I swallowed hard, refusing to respond to him.

"You killed him" — he leaned forward to hiss in my ear — "and you will pay for it. I will bleed you slowly, until you writhe in pain, until every last drop of your life belongs to me." I flinched when he ran a finger down my cheek, past my jaw, and down my neck. "Whether the king is right about your blood or not, I will use you and I will make you suffer for taking away the greatest creation I ever achieved, besides myself."

"Whatever you did to make yourself like this, it is no achievement," I spat back at him. "*You* will pay for what *you* have done, mark my words. I don't know why you aren't *Diūsh* yet, but you will be. That or worse. You will die a thousand horrible deaths for the horrors you've brought into our world."

His fingers curled to encircle my neck, slowly choking me. "How do you know that word? How do you know anything about such sacred knowledge?" His hand pressed against my throat, crushing my windpipe, rendering me unable to respond.

"*Evocon*, stop at once!"

The king's shout startled us both. The Summoner pushed his hand into my throat harder for a split second, but then he released me and stood up straight, turning to face King Armando. I gasped for air, my breathing reduced to a harsh, choking cough.

The king strode toward us, wearing all black as usual, his long robe tied with a sash of gold. The jewels in his crown flashed in the firelight of the burning altars, where two men in black robes bent over their work, wisps of smoke curling around their heads and rising to the ceiling high above us in the cavernous room.

"You killed my men." The king stopped next to the cot I sat on, reaching past The Summoner to pick up the sharp tube he'd taken my blood with. "You broke your word to me, and you helped prisoners to escape."

The icy talons of fear scraped down my spine at the cold fury in his eyes when he looked up at me. "And yet, you survived. You always do. You kill those far more powerful than you, and you always survive." He turned the device over so that the sharp point, still wet with my blood, was pressed into his fingertip. "Perhaps your blood will make me invincible, too." He pushed it harder, until his skin broke and his blood mingled with mine. A terrifying smile turned his lips up as he stared down at the crimson fluid dripping down his finger, a malicious expression that reminded me all too much of his brother, Hector.

"I'm not invincible. I've just been lucky," I replied.

His eyes snapped to mine and he lunged forward, shoving the sharp device beneath my jaw, into the bend of my throat where my blood pounded a drumbeat of terror against my skin, despite my attempts to seem unaffected by their torture and cruelty.

"Too bad the same luck didn't extend to your friend. Do you know what we did to his body?" The king's hot breath on my face made my stomach turn. "We dragged it outside the palace and left it to rot in the sun. We fed him to the *bitrius* — the birds who pecked at his flesh, tearing him away in bits and pieces until there was nothing left but bones."

I squeezed my eyes shut, turning my head away from King Armando, refusing to let him see the tears that burned for release. My chest heaved as I tried to control my breathing, to not let myself imagine Eljin's poor body defiled in such a horrific way.

But he hadn't said anything about Rylan — and that made me wonder if he'd managed to get away.

Suddenly, the king straightened, pulling the blade away from my throat. "We need more of her blood."

"I already bled her today, Your Majesty," The Summoner responded.

"We are marching out tomorrow. I need her blood *now*."

"Tomorrow, Your Majesty?" The Summoner sounded as

shocked as I felt at this announcement. What did that mean — was he marching on Antion? Was he going to fight Damian? Why the sudden urgency?

A horrible, grasping panic had seized my body, making my breath come harder and harder. My limbs felt as though I'd been running for hours, weak and trembling, and my heart raced.

"Get as much of her blood as you can without killing her. Then prepare to leave. She comes with us."

I opened my eyes to see the king drop the device on the cot beside me, and turning on his heel, he strode away.

⇥ TWENTY-NINE ⇤

ESPITE MY BEST intentions to stay alert, my head swam
from blood loss and dehydration, and I had to fight to
remain awake as I lay on the sandy ground where they'd tied me
for the night — the first night after marching out of the palace
earlier that morning. The ropes that were tied around my arms
and torso were almost tight enough to cut off my circulation —
assuming I had much blood left at this point — and then wound
around the tent pole behind me.

The size of the army King Armando had assembled was
beyond comprehension. From my vantage point, tied to one of the
smaller mares behind The Summoner's much larger mount, I
hadn't been able to see the beginning or the end of the line of
soldiers, horses, sorcerers, and other animals and people who were
marching toward Antion — toward Damian and the only people
left in the world whom I loved. There had been crowds of women
and children outside the palace, lining the stone street that wound
through the city made up of buildings the color of the sand with
what looked like some sort of clay tiles for roofs. The only color in
the city was in the curtains and blankets that hung from windows
and doors, dyed in vibrant hues, and the clothes the citizens wore.
The women and children all dressed in the longer robes Dansiians

seemed to favor, some in brightly woven colors, with silken scarves wrapped around their heads to protect them from the relentless sun, while others wore more drab colors, with plainer, rough-looking fabric wrapped over their heads. The rich and the poor came to see off their men, led by the mad king who ruled over them.

But once we'd passed through the city and left the river behind, with its verdant banks, there was only the sand and strange, straggly looking plants and bushes. Some even had spikes. I wished someone could have told me what they all were, but no one dared come close to me, let alone speak to me.

I was already woozy from blood loss when the trek through Dansii began, but as the day wore on and the sun continued to beat down upon us without relief, I actually grew nervous that I might faint. I couldn't even use my hands to lift my hair from where it stuck to my sweaty neck, because they were tied to the saddle. No one had given me a covering for my head, or any way to protect my face from the sun.

When the caravan stopped for a small break and some food, a sorcerer pulled me off my horse and forced me to sit on the ground, but no one brought me anything to eat, nor any water. Even the horses were given small bowls of water to lap up. It didn't look like nearly enough to me, but what did I know about Dansiian horses and their ability to withstand the dry heat?

"How do you intend to keep taking my blood if I die before you even reach Antion?" I dared ask The Summoner, my tongue swollen and my mouth as dry as the sand we sat upon, as he tilted a flagon of water to his lips.

He drank deeply before answering, the bump in his throat moving up and down as the water poured out of the flagon and into his mouth. Once he'd wiped his lips and closed the cap once more, he finally looked at me with his unnatural silver eyes, his pupils still abnormally large even in the sunlight. "Perhaps we've already gotten what we need out of you," he said.

"Then you wouldn't have made the effort to bring me," I retorted.

He was silent after that, standing and then turning away from me to await the signal to keep moving.

When the whistle blew, a familiar robed sorcerer was the one who came over to put me back on my horse and retie my bindings to the thin saddles they used in Dansii.

I didn't say anything when he pulled me to stand, gritting my teeth to keep my legs from swaying or flat-out buckling beneath the diminished weight of my body.

His eyes met mine when he lifted me up into the saddle, but then my gaze strayed to the side — to the dark bruise on his temple.

"I'm sorry," I finally said, my voice barely above a whisper.

Akio stood beside my horse for a moment longer, tightening the ropes on my wrists, making sure they were securely fastened to the metal ring on the saddle. Then he turned and walked away without a word.

I didn't blame him for being mad at me. He'd risked his life to bring me food, and I'd repaid him by knocking him unconscious. I could only hope that he realized I'd appreciated his kindness — that he was still alive because I did.

As the afternoon wore on, I grew dizzier and weaker. The heat in Antion was oppressive, but at least we had an abundance of water and vegetation — there was life thriving in every corner of my kingdom. The very air hung heavy with moisture. But here, the air was as dry as the bones of a corpse, all life sucked out by the relentless sun. There were hardly any plants, let alone wildlife, and water was the rarest treasure of all. When the wind kicked up, the sand pummeled our faces, stinging our skin.

Since no one would talk to me, I had nothing but my own thoughts to occupy me; my fears about Damian, the images of Eljin lying dead on the stairs, and Rylan separated from me in the dark tunnels, injured and frightened. I tried not to think of what had become of both of them, but it was impossible not to worry about Rylan or to think of the horrible way the king had dishonored Eljin's body.

As I lay in the tent that night, finally given the chance to rest after The Summoner had bled me again and then left me alone, taking my blood with him, I tried to think of some way to escape, to fight back, to do *something*. But I had almost no strength left. I wasn't sure how many times they'd bled me yesterday in The Summoner's cavern. I'd lost track after the fourth time. Or maybe I'd just lost consciousness. The last two times he'd taken a smaller amount, but it was still too much. *And for* what? I wondered. To have the sorcerers drink it? To sacrifice it on their altars? I didn't understand how The Summoner and his brother had managed to make themselves into what they were — or how they'd convinced so many sorcerers to become black sorcerers, to risk becoming *Diūsh*. Why didn't they suffer the same fate as the Blevonese sorcerers? I couldn't figure out how their experiments could have created Rafe and Vera and who knew how many others like them, with terrifying abilities and powers.

Unable to think of any way to stop the horrific battle that lay ahead, my thoughts turned to Rylan, hopefully making his way through the tunnels, somehow surviving and reaching Damian in time to warn him. A physical pain, as though my heart were being crushed, seized my chest when I thought of Damian. The urge to cry hit me when I remembered him standing in his mother's library, pressing his fist to his heart, watching me leave him and fearing that I would never return, but very little moisture actually filled my eyes because they were so dry.

He'd been right — over and over again. And now Eljin was dead because of my stubborn refusal to listen to him and stay at the palace. And Rylan probably was gone, too, if I was honest with myself. How could he have survived those tunnels, injured and in the dark?

I wasn't ever going to see Damian again to tell him how sorry I was. I had failed him — I had failed Antion.

Though I racked my mind, I could think of no way to fight back, to escape. Not when I was so weakened, and so thoroughly imprisoned. I couldn't even stand up on my own.

One lone tear finally leaked out when I squeezed my eyes shut, willing myself to sleep, to escape the horror and bleakness of my situation.

When I heard the flap of my tent lift, I forced myself to open my eyes once more, stiffening in preparation for being stabbed in the arm again.

But it wasn't The Summoner.

Akio crouched in the darkness, his dark eyes on me.

⇥ THIRTY ⇤

"SHHH." AKIO PRESSED his finger to his lips when my eyes widened at the sight of him, his head tilted as though listening for something. In his hands, he clutched a flagon of water. "I can't heal you completely, or they will notice. But I can do a little to help you regain your strength."

I stared at him, shocked into speechlessness.

"Drink some of this, but not too much, or you won't be able to keep it down." His voice was so quiet I could barely make out his words. He silently moved toward me and helped lift my head, and then tilted the flagon so that tepid water leaked slowly into my mouth. When I swallowed the first mouthful, I had to choke back a sob of relief. "That's enough for now. Lay back so that I can get to work. Quickly," he urged, pulling the flagon away after I swallowed twice more. "There isn't much time."

"Why?" I whispered. The thought of him getting caught helping me made my stomach cramp on the little bit of water I'd managed to swallow.

He shook his head, falling silent, and lifted his hands above my body. I lay back and closed my eyes, letting him work. He whispered in Blevonese, not Dansiian. I recognized the characteristic lilt to his words, though I didn't understand them. Who was this man — this Blevonese sorcerer — and how had he become part of the king of Dansii's household?

Within a few minutes, a surge of energy trickled through my body. I felt like I could breathe more fully than I had in days. The constant aching in my muscles and bones diminished, and the incessant throbbing of the wounds in my arms receded slightly. His hands centered over my shoulder, which was hidden by my tunic, and after a few more minutes the pain from the unhealed burns I'd received in the dungeons from the sorcerer's fire also disappeared.

There was a noise outside the tent, and my eyes flew open to see Akio grabbing the flagon and scrambling toward the fabric closest to me. He lifted it and rolled out of sight, just as the flap opened and The Summoner walked in. With him came the same chill I'd noticed in the dungeons in Antion with Manu.

He glanced at me lying on the ground, my eyes open, and shook his head.

"You should sleep while you have the chance," he said in his thick accent.

I didn't respond except to close my eyes and will my heart to calm. The sounds of him moving around the tent set my nerves on edge, and it took all my concentration not to tense. The newfound energy Akio had given me was an unexpected gift — but it also took away some of the exhaustion that had weighed me down and would have enabled me to sleep despite all the anxious worries clawing at my mind.

Finally, I heard him lay down. I hadn't realized he intended to stay in the same tent as me, and suddenly any hopes I had of sleeping were dashed. My heart kicked up a notch as a fresh wave of fear hit me. I cracked one eye open to see him lying on his side a few feet away, watching me.

I swallowed my gasp of fear and, with a shudder, squeezed my eyes shut again, forcing myself to pretend I was somewhere else — anywhere else.

"Sleep, Alexa. I won't touch you anymore . . . tonight." His soft, menacing words did little to comfort me.

It was difficult with my arms bound, but I managed to roll onto my side, turning my back to him. And then I pretended I was back in the palace with Damian. I imagined lying beside him, his arms securely wrapped around me. Another tear leaked out of my eye as the sounds of The Summoner's soft snores finally filled the tent.

The next day was exactly the same as the first, and the next few days after that, with no food or water for me, and The Summoner bleeding me at night before disappearing with my blood for a couple of hours. That's when Akio would try to sneak into the tent and bring me a little water or food, and heal me just enough to keep the worst effects of The Summoner's torture at bay. He said little and refused to answer my whispered questions.

As we traveled, the landscape began to change from the rolling, sandy hills to harder, flatter ground. We passed several small towns built around narrow, muddy streams. Some of the townspeople stood outside their homes, which seemed to be made of hardened mud, but others stayed as far away from the king's massive army as possible, peeking out from darkened windows as we passed them by. The closer we got to Antion, the more vegetation and water there was. The horses and soldiers and sorcerers alike were all given plenty.

Everyone except me.

But I made my face stay still, completely emotionless, staring forward as everyone around me drank their fill from the streams by which we'd stop for breaks. Though it was still hot, the air had grown more humid again, and clouds could be seen on the horizon more and more frequently as the days passed. Part of me was grateful for the relief, but the other part of me grew progressively more concerned. In the distance, I could see the massive Naswais Mountains, the jagged teeth of their peaks jutting far into the sky. We were getting close now — too close.

And then one afternoon, after days of travel, my horse plodded up and over a hill, and suddenly rising in the distance was the massive wall that separated our two kingdoms.

We'd reached Antion.

⊰ THIRTY-ONE ⊱

W E ARRIVED AT the wall as the sun dipped low on the western horizon, bleeding the light of day away into the darkness of the oncoming night. But rather than pressing on, the huge army came to a halt, making camp right next to the even-more-massive wall.

Every night had been the same, everyone moving quickly to do their jobs — very orderly. But tonight, something was off. Something was different. Soldiers rushed back and forth, seemingly distracted and perhaps even a little on edge. Normally, they were very cautious to remain silent whenever they were near me, but tonight, they spoke to one another, sometimes even yelling back and forth, without caring about me at all. It didn't matter though, since they spoke Dansiian. All I could decipher was that some of them seemed upset, and others seemed to be irritated.

The Summoner, whose tent had yet to be set up, seemed particularly annoyed when he finally dragged me off my horse and tied me to a tree without a word. He stalked off into the growing darkness, leaving me alone in the chaos. In his rush, he hadn't tied my bindings as well as normal, and if I worked at it long enough, I was confident that I could get at least one of my hands free from the rope and make an attempt at escaping. But did I dare try while it was still light, with the Dansiian soldiers and sorcerers surrounding me?

It didn't matter. I wouldn't get another opportunity to try, I reasoned. I was as good as dead anyway, so if I got killed escaping, perhaps that would just end my agony sooner.

I'd had my hands tied together in front of me on the horse, so they could secure the rope to the saddle, and rather than taking the time to change that, The Summoner had tied me facing the tree. I stepped closer to it to conceal the movement of my arms as I began to try to work my hand free. He'd also quickly tied my ankles together before leaving, but if I was able to get my hands free, it would only be the work of a moment to free my legs as well.

The sounds of the camp got pushed to the background of my mind, behind the dull roar of my pounding blood. My wrists were still a little raw from the manacles I'd worn for so long, despite Akio's rushed healings at night, and the rope quickly bit away at my irritated skin as I sawed my hands back and forth, trying to wiggle the little bit of give in the rope into just a little bit more so I could rip one of my hands free.

"Stop it right now." An angry whisper from beside me made me jump and twist to see Akio glaring at me, in between repeated glances over his shoulder.

"What do you mean?" I asked, feigning ignorance.

"I know what you're doing, and you have to stop."

All the adrenaline that had been surging through my body moments before — apparently keeping me from hearing his approach — drained away, and suddenly I could barely force myself to remain standing. I turned my head away from Akio, so he couldn't see the devastation on my face.

201

But rather than walking away or raising his voice to turn me in, he walked around me to stand in my line of sight again, purposefully turning his body partially away from me and barely moving his lips as he spoke. His voice was so quiet I had to strain to hear him.

"The king received word tonight that Antion is falling apart — his scouts believe that many people are fleeing the kingdom, despite the war with Blevon. There are even rumors that the king has disappeared."

Everything in me went cold at his words. Damian was gone? Where? Why? How? And why was he telling *me* this?

"King Armando is ruthless, as you know. I'm nervous about what he's going to do. But you can't try to escape right now — you won't make it past the wall."

Someone shouted something in Dansiian, and Akio ducked his head down, as though he was examining something on the ground, and then suddenly walked away.

I made myself stare forward, at the tree I was tied to, rather than craning my head to watch him leave. My heart pummeled my ribs, slamming my blood through my body. My head swam with the implications of what he'd said. Damian was missing. The people of Antion were fleeing — probably having heard that the Dansiian army was on the move from our scouts. King Armando was angry, which meant more suffering and death. But then, that last little bit . . . he'd said I can't try to escape *right now*. Not *I will let it go this time, but if I catch you again I will have you punished* or *The Summoner and King Armando will hear about this.* He'd stopped me because he said I wouldn't make it past the wall.

Did that mean he was hoping I *did* escape — once we were in Antion? Was that why he was helping me at night, trying to keep me from dying?

I finally dared turn my head, scanning the hastily erected camp, but there was no sign of Akio. He'd disappeared into the chaos.

When The Summoner returned, he was visibly upset. His skin was even more pale than normal, and his thin mouth pressed into a terse line that all but made his lips disappear. He strode over to where I was still tied to the tree, my legs aching from exhaustion due to lack of use and lack of food, and ripped the ropes free, then jerked me toward the tent that had now been set up for him — for us.

Once he'd tied me to the tent pole yet again, binding my arms to my body so that I couldn't struggle, he pulled out the device that I'd come to hate so much and yanked my sleeve up to remove the strip of fabric he'd tied around the open wounds that throbbed with every beat of my heart.

He muttered something in Dansiian as he attached the bottle already stained with my blood to the end of the metal tube.

"I don't speak Dansiian, you know. If you'd like to make conversation, you'll have to try Antionese." Though I risked his wrath by baiting him, it made me feel as though I still had at least a small bit of power over my situation — over him. He stole my blood, he was slowly killing me, but at least I could get under his skin and irritate him until the day I died.

Unless Akio really was going to help me escape.

His eyes flickered to mine, and I quickly looked away. "We need more," he said in my language, his voice mocking. "We need *all* of your blood."

"But you haven't even made it into Antion yet. How long will the effects last?" I didn't believe my blood would do anything to help any of them, but there was no proof, since they hadn't had to battle yet. Still, his words had sent a sudden schism of terror through my fragile hope. If he intended to take all my blood tonight, then this was it for me. Wall or no wall, I wasn't going to survive until morning to cross through it.

Akio should have let me take my chances.

"I'm not going to take it all *now*, you fool girl," he responded, and I released a shuddering breath of relief. "But soon. Soon, I will." He stared down at the device, turning it over in his hands. I cringed, waiting for the blinding pain that would come when it gouged my skin and entered my veins. But instead of shoving it into my arm, he abruptly stood up and strode out of the tent.

I sat on the hard ground, trying to hold back the sudden sobs that threatened to rack my body. I'd been sure this was it. Though I knew my death was imminent, some part of me still had managed to cling to the hope that I would be able to escape. And now, after Akio's strange interference with my one chance to try, that tiny seed of hope had blossomed into a pulsing root of belief that perhaps I truly could — that maybe I had somehow found an ally in this terrifying kingdom of black sorcery and blood-power and violence. The Summoner's words had stolen all of that from me, leaving me shaken and struggling to breathe normally. *Not tonight,* I reminded myself. He said he wasn't going to take all my blood tonight.

But *soon*, he would. The battle King Armando had been planning for decades — the fight to take control of our entire world and the hidden power Blevon still controlled — was looming in front of us.

If I didn't escape, he was going to have The Summoner bleed me to death to try and ensure his victory.

⊰ THIRTY-TWO ⊱

A KIO SLIPPED BENEATH the tent right beside me only
moments after The Summoner had left.

"He didn't bleed you tonight?" he whispered, his voice quiet
but urgent.

I shook my head.

Akio glanced at the tent flap in alarm. "Then I have no idea
how long he will be gone." He reached beneath his robe and
pulled out a flagon and a small piece of cheese. "Here, hurry
and eat this."

I practically inhaled the cheese, which barely touched the
gnawing, all-consuming hunger that made my belly burn all day
and night, then I took three huge swallows of water from his
flagon. The whole time Akio crouched beside me, his head cocked,
listening intently for any warning that The Summoner was coming
back. He'd just taken the flagon back when we both stiffened at
the barely decipherable sound of boots crunching across the rocky
patch of ground the tent had been set up on.

Akio lunged for the edge of the tent, rolling underneath it as
quickly as he could, but the flap opened before he'd made it completely. My heart jumped into my throat when The Summoner
marched in, but through a twist of luck, his head was turned back,

206

looking at someone behind him rather than forward at the interior of his tent. Akio slipped away without discovery.

But my focus was now on The Summoner, who was no longer alone. Directly behind him was King Armando.

The king slowly made his way toward me, his piercing blue eyes studying me the way a predator inspects its prey before devouring it.

"You're right," he said at last, making me wonder what on earth I was right about — until he turned to face The Summoner. "She's not going to last the week like this. We need to conserve her blood — for now. Until the opportune moment."

I glared up at him, keeping my face emotionless. He wore all black again, except for his usual sash and the golden crown inlaid with many large gemstones that glittered, even in the darkness inside the tent.

"You'd best start giving her water — just enough so that her blood supply will rebuild." The king's eyes narrowed as he bent down to grab my jaw. "Your blood had better not fail me." His voice was deadly quiet.

I remained silent, clenching my teeth against the bruising force of his fingers on my skin.

Finally, he shoved my head back, slamming it against the pole behind me. Armando straightened and turned to The Summoner. "We're almost there," he said. "Soon, you will have your ultimate reward."

The Summoner nodded, bending his head and bowing to the king as Armando strode out of the tent, leaving us alone once more.

The Summoner almost seemed angry when he uncapped his flagon and pushed it against my lips.

"Drink," he commanded, as if I needed his urging.

I swallowed as much as I could before he yanked it away and wiped it off, then recapped it. Apparently, my blood was fit to be consumed, but he couldn't bring himself to drink out of the same flagon that I had without cleaning it first.

Though I was still starving, the water and the small bit of cheese at least filled my stomach with something as I rolled onto my side, away from The Summoner's disconcerting stare, to try and sleep that night. But even though I knew I was safe from him once his usual soft snore began, I still couldn't relax. Too many questions, too many fears, and too many hopes all conspired to keep me up most of the night. The worst one of all was wondering what had happened to Damian. When I'd left, Blevon had just declared war on Antion again, through General Tinso. What if Blevon had invaded and this time succeeded in defeating Antion? What if Damian was . . .

I couldn't even let myself finish the thought. He was alive. He had to be alive.

I repeated it to myself for hours until, finally, I drifted off to sleep only a short while before dawn.

The next day, we woke to a storm, the first I'd seen in weeks. The first bit of rain broke as I slumped in the saddle upon my horse, tied to the metal ring as usual, my feet tied to the stirrups as well this time, waiting in the huge line of soldiers and sorcerers that made up the Dansiian army as it slowly passed through the one opening in the wall that would allow us into Antion. I'd never gone this long without food, and despite Akio's attempts to help me, I could barely sit up in the saddle. But the rain had a rejuvenating effect on me. I opened my mouth and let it drip onto my teeth and tongue, running down my throat.

Those little droplets of water plopping on my skin, rolling down my cheeks and neck and arms, made me realize how much I'd missed the jungle. I'd spent my whole life hating it — fearing it — but now, after my time as a prisoner in Dansii, I realized just how much I loved Antion. It was dangerous, yes. But it was also beautiful, and lush. Water was never in short supply, and the heat was tempered by the steady storms.

It hadn't been that long when soldiers began shouting at us all in Dansiian, pushing the line back rather than forward.

"What's going on?" I asked, craning my head to try and see what was ahead of us — why they were suddenly in such a rush to get further *away* from the wall, rather than closer.

When Akio went riding past us on a large white stallion with the longest mane I'd ever seen, I shouted my question again.

He wheeled his horse around and called back, "The Antionese are gone — the city is deserted on the other side of the wall. The king has ordered it taken down to speed up our passage."

The Summoner, who had ridden ahead, turned in his saddle when he heard Antionese from one of his men, and when he saw Akio riding away, his eyes narrowed. A slice of fear cut through me at the look on his face. I was suddenly afraid that by answering my question, Akio had just given The Summoner reason to suspect him.

I tried to brush it off, to convince myself that there was absolutely no reason for The Summoner to suspect Akio, but that pulsing instinct I'd learned to trust long ago warned me that Akio was in danger.

I glanced over my shoulder, but he'd already ridden out of sight, spreading the message to back away from the wall. What had he meant by having the wall *taken down*?

The Summoner rode back to where my horse stood a short time later and grabbed her reins to pull her back with the rest of the remaining army still in Dansii. Once I was sandwiched between two huge soldiers dressed in black and red, who were also on horses, rather than on foot like the majority of the non-sorcerers, he barked something at them in Dansiian, and they nodded quickly, murmuring their responses. One of them reached out and grabbed the reins of my horse, and the other urged his horse closer so that his leg was almost pressed against mine.

Once The Summoner seemed satisfied that they had complied with his order, he wheeled his horse around and sent him charging forward — toward the wall.

I glanced around, blinking against the rain that had grown steadily more insistent, wondering if anyone else was questioning why he was going the wrong direction, but no one seemed concerned.

A few minutes later, a colossal *boom* nearly deafened me and made the very earth beneath my horse's hooves tremble. She tossed her head, prancing in fear, as did the mounts of the two men on either side of me. As they struggled to keep the horses from spooking and bolting, I just focused on trying not to fall out of the saddle and get trampled, since I was tied to my horse.

Another massive *boom* shook the ground again, and then an even louder and more terrifying sound rent the air. I stared in shock as a section of the wall began to crumple to the ground in front of us, the stones and rocks collapsing in on themselves, sending an immense cloud of dust and debris into the air.

⇥ THIRTY·THREE ⇤

A SHORT TIME AFTER the wall was demolished by the power of Armando's sorcerers' joint efforts, The Summoner came back to get me. The entire army was surging forward, toward the gaping hole. There was a massive pile of debris that still smoked in places, despite the rain, probably from sorcerer's fire if I had to guess, but the men just climbed over it. The horses were another matter, and The Summoner led me toward a particular spot where the rubble had been lifted away, making a narrow path of flat ground for the horses to use.

Before I knew it, we'd crossed into Antion, leaving Dansii behind us. I blinked hard when I saw Bikoro, the large city Eljin and I had avoided on our journey to Dansii.

I'd forced myself to push the pain of his death to the back of my heart, with the rest of those I'd already lost, knowing I couldn't afford to mourn him — not yet, not now. Just as I'd had to force myself to continue on when my parents died, just as I'd had to pretend I was fine after Marcel's death. I knew how to shut it off, to do what I must to survive. But in that moment, as I stared at the now-abandoned city and the thick green line of the jungle stretching across the horizon in the distance, the sharp pain of his loss surged up, stabbing through me as though the barbs from the whip King Armando had framed in his library had somehow found their way inside of my body and were digging into my belly and lungs and heart.

After passing through the destroyed wall, The Summoner grabbed my horse's reins and tied them to his saddle as he usually did for the long treks during the day, rather than holding them. King Armando must have been very certain of his victory, if he was confident enough to tear down such a huge undertaking for the sole purpose of letting his men through faster. The army was rushing forward into the city, breaking into the closest homes and shops, pillaging for anything of value. The sounds of their destruction sent a spike of fury boiling through me. It was good that these families had fled, that they weren't being killed by Armando's army. But it still broke my heart to see their homes, their gardens and belongings, being torn apart, set on fire, or stolen.

As we passed through the city, I made myself turn away to stare at the massive Naswais Mountains, which jutted up into the sky above the rooflines of Bikoro, far beyond the destruction I was being forced to witness. The peaks disappeared into the dark, roiling clouds of the storm that still spat rain down on us. In the distance, a lone bird of some sort circled in the sky, its wings spread wide, nearly touching the clouds. For a moment I imagined I was that bird, free to soar away from everything.

Before long, the army had completely taken over the city, filling it like dark ants, with their black hoods pulled up against the rain. The Summoner rode to the end of the houses, where King Armando sat upon a massive black stallion. The horse's nostrils were flared and he kept tossing his head, especially as we drew closer to him.

"We will stay here tonight," King Armando said in Antionese, for my benefit. "Let the men feast on their spoils and enjoy roofs over their heads."

The Summoner nodded. "They will enjoy that, Your Majesty."

The king laughed, a sound tinged with viciousness. "I don't care if they *enjoy* it. I just need them full and rested, because tomorrow, we are burning down a jungle."

I forced myself to stay still, to not reveal my shock. "Your Majesty, there's a road — just there." I tilted my head toward the muddy path that wound away from Bikoro and on into the jungle, since I couldn't lift my hands to point — the same road that would take them directly to Tubatse and the palace if they followed it long enough. "There's no need to burn the jungle down."

King Armando's gaze fell on me and he smiled, a cruel twist of his mouth. "Do you think I honestly care about protecting this horrific excuse for a kingdom? Why do you think I sent Hector to be king of this one, rather than letting him have Dansii, even though Antion is closer to Blevon?"

I clenched my jaw, refusing to respond to him. It had been foolish of me to say anything to begin with. Now he would only be more determined to destroy Damian's kingdom — my home — if only to make me suffer.

"I let him fight the battles for me, to weaken Antion and Blevon, while I worked to create sorcerers who were powerful enough to accomplish my ultimate goal."

I thought about what Rylan had overheard — the rumors that he'd grown nervous and impatient because I'd killed some of his most powerful sorcerers. The ones he'd spent so long creating. Was that why he was suddenly moving forward now?

"For years and years, I worked and waited," he continued. "It takes time to destroy kingdoms, but I was patient. And now, finally, I will take what is mine." His smile slid away and his voice turned cold. "We will burn it *all*."

I stared past him to the jungle. His black sorcerers could do it, with their unnatural fire. Even if I did escape, there was no way to stop him from destroying Antion.

"Keep her with you," the king said to The Summoner, brushing us off. "And make sure you get some rest tonight as well. I need you in the morning."

The Summoner nodded. "Yes, my king." Then he turned his horse back toward the city, taking me with him.

The Summoner found one of the bigger houses to stay in for the night. He released our horses in the fenced corral out back, letting them graze. The rolling expanse of grass was probably more green food than either of them had ever seen before. He dragged me inside, into one of the bedrooms with a large bed. The blankets had been removed, but the straw mattress remained. The Summoner forced me to lie down on the bed. He tied my arms above my head, to the hand-carved wooden headboard, then moved down my body to tie my feet to the bottom of the bed. I was forced to lie there on my back, staring at the ceiling for hours after he disappeared, listening to the rain plink against the rooftop above me, trying to distract myself from the pain in my hands and arms as the blood drained out of them by wondering what family had lived here. I imagined an entire scenario, a husband and wife, and their three children. They had a family horse, and the father would carve wooden toys for the children to play with. I forced myself to keep my mind walled into the pretend scenes, rather than letting myself think about Eljin or Rylan or Tanoori, or anyone else from Antion — especially not Damian.

Sometime later, when the light outside the one window in the room had grown even darker than the dreary grayness that had lasted all day as the storm continued, The Summoner returned. He smelled of fire and blood as he came to stand over me, staring down at me tied to the bed like an offering.

I turned my face away from him, trying to keep my pulse from speeding up in fear. I wouldn't let him scare me. I was stronger than that.

"Here," he said at last, and when he touched my head, I jerked away from his touch. "Here," he repeated angrily, grabbing my jaw and forcing my head toward him. When I saw the flagon he held, I stopped struggling and reluctantly allowed him to help me drink.

The water sloshed in my empty stomach, making it cramp. "I need more than water to live, you know," I said quietly.

He ignored me, standing up and walking out of the room again.

A short time later, the door creaked open again and I stiffened, but when Akio crept in, I relaxed slightly — though I glanced past him in alarm. Where had The Summoner gone, and how soon would he return?

Akio hurried to my side and lifted my head so I could eat the roll he'd brought me.

"There are soldiers still up celebrating in the streets. Wait until it's been dark for many hours and the noises outside have ceased. Then tell The Summoner you need to go outside to relieve yourself." Akio spoke in a rush as I chewed. "I'll wait outside, behind the home. When you come out, I will attack him, and you must take one of the horses and flee. It will be your only chance to escape."

I nearly choked on the last bite of my roll; my eyes widened in shock. "Why are you doing this — why are you helping me?"

Akio glanced over his shoulder, his entire body tense, prepared to flee. When the house remained quiet, he glanced back at me, his dark eyes sad. "I was born in Blevon. I trained to be a sorcerer there. But my father . . . he was greedy. He'd heard rumors of greater power in Dansii. He convinced himself that the Blevonese leaders were lying to us — to keep us from becoming stronger. He hated the *Rén Zhúsas*, mostly because he was jealous of their enormous power. He forced us to sneak through Antion and go to Dansii. He offered our family to the king in return for his help in making him more powerful. Armando agreed, taking my mother and sister and forcing them to become servants in his palace. Since I was a sorcerer, I was allowed to come with my father when he made his first sacrifice, to transform himself into a black sorcerer. Instead, he became *Diúsh*." Akio spoke quickly, his voice low with grief and pain. "He was dead, but not dead. Alive, but not alive. I had to stab him in the heart, to release his body from what he'd done. But his spirit will be cursed forever because of his greed."

I could do nothing but stare at him as he told me his story, unable to move my hands or reach out to him. I couldn't imagine what he'd been through because of his father.

"Armando refused to let us leave when I begged him to release us from my father's bargain. We knew too much. So I was forced to become a healer for him. I refused to try his experiments, and he left me alone after what happened to my father. He told me that

Blevonese sorcerers couldn't handle the change because we were weaker than Dansiian sorcerers. He claims that a Dansiian king actually discovered the golden waters hidden in the mountains of Blevon when he was visiting his friend, the king of Blevon. Dansiians believe that their king is the one who was first made a sorcerer, and that the Blevonese king was jealous when he discovered what had happened and went to drink some for himself, but because he and his brother drank second, they became weaker sorcerers, unable to tolerate the greater power gifted to the Dansiians by the Gods of the Underworld."

"The demons," I said quietly.

"Yes." Akio glanced over his shoulder again. "I don't know why the Dansiian sorcerers don't suffer the same fate we do, but I know their story is false." He paused as if considering, then rushed on. "Do you know why The Summoner is able to do the things he can do?"

I shook my head.

"He was a black sorcerer already, but he wanted even greater power. He sacrificed his own parents to the demons. He made his brother, who wasn't a sorcerer at all, help him. They were given their powers in return for their horrible deed."

My mouth fell open as a wave of horror washed over me. Their own parents? For power? The water The Summoner had given me felt like poison in my stomach.

"The Duke of Montklief sacrificed his own children to the king, to be used as experiments, and they were given their terrible power to control others' minds because of it. The demons reward sacrifice with power. But the twins are not all-powerful, as they believe. Their powers only last for a time on true sorcerers' minds.

217

After a few days, sorcerers can break through the twins' hold on them unless they repeat the command."

"But a regular person like me?" I asked, my stomach sinking, already knowing the answer.

"It's permanent. Unless the twin dies or rescinds it."

Which meant I had no hope of breaking through Rafe's control on my mind — his command that I couldn't hurt him and had to defend him if he was in danger. But it did explain why Damian had been able to fight through Vera's control on his mind.

Akio tensed as though he'd heard something. "I've stayed too long; I have to go. He could return at any moment." He hurried toward the door.

"Wait — you still haven't told me why you are helping me."

He paused and turned back to me. "Because my mother told me she believes all this — all the pain and suffering — had a purpose. I've prayed to the Unseen Power I learned about in *Sì Miào Chán Wù* before we came to Dansii to understand what purpose I could possibly serve, and I was told that there would come a time when I would be able to help save my people from destruction. I believe Armando's father. I believe you are the one no sorcerer will be able to stop — I believe you are the one who can help my people defeat Armando. That's why I'm helping you."

And then he slipped away into the darkness of the home, leaving me to wait for The Summoner to return and for the hours to pass until the soldiers had finally all gone to sleep, so that I could try to escape.

≼ THIRTY·FOUR ≽

WHEN THE SUMMONER returned again, shortly after Akio had left, he looked angry.

"Why aren't you sleeping?" he bit out at me.

I didn't respond, watching him warily as he moved toward the bed where I was tied up. The sounds of celebration outside the home were beginning to die down as nighttime swallowed up the daylight completely.

"I must rest, as you heard. I have a big day tomorrow."

He walked around the bed and then stretched out beside me, only a foot away from my body. The unnatural chill in the air from his presence grew even more pronounced by his proximity. I inhaled sharply, terror and disgust roiling through my body. Akio's words repeated over and over in my mind. He had the powers that he did because he'd sacrificed his own parents — killed them, with Manu's help.

I lay there stiffly for what felt like hours, waiting for the soft snores I'd become accustomed to, but they never came. My arms ached from being forced to remain above my head for so long, and I was afraid my numb hands would be completely useless because they'd been bloodless for so long. The roll Akio had given me had quelled my hunger a bit, but not enough to give me the strength

I'd need if I had to fight The Summoner. I'd seen what Manu was capable of — how the vial of crimson fluid had exploded into a cloud that made us see our own worst fears, allowing him to kill at will. What could The Summoner do if provoked — the one who was already a sorcerer and had orchestrated the sacrifice, not just aided in it?

As the hours passed, I grew more and more alarmed and tense. Finally, I couldn't take it anymore.

"I need you to take me outside," I said into the silent night. The rain had let up shortly after he'd come back into the room, and the white glow of moonlight chased the shadows of the clouds across the walls as the storm broke apart above us.

When he didn't respond right away, I repeated myself. "I need to go outside to relieve myself. The water you gave me . . . It can't wait."

He still didn't say anything, so I hazarded a glance toward him, only to find him lying on his side, staring at me, his eyes wide open. I swallowed a scream of terror and jerked my head back.

"No," he whispered, his voice silky.

Sudden terror clawed at my chest as he slowly sat up and inched closer to me. I struggled against the ropes that held me in place, futilely yanking to free myself.

The Summoner lifted one hand to stroke my cheek, and I choked down a sob of desperation as I jerked my head away. *Akio,* I begged in my mind. *Akio, save me, please.* There was nothing I could do to stop him, not with my feet and hands tied. The only weapon I had was my teeth.

"You have fire in you. Different fire than I or the sorcerers I create have. Your blood isn't working, but the king won't admit it.

Even though I killed one of his sorcerers today to prove I am right." As The Summoner spoke, he suddenly rolled to his knees and moved so that he straddled my body, his hands on my arms, pressing them down into the bed. Despite the uselessness of it, I continued to struggle against him. "Maybe if *I* take you, I will be able to claim your fire for myself. Then *I*, and I alone, will be invincible."

"No," I screamed when he bent toward me, thrashing violently, my mind racing for some way to stop him, to protect myself. "Stop! Help me!" I screamed again, but he just grinned, a horrible flash of teeth in the moonlight.

He lifted one hand from my arm and reached back into his robe. "I will sacrifice you to my Maker and become the most powerful being to ever walk upon the soil of this world." And then he pulled out the device he'd been using to torture me. The metal glinted in his hand.

He was going to kill me, I realized.

"But perhaps, I should indulge first. The fear in your eyes is quite delicious, I must say. The taste of it on your body would be intoxicating." He bent toward me again, and though I screamed and thrashed, he was able to reach my face, to lick my unscarred jaw. I slammed my head forward with a satisfying crack against his. The pain was worth the shock on his face as he jerked back with a sharp yelp.

"Enough," he growled, and then he climbed off me to stand next to the bed. He lifted his hand and used the device to cut a thin line across his own palm, so that his blood bubbled up. And then he turned it so the blood dripped to the floor. I continued to yank on the ropes, tearing my skin and making myself bleed in my desperation to escape.

"Help!" I screamed again, hoping Akio would hear me.

The Summoner closed his eyes and let his head drop back. When he snapped it forward again, his eyes flared blood-red. Just as a stream of flames burst from his hand to light the crimson line on the floor beside us on fire, the window shattered, and Akio leaped into the room.

❧ THIRTY-FIVE ❧

The Summoner's head swiveled toward Akio, and a malicious grin lit his face. He turned his palm toward Akio, sending the stream of flames at my only ally.

"Akio!" I screamed, but he threw himself to the floor, rolling quickly toward the bed. The Summoner had forgotten about the fire behind him when he attacked Akio, and when I glanced at him, he'd stepped backward toward the flames. His robes caught fire, and he spun around in shock.

Akio took the moment of distraction to leap up from the ground and in the blink of an eye slashed a curved sword at my bindings, narrowly missing my head, but freeing my hands. My arms dropped to either side of my face, pain shooting through my body as blood rushed back down to my fingers.

The moment my arms were free, Akio sprang past me toward The Summoner, knocking him to the ground.

Ignoring the agony in my arms and hands, I forced myself to sit up and frantically pulled at the ropes on my ankles with my numb fingers as Akio and The Summoner rolled across the floor, both of their robes burning now. Akio had lost his sword. It lay next to the bed, reflecting the hungry flames that were now moving toward me. I heard a howl of pain but didn't let myself pause to look and see what was happening. Instead, I leaned over the bed, grabbed the sword, and, sitting back up, slashed my feet free.

I snatched up the device The Summoner had used to bleed me in my left hand and clutched the sword in my right as I jumped up from the bed, leaping over the growing fire to see The Summoner lying on his back, gripping Akio by the throat. Akio's body was convulsing. I ran toward them, but just before I would have swiped the sword across The Summoner's throat, he threw Akio toward me, sending us both tumbling to the ground, too close to the flames that were spreading around the room. The sword fell out of my tingling, still half-numb hand, leaving me with only the metal tube to defend myself as I scrambled back to my feet.

Akio lay unmoving on the ground, but The Summoner stood at the end of the now-burning bed, his palm stretched toward me.

"You must bleed first," he said, his voice burning my ears like the flames that filled the room with unbearable heat and a thick, cloying smoke. "Then you will die." He lifted his hand, but before he could do anything to me, Akio suddenly moved toward him, wrapping his arms around The Summoner's legs and knocking him to the ground again.

I didn't have time to wonder if he'd been pretending to be unconscious or how he'd been able to recover so quickly. It was my only chance to kill The Summoner and escape.

I rushed toward them just as The Summoner rolled away from Akio and lifted his hand. I screamed Akio's name as I lifted the device above my head and leaped toward The Summoner. The jet of fire burst from his hand to hit Akio in the same moment that he turned and saw me throwing myself toward him, slicing the sharp metal through the air toward his throat. He threw out his other hand, and it felt as though I'd been slammed by one of Deron's hardest hits, straight to the chest, throwing me back onto the ground again.

"Kill him!" I heard Akio's agonized scream as I rolled to my knees and forced myself to my feet only to have The Summoner grab me from behind and bring the sword up to my throat. I stiffened.

"Now you shall bleed," he said as he pushed me toward the fire that consumed half of the room, the smoke chugging into the air, choking me. As soon as I breathed it in, I realized his voice had changed, and it was Damian who said, "And then you will die."

Panic seized me, but I forced it down. *It's his blood,* I realized. The smoke from the flames that had burned up his blood was causing me to hallucinate, like the cloud Manu had created. The demons must have given their blood extra power. *It's not Damian,* I told myself. *It's not Damian.*

He held me so tightly, expecting me to fight back, that he wasn't prepared for when I let my body slump forward, my entire weight suddenly pulling on his arms. He lurched forward, his grip loosening ever so slightly as he stumbled to regain his balance. But that was all I needed. Using every ounce of strength I had in me, I twisted, ripping my arm free. Swinging it around before he could lift his hand to stop me, I stabbed the metal device straight back above my head — directly into his throat.

The Summoner's arms convulsed around my body as he let out a gurgled cry of agony before dropping them completely. He stumbled back, and I spun around, yanking the device out of his neck as I did. But when I saw Damian standing there, his blue eyes wide and glazed with pain and shock as the blood rushed down his throat to coat his black-and-white robes, I had to choke back a scream of shock. I shook my head and stepped forward, out of the cloud, and when I blinked, I no longer saw Damian, but The Summoner, swaying on his feet.

"No," I said, stalking toward him and shoving him to the ground, holding him down with my foot on his shoulder. "*You* will bleed, and then *you* will die. And then your master can take what's left of your soul for himself." I lifted the device above my head and sliced it down through the air, straight into his heart — if he even had one anymore.

His mouth opened, and he tried to say something, but blood filled his throat, and with a final shudder, he became still and his eyes grew glassy.

Trembling now that it was over, I spun and dropped to the floor to avoid the hallucination-inducing smoke, searching for Akio on my hands and knees.

"Akio!" I called out, hurrying forward, away from the flames that were quickly reaching for The Summoner's body. "Akio!"

I heard a quiet sound, not quite a word — more of a coughing gasp — and I rushed toward it to see Akio lying on the ground, half of his body charred and bleeding, his eyes squeezed shut against the pain.

I dropped to my knees beside him. "Akio," I murmured. "Can you heal yourself? Can you stand?"

His eyes opened, searching for me. When he saw me leaning over him, he jerkily shook his head. "Go," he managed to whisper, his voice gravelly with pain. "Stop . . . him . . . he will destroy . . . the whole world . . . stop him. . . ." he gasped the words until I

226

reached down and clutched his unburned hand. Tears stung my eyes as I stared down at Akio. "Go . . . before . . . they come. . . ."

"Thank you," I said, bending forward to press a kiss to his forehead. His eyes closed, and with a soft sigh, the air released from his lungs, and he didn't breathe again.

I let my forehead rest against his for a brief moment as a tear slipped out and dripped onto his charred skin. "I'm sorry," I whispered.

And then I stood and rushed toward the open window and freedom.

⪢ THIRTY-SIX ⪡

*T*HOUGH THE SUMMONER's horse was bigger, I didn't want anything that had ever been his, so I hurried up to the mare I'd ridden the whole time I'd been captive on this trek. The Summoner had left the saddle and bridle on both animals, so it only took a moment to swing myself up into her saddle and gather the reins as Eljin had taught me to with Mira, after wiping the grit and tears from my eyes. She needed little urging to hurry away from the burning home, where the flames were now bursting out of the window and licking up toward the roof.

I'd opened the gate, and when my mare galloped through it, The Summoner's horse lifted his head and followed after us for a bit before slowing to a trot and then stopping again, once he was away from the fire. Exhaustion and weakness threatened to drag me under as we galloped away from Bikoro and King Armando toward the jungle. I hadn't exerted myself like that in far too long — and I also hadn't had enough nourishment to sustain that kind of energy for the same length of time. I had to force myself to hang on until we had put as much distance between us and the Dansiians as possible. The moment The Summoner's death and my escape were discovered, King Armando was sure to drive his men into the ground to pursue and recapture me. My defeat of his most powerful sorcerer would most likely only solidify his belief that I could make him and his men invincible, even though The Summoner had apparently proven to him today that it wasn't the case.

The sound of my horse's hooves pounding against the muddy ground seemed unbearably loud in the quiet night, and I kept glancing over my shoulder, expecting to see Dansiian sorcerers coming after me, but the city remained quiet, save for the homes that were burning. The one I'd been kept in wasn't the only one to go up in flames. The pillaging had resulted in many houses being burned down, though that had stopped after the king's order that they spend the night in Bikoro had been circulated.

I turned back to face the jungle again, forcing my trembling thighs to grip the mare's sides as I urged her to go even faster. Her legs ate up the ground, practically flying toward the protection of the jungle — almost as if she knew the danger we were in.

But even as fast as she was going, it felt like forever before we finally raced past the treeline and plunged into the arms of the jungle. The moment the lush vegetation encircled us, I heaved a huge sigh of relief. I pulled back on the reins slightly, slowing her a bit. I didn't want to risk having her trip or get hurt on the rutted road in the darkness, or my escape would be short-lived.

We pressed on for what felt like hours, galloping down the road toward Tubatse and the palace. Were the rumors true — would everyone be gone when I got there? Panic and fear beat in time with my blood as the night wore on. But every time I glanced over my shoulder, there was nothing there except for trees, flowers, bushes, and the prints of my mare's hooves in the muddy road. I could only hope a storm would work its way up again and wash away the evidence of our path before King Armando entered the jungle. Would he still burn it down if he was searching for me?

Finally, just before dawn, it began to rain again, and I knew if I kept going, I would end up falling off the mare. I had absolutely no strength left. I had to stop and rest and find something to eat. Though I didn't dare let myself sleep. If King Armando still decided to burn the jungle down, I wasn't sure I'd put enough distance between us to outrun the flames that would be coming in a few short hours' time.

When I dismounted, my legs nearly gave out on me, and I had to grab the saddle to keep myself from falling to the ground. I hated how weak I was. Tears struggled for release as I let my head fall forward to rest against the leather saddle I'd been tied to for so many days. So much death and destruction . . . it left me breathless with grief. Contrary to Armando's belief, I was far from invincible; I'd been extremely lucky up until this point to have survived my battles against so many sorcerers so much more powerful than I could ever dream of being. So many had sacrificed their lives to help me defeat them — without their aid, I wouldn't ever have succeeded. Without Jude, and Eljin, and now Akio.

As if she could sense my distress, the mare swung her head around to nip at my arm softly, with just her lips. I reached forward to scratch her chin, though my arm shook from the effort and the painful wounds from the bleedings throbbed even harder.

"It's not your fault," I said. "You can't control who owns you."

I took a deep breath and straightened. There was no time for this. I had to find food and water. I could sit for a minute, to rest and let the nourishment take hold. And then we would keep going.

I had to get to Damian. I had to prove that I kept my word — I was coming back to him.

I lost track of how many days — or weeks — we'd been traveling, barely stopping to sleep, scrounging for fruit or roots to survive on, pushing forward as fast as possible to continue to outrun King Armando, when I finally pulled the mare, who I had named Nia after my mother, whose name had been Nialah, to a stop. There, in the valley before us, carved out from the belly of the jungle, was the city of Tubatse. And above it, on the hill across from us, rose the walls that surrounded the palace.

I stared at my former home, straining to see any sign of life. Heavy, dark clouds, pregnant with rain, strained above us, preparing to unleash their load at any moment. But after waiting for long minutes, hoping to see something — anything — that would defy the rumors, I had to accept what I was seeing.

The capital city and the palace of Antion were completely abandoned.

❧ THIRTY-SEVEN ☙

*T*HE GATE TO the palace wall was already open when we rode up to it after crossing through the empty city, passing one abandoned house after another. The only consolation was that it appeared to have been voluntary. There were no signs of fighting or destruction.

I urged Nia past the wall, just to make sure. I had to be absolutely certain that no one was in the palace before I moved on. I didn't even know where to go now. My whole focus had been to get here — to get to Damian. But as we circled the empty grounds I had to face the reality that no one was there, including the king.

Weeds had already sprung up everywhere, the tenacious jungle reclaiming its ground as quickly as possible now that there was no one to hold it at bay. I guided Nia over to the stables where Damian had kept his horse, but it, too, was empty. I dismounted and let her eat what little bit of food for the horses was left.

While she ate, I turned to face the palace. The silence was strangely deafening — and unnerving. The tent city of displaced women and babies was gone; the army and guards were all gone. No sounds of sparring, or sentinels changing shifts. There was no movement behind the windows of the palace. Only the dark reflection of the storm building in the sky above us.

I looped Nia's reins over one of the bars inside the stable and then strode across the hard ground toward the palace, just as the first few fat drops of rain plopped against my face and arms. I broke into a run, but the storm broke faster, turning into a deluge in mere seconds. I was completely soaked by the time I rushed up the stairs — the same ones where I'd fought Iker — and then stopped in front of the massive door that filled the main entrance to the palace. I hesitated for some reason, but then forced myself to reach for the handle and try it. The door ground open; they'd left it unlocked.

Once inside, I left the door ajar so more light would illuminate the dark, empty palace. There were no candles, no torches or fires, to break up the gloom from the storm. Despite the thick humidity in the air, I couldn't keep from shivering. The wounds that were finally almost healed in the crooks of my elbows still caused a ping of pain when I bent my arms to wrap them around my body and walked purposefully forward.

There was no reason to be afraid, I told myself. No one was here. I'd hurry and get what I needed and then continue on. Surely, so many people trekking through the jungle would leave a distinct path, despite the constant rain that would have washed away their tracks. But where on earth could they have gone?

Shaking off my paranoia, I hurried toward the stairs and ran up to my old room, pushing the door open and then striding straight over to my guard uniforms. I practically tore the Dansiian clothes from my body in my rush to get them off. Once they were in a wet pile on the ground, I reached for the dry, familiar clothes I'd worn for years as Damian's personal guard. I paused after pulling on my pants, before yanking the shirt over my head, to stare down at the scars on my arms. The slashes where The Summoner had punctured my skin with his disgusting device were red and angry looking, but at least they didn't appear to be getting infected as they healed. Akio had managed to heal my shoulder completely, my new scars blending in with the old ones Iker had given me. Thinking of Akio reminded me of that horrible night in Bikoro, and his death. I shook away those memories, forcing them to the recesses of my mind as I finished dressing, pulled on the extra pair of boots I'd kept in my room, and then picked up the wet clothes and walked out of my room toward Damian's.

As soon as I opened the door to his actual room and saw his bed and desk and everything else left untouched, abandoned, I forgot for a moment why I'd come in there. I froze in the doorway, staring at the shadowed, empty room. Something inside me lurched when I glanced toward the window where Damian had stood when I came to tell him I had to go after Rylan. Had he left the palace thinking I was dead?

Lightning flashed, blinding me momentarily and making me flinch, and then thunder roared across the jungle, rattling the windowpanes. Shaken from my painful thoughts, I remembered the wet, cold clothes in my arms and rushed toward the fireplace and tossed them down on top of the ashes. I never wanted to see them again — didn't want anything left to remind me of that horrible night or all the things that had led up to it. I knelt down in front of the hearth and picked up the stone and flint to start a fire. There were only two pieces of wood and a tiny bit of kindling, but after some effort, I was able to get the fire going. The clothes were too wet to catch easily and thick, viscous smoke chugged into the air as the flames from the logs attempted to spread to the pile of soggy fabric.

I waited, staring at the fire until finally, the fabric began to curl and turn black, slowly burning away to ash despite the moisture in the threads from the rain. Only once they were completely gone — destroyed — and the logs nearly burned down to nothing did I stand and turn to face the empty room again.

And that's when I noticed the parchment lying on the desk, with an unfamiliar ring lying on top of it.

A strange echo of my heartbeat pounded in my belly as I walked hesitantly toward the desk to see Damian's familiar handwriting on the parchment beneath the beautiful ring.

It was a letter . . . addressed to me.

⇥ THIRTY·EIGHT ⇤

MY HANDS SHOOK as I picked up the ring so I could get to
the letter. It was much smaller than something that would
have fit Damian, and in the center of the band was a large, stunning blue gemstone that reminded me almost perfectly of the color
of Damian's eyes, cut into a rectangle, with smaller glittering diamonds inlaid on the band to either side of the center stone.

I carefully set the ring down on the desk to pick up the letter.

My Dearest Alexa,

If you are reading this, then my pleadings for a mira-
cle have been answered, and you have somehow survived to
return to the palace. I know there is no reason to hope for
such a miracle, but hope is the only luxury I have left to
keep me from giving up entirely and just succumbing to
the continual horrors fate seems to yet hold in store for me
and my people.

The ring I left is the ring I told you about — my moth-
er's ring, the one I hoped to give you to formally secure our
engagement. There is no one else I could ever give it to, so I
left it behind, as a token of my faith that miracles can

occur. That perhaps, they might even someday occur for me. Though I have little reason to believe that, I suppose.

I am rambling and must close this pointless letter, as General D'agnen has assembled everyone from the palace to begin our long journey to Lóngshāndū, the capital city of Blevon. But, you wouldn't know — I made Deron the new general over all my armies and have promoted Rylan to captain of my personal guard. At least you were successful in your mission. You saved Rylan. Only to be taken captive yourself, and most likely killed by now.

No, I refuse to lose hope. If you do return to find the palace empty, come to me in Blevon.

Eternally Yours,

Damian, King of Antion

The words of his letter blurred through my tears. Deron had been made general. Rylan had survived — he'd returned to Damian. He must have given Damian my warning and convinced him to retreat to Blevon as I'd said, to join forces with King Osgand, despite the declaration of war. But they all believed me dead. Even though Damian had left the ring and this letter behind, I could hear the desperation behind his attempt at retaining hope.

He, too, thought I was lost.

My hands trembled as I picked up the ring and shakily slid it onto my finger. I picked up the letter to read it once more, but this time I noticed a second letter beneath it, this one written in a different language — Blevonese. I couldn't understand any of it, except for who it was addressed to, *Damian*, and part of the signature:

Osgand.

The king of Blevon had written Damian personally.

When I returned to the stable, still wearing my ring, and with Damian's letter tucked into the leather satchel at my side, Nia was standing with her head lifted and ears cocked. I unwrapped her reins from the bar and led her outside, where the storm had wound down, only sprinkling little flecks of water toward the earth, barely enough to do more than mist the air. I'd managed to scrounge up a bow and a quiver of arrows, as well as an old sword. It wasn't the sharpest blade I'd ever used, but it was better than nothing. I also had a knapsack packed with every little bit of food I could find that had been left behind. I attached it to the saddle, to the very metal ring that I had been tied to for so long, and then put my foot in the stirrup and swung up and over Nia's back.

As we trotted back out the gate toward the main road that would take us away from Tubatse and continue on toward Blevon, I glanced over my shoulder at the palace one more time. It rose into the roiling clouds, a massive, sprawling sentinel that had stood for centuries, housing the kings and queens of Antion until the day Hector and Armando had killed them and placed a Dansiian on the throne. Though I hated them for what they'd done, and all the deaths and suffering they'd caused, I had to acknowledge that without Hector's atrocities, there never would have been a Prince Damian for me to guard and eventually fall in love with. And this had been his home, too.

For some reason, as I stared up at the empty windows a dark foreboding washed over me — a feeling that I would never see the palace again.

For days we rushed toward Blevon without a sign of human life —
though we ran into plenty of *other* life, including birds, monkeys,
an unfortunate scare with a massive snake winding its way across
the road, and the sound of a jaguar's throaty roar much too close
for comfort, but luckily without any situations in which I had to
use either of the weapons I carried. Though there weren't any boot
prints left, there were some indicators that a large group of people
had passed through Antion by way of this road recently: trampled bushes on either side of the path, broken branches, and trees
stripped bare of their fruits, making it so that I had to trek farther
away from the road, deeper into the jungle, to find any food for
Nia and me once the few supplies I'd managed to scrounge up in
the raided kitchen were gone.

I only stopped to eat a couple of times a day and forced Nia to
keep going long into the darkness of the nights, until I was so
exhausted I couldn't stay upright in the saddle any longer. Then I
would finally pull Nia to a stop and allow myself to sleep, my arms
wrapped through her reins, hoping she would wake me if she
sensed any danger.

As we neared the border between Blevon and Antion, I grew
increasingly anxious and determined to keep moving quickly. So
far, I'd managed to outpace King Armando and his massive army,
but every morning I jerked awake at first light — sometimes even
before dawn — my heart racing and my nightmares making my
skin cold with sweat, expecting to open my eyes to a sea of flames,
or worse, to Armando leaning over me with a sword to my throat.

Finally, the jungle began to thin out and the tall grasses and sparser trees of Blevon took its place, but the road I'd been following also narrowed and turned into little more than a cart path after a day of traveling through Blevon. I hadn't seen any towns yet, but I wasn't sure what I would do when I reached one, since I didn't speak their language. Was Antion still considered an enemy? I desperately wondered what the letter from Osgand had contained. I didn't know where I was, or how to get to the capital city of Blevon, where King Osgand lived, but I was easily able to pick out the path the people of Antion had left — a wide swath of trampled grass and broken bushes. I was even able to find where they'd made camps from the mounds where fires had been built and the flattened grass where tents had been erected.

For four more days, I followed their trail, which wound over the hills and through the strange, thin trees I remembered from my last trek into Blevon, but never once spotted a single town. I wondered if Damian had someone helping him avoid them on purpose, or if they were just hoping they were heading in the right direction. Eljin could have guided him, but he had come with me. And now he was gone forever.

The deeper into the kingdom Nia and I traveled, the cooler the temperatures grew, especially at night. The ground also grew harder and drier, but not in the hot, parched way of Dansii's. Blevon was a wilder kingdom, with thin grasses and tall trees that clumped together in bunches, most of their strange and brightly colored leaves littering the ground, rather than staying attached to the trees. I remembered Eljin's story — that Blevon had been cursed because of Prince Delun's atrocities in becoming a black sorcerer and attacking his brother to try and take his throne — and wondered if that was why it was so cold at night, and why the soil was like a massive, unending rock beneath Nia's hooves the farther we traveled through the kingdom. It also led me to wonder if the even harsher climate of Dansii was yet another curse — an even more powerful one, because of their horrific, ongoing atrocities.

The hills that had started out as rolling, grassy knolls grew larger and larger with each passing day, turning into steep, rocky inclines that would suddenly pitch down again toward wide, gaping valleys where small streams gathered into paltry lakes that reflected cloudless skies. And surrounding the lakes were towns.

Towns that were abandoned — completely empty. We rode past silently as I fought a chill of dread. What had happened to make all these people — Antionese and Blevonese alike — leave their homes and flee to King Osgand?

⇥ THIRTY-NINE ⇤

A MASSIVE MOUNTAIN RANGE had begun to take form on the horizon a few days into our trek through Blevon, and I quickly realized the path I was following in the wake of the Antionese exodus was heading straight for them. I knew I was traveling somewhat northwest, and that made me wonder if the peaks I could see jutting up into the sky in the far distance were part of the Naswais Mountains, which divided the border of Blevon and Dansii, or if these were an entirely different range.

The path we were on turned into more of a rocky trail the closer we got to the massive mountains, and though the ground continued to rise and fall into peaks and valleys, we seemed to be moving up a steady incline. I imagined it would have been difficult to get such a large group of people and animals to move as quickly on the narrower road — I could only hope it would slow King Armando down. I was continually looking back, searching the sky for smoke or dust or any sign that he was getting close, but so far, there had been no sign of him gaining on me and Nia.

After six or seven days in Blevon, with food options growing scarcer and scarcer, I could feel myself weakening again. I needed to hunt, but I didn't dare take the time, too afraid of King Armando drawing closer. Nia bravely pushed on, but we were no longer galloping. Instead, Nia plodded up the steep inclines and then braced herself as her hooves threatened to skid down the declines on the other side of the summits we traversed.

The night of the seventh day, the air was bitingly cold. My fingers were almost numb as I clutched the reins, and Nia's breath plumed into clouds in front of her face as she huffed her way up yet another steep incline. The mountain peaks were close now, so close; if I'd had to guess, I was fairly certain we would reach them in two days' time.

Assuming I survived that long.

I'd found a stream for Nia to drink from earlier in the day, and I'd replenished my flagon, but though Nia had found some dried-up leaves to munch on and a little bit of thin grass, there had been nothing for me to eat, except a few shriveled mushrooms at the base of a tree and a couple of hard, round nuts of some sort that seemed to have fallen from the tree itself. I was nervous to eat the mushrooms, not sure if they would be safe or not, but finally desperation won out, and I bit into one. It didn't taste harmful, so I quickly ate the rest. But within a few hours, my stomach began to cramp, and I ended up stopping Nia so I could lean over and vomit my meager lunch back up again.

"Keep going, girl," I murmured to her, half to keep myself from slipping into sleep and half to force my frozen lips to move. The cold was so intense; I'd never felt anything like it, not even on the coldest night in Dansii. The air had a crystalline feel to it, and the slate clouds that hung low in the sky, concealing the peaks of the mountain range in the distance, were different from any other clouds I'd seen before. I'd heard of snow, but I'd never seen it in person, except from a distance on the tops of the Naswais

Mountains. I had a sinking feeling I was going to get firsthand experience with it very soon.

Nia dipped her head down as she reached the summit of one of the rolling hills, and I pulled back on her reins to let her pause and rest for a moment before continuing on to find somewhere we could sleep for the night. But when I looked down into the massive valley below us, my heart suddenly leaped into my throat, choking the breath out of me.

Hundreds of fires dotted the darkness with light. And in the distance, spreading across the far hills to the north of where Nia stood — hills that rose up into the massive mountain range — a huge city sprawled. It was a city full of people, judging from the tiny specks of glowing windows that gave the buildings a golden hue beneath the cloud cover. And rising above it all, built on an outcropping that jutted straight out from the base of the tallest mountain, stood a huge castle, its pearlescent walls so white, it was visible even in the darkness, even from all the way across the valley.

"Damian," I whispered. Tears stung my eyes as I squeezed my ice-cold legs against Nia's sides, urging her to hurry down the hill.

We'd made it. Somehow I'd done it. I'd escaped; I'd *lived*. And I'd made it back to him.

"Damian," I repeated as Nia struggled down the steep, rocky path toward the valley below. Her hooves slid through the shale and rock, but she kept her footing and continued her stiff-legged descent toward the glowing fires and the thousands of tents that filled the valley.

I clutched the reins, sitting tall in the saddle and searching the darkness, straining to see if I could spot him, even though I knew it was irrational to hope that he would be staying on the outskirts of this tent city.

Nia picked up the pace the moment the trail began to level out slightly, as if she could sense my urgency, and trotted toward the massive camp.

It was so late, the fires were all burning low, and only a few shadowy bodies milled about while everyone else slept.

As soon as we reached the bottom of the trail, Nia broke into a full gallop, racing toward the tents.

A shout of alarm went up, but I didn't care; I urged her to go even faster.

"Damian," I cried out, quietly at first, then louder and louder, my voice rough with desperation. "Damian!"

The tents were only a few strides away when a Blevonese soldier on horseback rode into our path, lifting his sword, and shouted, "Halt!" in heavily accented Antionese.

I didn't recognize him, so I wheeled Nia to the right and kicked my heels into her sides, leaning forward to knead my hands along her neck, urging her to go as fast as her legs would carry her. Let the soldier come after me; I didn't care. If he was a sorcerer, he could try to stop me, but at least I knew he wouldn't be flinging fire at my back.

"Damian!" I shouted, the wind tearing my voice away as Nia plunged in between two tents and we began to race our way through the makeshift city, toward the actual city rising on the hills above what suddenly seemed to be a never-ending valley.

There were more shouts, and I glanced over my shoulder to see three men in pursuit of me now — but this time, I did recognize one of them.

I sawed back on Nia's reins, and she ground to a sudden halt, dirt clods kicking up in the air from her hooves digging into the ground.

"Mateo! Mateo, it's me!" I shouted out to them as they barreled down upon us, even though I'd stopped.

When he heard his name he leaned forward, and then he jerked back in his saddle, yanking on the reins of his horse as his eyes widened in shock. He lifted one hand to wave some sort of signal to the other men, and they all pulled their mounts back to a slow trot before stopping a few feet away from me.

"*Alexa?*" Mateo was still gaping at me. "It can't be. . . . Rylan said . . . you . . ."

"Where is he?" I cut him off, urgency burning through my blood.

"Wh —"

"Where is Damian? *Where is he?*" My voice grew frantic.

"He's over there — we just got here and we haven't made it all the way to —"

I didn't wait to hear the rest of whatever reason there was that Damian wasn't at the castle in the distance yet. I spurred Nia into a gallop again, heading in the direction Mateo had pointed.

⊰ FORTY ⊱

D AMIAN!" I SHOUTED, heedless of all the people sleeping in tents as Nia charged through the camp. "DAMIAN!"

"Alexa?" When I heard his responding shout, my heart nearly stopped.

"Damian." His name turned into a strangled sob as he burst out of a tent just ahead of us, barefoot, wearing only his pants and a loose tunic.

"Alexa!" His eyes went wide with astonishment when he saw me, and for a split second he stood frozen. But then he broke into a run, racing toward us. I pulled on Nia's reins, but didn't even wait for her to completely stop before throwing myself off the saddle and into his arms, just as he reached her side.

"Damian," I cried out hoarsely as he grabbed me to him, squeezing me so tightly I could scarcely breathe. But I didn't care. It was him. It was *Damian* — holding me in his arms again. Tears blinded me, rushing down my face as I clung to him.

"Alexa," he choked out. His mouth pressed to the groove where my neck met my shoulder. He hadn't even let my feet touch the ground yet. "You're alive. You're *alive*." His voice cracked and he broke down into sobs, his whole body shaking violently beneath my arms.

I reached up to grasp his hair, holding his head against my body. "I promised I'd come back to you. I promised." I couldn't stop crying, taking great, heaving gulps of air as we clung to each other, hardly able to believe this was real.

Suddenly, he pulled back to stare into my face, finally setting me down on the hard ground. His eyes were still full of tears and his cheeks were wet. "I can't believe it," he whispered. "I can't believe you're really here. You're alive. You're alive." He kept repeating it as he stroked my hair back from my face, over and over.

And then he bent down, crushing his mouth to mine, his arms encircling my body once more, pulling me in to his chest. I pressed myself in to him, winding my arms around his back and clutching his tunic as his lips moved on mine. Desperation, love, and grief melded together into a tide of emotions that consumed me — body and soul.

"I love you," Damian said against my mouth. "I love you, *I love you*." He pulled back just an inch or two, so that his forehead rested against mine, his eyes squeezed shut. "I'm going to tell you every minute of every day until we both die."

"As much as I enjoy hearing you say it, I'm not sure everyone else would care for hearing it thousands of times for the rest of our lives," I teased gently, smiling for the first time in weeks — maybe even months.

"I don't care what anyone else thinks," he responded gruffly. "You *died*. Rylan was sure you'd been killed. I lost you, Alexa. I've been mourning your loss this whole time, ever since Rylan showed up at the palace, sick and injured and alone." He leaned back so that his piercing blue eyes could meet mine — so similar to his uncle's and yet so very, *very* different. "What did they do to you in Dansii? How did you ever escape?"

Images of the dungeons, of The Summoner and Akio and Eljin and King Armando and more began to fill my mind until I shook my head, swallowing everything down, deep into the depths of me. I didn't want to talk about it, not now. Maybe not ever. "I can't," was all I managed to force out.

Damian's arms tightened around me, and his gaze darkened slightly, but he responded, "It's all right. You don't have to talk about it. You're here now. I can't believe it's true, but you are."

"I promised," I whispered, trying to hold myself together, to keep everything locked inside of me. My only thought had been to find him, to keep my word. And somehow, against all odds, I'd done it. But now that I had, everything I'd been holding in for so long threatened to shatter me into a million pieces.

"I should have had more faith, but after Rylan explained what he'd been through and overheard, it just didn't seem possible. . . ." He trailed off with a shake of his head. "I've never felt pain like that in my entire life — not even when my mother died, because I *could* have saved *you*. Instead, I ignored my instincts, and I let you leave and go to your death. When Rylan told me what had happened when you tried to escape, I didn't want to go on; I didn't want to fight. But I love my people, too, and I know my duty. So I planned; I led them here, all the while hardly able to force myself to eat anything or get up each morning." He reached up to cup my face, his fierce expression softening. "But then, I heard you shout my name. I thought I was dreaming. I thought perhaps I *had* finally died. But I'm not dead, and somehow my prayers were answered — because you're *here*. And if I want to tell you I love

249

you every minute of every day for the rest of our lives, *no one* is going to stop me. Least of all you."

I was smiling and crying all at once as I stretched up to press my lips to his again.

"All right, you win. You can say it as much as you like. I should have known better than to argue with the sorcerer King of Antion."

He laughed once, a tiny burst of happiness, against my mouth.

"Your Majesty, I apologize for interrupting. . . ."

We broke apart and turned to see Mateo standing a little way off, holding his horse's reins in one hand and a plate in the other.

"I thought Alexa might be hungry after her ordeal getting here. I brought her some food."

My eyes dropped to the plate with sudden interest, to see what looked like some sort of meat and fruit along with a roll. The adrenaline of being reunited with Damian began to drain away as the exhaustion and hunger that had held me in its grasp for so long surged back up.

"Thank you, Mateo." Damian kept an arm around my waist, pulling me with him when he stepped forward to take the plate. "Will you please take Alexa's horse and see that she is fed and rubbed down as well?"

Mateo nodded, handing off the plate, then guiding his horse toward Nia and reaching out to grab her reins. Her flanks were flecked with white, and her nostrils still flared when she breathed, from galloping toward Damian after a full day and half a night's travel without much of a break.

"Her name is Nia," I said, gazing fondly at the mare I now considered mine. She and I had been through a lot together.

As Mateo led her away, I turned back to Damian. "I didn't know Mateo knew how to ride."

"He didn't. We've all had to learn a lot to survive the last little while," Damian replied, guiding me toward his tent. It was no bigger than any of the others, and there were no extra embellishments to denote that it was the tent of the king of Antion. But when he pulled the flap open for me, the sight of the thick blankets and furs that made up his bed on the ground was almost enough to start me crying yet again. I couldn't remember the last time I'd slept in any semblance of comfort.

"You must be freezing," he observed as I stood there, staring at his bed. "Here, sit down and start eating."

I did as he suggested and sat on the edge of the blankets, taking the plate from him and lifting a piece of the meat to my mouth. Damian knelt down beside me and wrapped one of the furs around my shoulders.

I tried to eat quickly, watching him the whole while, as if the very act of staring at Damian would make it seem more plausible that I was sitting in a tent next to him. I noticed his eyes drop to my hands, and he exhaled softly.

"You found it." Damian reached out and hesitantly ran the tips of his fingers over my knuckles and the ring I wore — his mother's ring.

That tiny touch sent an explosion of sensation rushing up my arm and straight into my lungs, where my breath caught. His eyes lifted to mine again as his fingertips slid up my arm, gently pulling me toward him, the almost-empty plate forgotten.

"So does this mean you still want to be my queen?" he asked, his eyes on my lips as he rose to his knees and crawled closer to me, sliding his hand over the top of my shoulder to the back of my neck.

"No," I replied, and he drew back, his eyebrows lifting. "I've never wanted to be a queen. But I *do* want to be your wife. And I suppose being the queen is an unavoidable consequence of that desire."

Damian laughed, shaking his head as I rose to my knees as well, so that we were only a foot apart. His thumb stroked up and down the tendon behind my ear. When our eyes met again, his smile died.

"I can't believe you're truly here," he whispered, closing the gap so that our bodies nearly touched. He wound his other arm around my waist and drew me in so close to him that I had to pull my head back and lift my chin to look up at him.

I reached up to cup his face in both of my hands, pulling him toward me, until his mouth brushed mine. He paused, as if savoring the moment of anticipation, his breath warming my still-cold lips. I let my eyes close and wrapped my arms around his neck, my heart flying beneath my ribs.

"This isn't a dream, is it?" he asked softly.

I shook my head, my eyes still closed. "If it is, you need to pick a better location for your next dream."

He laughed again, a soft, low sound that delved straight through me, deep into my belly. Then suddenly, he was kissing me, any teasing forgotten in the face of an all-consuming need that swooped up and threatened to pull us both under. He clutched at me, pressing his body into mine, and I pushed back just as hard, clinging to him as his lips moved on mine. The hand he still had on my back tightened around my tunic, lifting it so that his fingertips brushed my bare skin. The combination of the cold air and his heated touch sent a delicious shiver down my spine, and I had the sudden, wanton desire to pull his shirt off, to feel his skin against mine.

Almost as if he could sense my need, he bent forward, pressing me down toward the ground, until I was laying on the bed of furs, with him beside me, his kiss growing even more heated, one hand teasing my hips, my spine, the lower edge of my rib cage, while the other cushioned my head.

Our legs tangled together as I reached beneath his shirt to explore the muscles of his back with my fingertips. His mouth left mine so that he could bend his head and kiss my neck, working his way toward the groove behind my collarbone. I was gasping for air when I arched my head back to give him easier access. My eyes opened to see the fabric ceiling above us, and the reality that we were in a tent, in the middle of a massive camp, suddenly hit me like a cold rain that stole the heat of a fire, dousing its flames.

"Stop," I managed to say, my voice hoarse.

Damian immediately stilled, lifting his head to look at me inquisitively. But before I could explain my thoughts, he said, "You're right," and pulled my tunic back into place. He reached up to brush some hair off my cheek, before lifting himself up onto one elbow so he could look down at me. "I apologize for getting so carried away."

"No apology necessary." I was sure my cheeks were bright red — both from the cold and from what he'd just done to me. My lips throbbed, and I was already chilled without his body pressed to mine. He must have noticed my shiver, because he immediately got to his knees and bent down to grab some of the blankets and pull them over my body, tucking them around my shoulders. I noted that he didn't cover himself with the blankets, though.

When he noticed my questioning frown, he smiled ruefully. "I don't want anyone to ever question your honor or purity. I will go sleep with some of the other members of the guard. It's a cold night; they won't mind the extra body heat, I'm sure."

"I . . . I don't . . ." I trailed off, uncomfortable and embarrassed, especially after he had just been so kind as to think about my *honor* and *purity*. I, who had been living with men for the majority of the last few years.

"What is it?" he prompted, still kneeling beside me, his vibrant blue eyes still slightly darkened with need and his breathing ragged, which made me think that he might not have been quite as cool and collected as he seemed.

"I don't want to be alone," I finally admitted.

His gaze softened, and he reached down to brush his fingers across my jaw, sending another shiver of want through me. "How about if I lie with you until you fall asleep, and then I'll go."

"But you need to sleep, too," I protested.

"Not tonight, I don't." He lifted the blankets and stretched out beside me. I turned my back to him, so he could wrap his arm around my waist and pull me in tight to his chest, curling his body around mine.

We were silent for a moment, so that all I could hear was the thud of my heart echoing through my head, pulsing in my ears. Perhaps this hadn't been the plan most conducive to helping me sleep, I realized. Despite the exhaustion that weighed me down, all I wanted to do was roll over and kiss him again and, this time, never stop.

"Why did you come here?" I asked to distract myself. "What did King Osgand's letter say? I thought Blevon declared war on us."

Damian's arm tightened around me, and he sighed against my hair. "General Tinso's missive did, yes. But I'd already sent someone to King Osgand to ascertain his thoughts on the situations we'd heard about before that — the attacks on the villages, supposedly made by the Blevonese army combined with black sorcerers. I received the letter back from him a couple of weeks after you left, shortly after my scouts had returned to tell me that they couldn't find General Tinso, that his castle was abandoned and the town outside of it ransacked and pillaged, confirming my fears that something else was going on, beyond what we knew.

"King Osgand first wrote to tell me that he feared Dansii was bringing great evil through the jungles of Antion to Blevon, and that he had reason to believe my uncle was preparing to attack us very soon. He told me what I already knew through you — that no black sorcerers would ever have come from Blevon, which meant that Dansii was behind the attacks, disguised as Blevonese soldiers, probably just wearing their uniforms, or forcing the Blevonese soldiers to act on their orders on pain of death."

I wove my fingers through Damian's, squeezing tightly as he spoke.

"The letter you saw, beneath the one I left you, was the second missive he sent me. I had responded and told him of the declaration of war from General Tinso and what Rylan told me when he returned — that Armando was amassing his entire army to march through Antion and destroy us before moving on to Blevon. He recommended exactly what you had — that I send notices to my people to evacuate to Blevon, and to bring my armies and those who wished to fight to his castle and there make our stand against Dansii together. I'd already done as you suggested and had as many of my people who were willing come to Tubatse, where I could more easily protect them. It took a few days, but I eventually convinced them that Blevon was not our enemy, and that we needed to do as King Osgand asked. Our only hope of surviving this is to join our forces together."

"These tents . . ."

"Are for the many soldiers from both Antion and Blevon. Those who didn't wish to fight have fled to the farthest reaches of Blevon, into the mountains or to the southwest, far from the castle and *Sì Miào Chán Wù*."

The temple that Armando wanted to take possession of — where he believed he would be able to claim the ultimate power for himself and his people by drinking from the golden waters.

"We will stop him," I said, though a pulse of fear beat low in my belly.

Damian squeezed me tightly. "Yes, we will."

I wondered if he, too, was ignoring the worry that we were both wrong.

⇥ FORTY-ONE ⇤

HE SOUND OF shouting outside jerked me awake the next day. After our discussion of King Osgand's letter, we'd both fallen silent, and eventually I'd relaxed into the warmth and strength of Damian's arms and drifted off to sleep. But when I lurched up, gazing wildly around the tent, I realized he'd stayed true to his word and left during the night.

I was alone.

The air was still bitterly cold, even though it was daylight outside. The tent was lit by a muted glow that could only have been from the sun. I quickly stood up and ran out of the tent to see hundreds of men and even some women rushing back and forth. I recognized a few of the Antionese soldiers, but none by name. A strange panic seized me, clutching at my lungs until I could barely breathe. I spun in the direction Nia and I had come from last night, positive I was going to see Armando's armies on the summit we'd traversed. But the rocky incline was empty, save for some scraggly trees — and a fine coating of snow, painting the entire scene white.

Where I stood in the valley, the ground was frozen hard, but there was no snow. Yet. I turned back toward the camp, searching for anyone I knew, when I heard a voice from behind me that I'd been positive I'd never hear again.

"Alex!"

I spun to see Rylan running toward me, pulling Nia behind him.

"Rylan!" I met him halfway, letting him scoop me up with one arm — his uninjured one — pulling me against his chest. "I can't believe you made it! I was so afraid that you'd died in those tunnels."

"You can't believe *I'm* alive? Of course I made it." He sounded insulted. "*I* can't believe *you're* alive."

"It was a close call," I admitted.

"I'll have to tell you someday about how I killed a black sorcerer by pretending to be one myself and then barely made it through that gate alive by hiding in the back of a cart, but for now, the king needs you." He handed me Nia's reins, and I eagerly stepped forward to rub her nose.

"Hey, girl," I murmured. I hadn't been separated from her for more than an hour or two since we'd escaped from King Armando until last night, and it was a relief to be with the small, tenacious mare once more. "Where is he?" I asked, turning back to Rylan.

"He's waiting for you up there." He pointed down the path between the row of tents where we stood. "Our outer scouts have spotted the Dansiian army. They got here more quickly than we anticipated, and King Osgand and King Damian have both ordered their armies to retreat to the city and the mountains surrounding the castle. We'll be target practice for the sorcerers out here."

I threw Nia's reins over her head and hurried to her side so I could swing myself up into her saddle. "Are you coming, *Captain*?" I asked once I'd settled into my seat.

Rylan smiled ruefully as he looked up at me, the flecks of gold in his brown eyes more prominent in the sunlight. "You weren't here to claim the title. I was the best of what was left, I suppose.

And to answer your question, no, not yet. I have to help organize this chaos and get our men where they need to be. And women," he added, looking past me.

I twisted in the saddle to see another familiar figure standing a little way off, arguing with an Antionese soldier I didn't know. She looked different — her hair was cut short, just above her shoulders, and she wore tight pants, boots, a tunic, and a vest. But when she glanced up and her eyes met mine, almost as if she could feel the weight of my guilty stare, Tanoori's face broke into a smile. I saw my name form on her lips, though I couldn't hear her voice, and then she waved the man off and hurried over to us.

I had to dismount so I could throw my arms around her, biting down on my tongue to keep from crying.

"I can't tell you how glad I am that you made it," Tanoori said as she hugged me back tightly. "When I heard the news this morning, I couldn't believe it."

I pulled away to brush hastily at the tears on my cheeks. "I'm so sorry," I whispered, my voice choked.

Seeing her brought back all the grief and guilt that I'd tried to bury after Eljin's death. Because of me, the man she'd allowed herself to fall in love with was gone.

She took my hand in hers, gripping it tightly, her smile slipping away, her dark eyes bright with unshed tears. "I am, too."

"If I'd only been able to —"

"Stop," Tanoori cut me off. "It wasn't your fault. Rylan told me what happened. You did the best you could. He went with you willingly, to protect you. And he did his job." Her voice wobbled slightly, and she squeezed my hand one more time before letting go and wiping at her eyes brusquely.

I shook my head, unable to speak.

"Go," she urged me. "The king is waiting for you. I have to help here."

I nodded and turned back to Nia, climbing into the saddle once more. "I'm glad you got your wish," I managed to say. "To fight," I added when she looked at me with her eyebrows lifted.

She gave me a rueful smile as her hand dropped to rest on the hilt of the sword at her hip. "I'm not nearly good enough yet, but at least I'm not entirely helpless any longer."

"Just remember that being small actually gives you an advantage — you're quicker and harder to catch. Use that."

Tanoori nodded. "Thank you, Alexa. Good luck to you."

"And you," I replied, knowing she meant in the upcoming battle.

With a final glance toward Rylan, Tanoori turned and headed back the way she'd come. He'd stood there the whole time observing, but now he came forward.

"It wasn't your fault," he repeated, gazing up at me, his hand resting on Nia's powerful shoulder muscle, near my leg. "We knew that if it came down to choosing to sacrifice ourselves so you could escape and survive, that we would do it. You were the one who had to get back to Damian. He needs you, Alexa."

I clenched my teeth, staring off toward the mountains in the distance as I tried to control my emotions. The sky was a cloudless expanse of crystalline blue, frigid and endless over the rugged peaks that soared high above us, their alabaster perfection slashed by tears of black where jagged rocks cut through the blanket of snow. Rylan hesitantly touched my calf, and I forced myself to look back down at him.

"You should go," he said. "We have to hurry before Armando gets here."

I nodded, but when he turned to walk away I burst out, "Rylan, wait."

He faced me once again, but kept his distance. I hurried to dismount once more, my heart racing beneath my ribs. Armando was coming, and I didn't know what the future held for any of us. I walked up to him and wrapped my arms around him one more time, squeezing him tightly. He hugged me back, his strong arms enfolding me against his body. He sighed softly when he let his head drop to rest against mine for just an instant. And then he pulled away.

I stood there for a moment looking up at him, my throat tight. Finally, I reached up to cup his cheek. The ring Damian had given me glittered in the sunlight.

"I love you, Ry," I said softly. "You know that, don't you?"

He nodded, swallowing once, hard, his eyes never leaving mine. "I know you do." He lifted his hand to cover mine. "And you know I do, too."

I searched his eyes for a long moment, but for the first time since I'd found out that he knew my secret, I saw no jealousy, no bitterness in his gaze. I pulled my hand back and he let it go. But before I turned away, I stretched up and quickly kissed his cheek.

"Thank you," I whispered against his ear.

"Go," was all he said.

I gazed at him for a moment longer, and then I hurried over to Nia, remounted, and, wheeling her around, kicked her sides and rushed to where Rylan had told me Damian waited for me, leaving him standing there, staring after me.

⊰ FORTY-TWO ⊱

IT TOOK TWO hours to cross the valley, make our way through the streets of the city, and then finally pass the gate into the courtyard of King Osgand's castle. Damian rode his stallion, a dark black horse that was at least a couple of feet taller than my small mare, but he kept me at his side the whole time, followed by Deron — now General D'agnen — and some of Damian's personal guard. He'd ordered Rylan to come, as well as Jerrod, Asher, and Mateo. But the rest had stayed behind to help move everyone to higher ground and prepare for battle. Everyone knew about our engagement now, apparently, as many people congratulated us and bowed to both the king and me, though I noticed more than one person's eyes straying to the scars on my face before they bent their heads.

As we made our way through the city streets, I glanced over my shoulder to see the endless tent city completely disassembled and a sea of men, horses, and even women surging toward the mountains behind us. The city was already empty of women who did not wish to fight, children, and the elderly. They'd all been sent a week ago to the southwestern cities, far from where King Osgand anticipated the battle to take place, Damian explained as we rode through the valley. He'd also sent the women, children, and elderly of Antion — including Lisbet and Jax — to the south-western reaches of Blevon, hoping to keep them safe. He also told me how many of the men and boys who had chosen to return to their homes at the end of the last war had changed their minds, volunteering to stay with him and fight. They'd actually all arrived only a day before me, which was why he'd still been in the tent when I'd found him the night before.

It amazed me how close he'd come to having his people massacred by Armando. If he'd waited even a day or two more to abandon his palace and take his people to Blevon, Armando might have caught them and slaughtered them.

Once we went through the gate and saw King Osgand waiting for us, flanked by ten men on either side of him in full armor, I had to grip the reins harder to keep my hands from trembling.

"Welcome, King Damian. And, Alexa, I'm very happy to see you here as well. My informants tell me that you've endured quite an ordeal. But it sounds as if we are in your debt — yet again." King Osgand strode over to take my hand and assist me as I dismounted.

"Thank you, Your Majesty, but I don't know how you could possibly be in my debt," I disagreed.

King Osgand's dark eyes flickered to Damian, who watched us intently from his stallion, then back to me. "I was told that you are now responsible for killing not only the black sorcerer who did this to you" — he gestured to my cheek and neck — "but also the two men who King Armando called *Manu de Reich os Deos* and *El Evocon*."

"*El Ecovon?*" Damian repeated, his expression inscrutable in the bright sunlight as his eyes met mine.

"The Summoner," I translated, the memories of that horrible night surging once more. "Yes, I did kill them both." But how could King Osgand have found out about The Summoner?

When I didn't say any more, King Osgand inclined his head slightly. "The *Rén Zhŭsas* were told of his passing. A great evil has been removed from this world, and we are all indebted to you for that." And then he turned, gesturing for me to follow him. "Come, we have much to do and very little time to do it. Armando and his army of abominations could be here by the middle of this night if he marches through the darkness as well as the day."

I stared after him, wondering who had told the three powerful sorcerers who lived in the temple. Had it been the Unseen Power? Damian quickly dismounted and handed the reins of his stallion to a waiting stable boy. There were very few people in the courtyard, but the tension in the air was palpable as Damian came to my side and together we followed King Osgand toward the tall wooden doors painted red and carved with intricate twists and curls that would admit us into his castle.

"The Summoner?" Damian finally questioned under his breath.

"If we survive this battle, I'll tell you everything, I promise. But right now, the only important thing to know is that I lived and he didn't, and his death was probably a fairly large blow to Armando." I spoke rapidly, my voice quiet.

He glanced down at me but didn't say anything else. Instead, he reached over and took my hand in his, and together, we stepped through the doors and into King Osgand's castle.

It seemed like hours later, but in reality probably only an hour had passed when we reemerged and looked out at the now mostly empty valley. The majority of the two armies swarmed the city below us or hid in the mountains and trails surrounding the city and palace. King Osgand had instructed his generals and captains who could speak any Antionese to help divide Damian's men between their own companies of soldiers and sorcerers and then guide them where to go. The Blevonese knew this land and were able to tell Damian's people where the best places were to defend and fight the oncoming enemy. But I still felt a terrible foreboding as I stood on the castle steps and stared down at the land that was quiet and peaceful. Tomorrow, would the streams run red as they tumbled out of the mountains and through the city down into the valley, stained with the blood of both of our people, while Armando looked on in victory?

Osgand had given Damian and me fur-lined capes; Damian's was black on the outside and mine was a lighter silvery gray. I pulled it tighter around my body as we followed the king of Blevon around the side of the castle, toward a small iron gate that had three locks on it. He used a keychain attached to his hip to unlock two of the three — the last was a key that he wore around his neck, beneath his clothes — and then opened the gate, and Damian, myself, Rylan, Mateo, and Asher all followed him and his guards onto a narrow, snow-dusted path that wound up and away from the castle, deep into the mountains.

There were two ways to reach *Sì Miào Chán Wù* — the Temple of Awakening to Truth, where the golden waters were hidden and the *Rén Zhùsas* lived — King Osgand had explained to us. A large contingent of his army was placed along the other, easier-to-find

265

path. This second path was narrow and more easily defended, so there were a few soldiers spread out along the trail as we hiked farther and farther away from the castle, but not nearly as many as we'd been told were positioned along the other parallel path that we couldn't see from our location.

The trail twisted through the unfamiliar trees of Blevon and around massive boulders, sometimes rising steeply before flattening out again. It wound around a sharp outcropping of rock and then plunged deeper into the mountain range, taking us into a canyon. The sides of the mountains rose sharply above us, sheer and terrifying. A glittering layer of snow lightly dusted everything, but the higher up the mountain we climbed, the thicker the snow became, until we were tromping through several inches of it. My feet were cold; my hands were cold; my nose was frozen. Was the curse placed on Blevon because of Prince Delun truly why the terrain and weather were so different — and miserable? And if so, what would happen if we managed to defeat Armando and his horde of black sorcerers? What kind of curse would the land suffer this time?

I didn't dare ask.

The sun had begun to arc down to the earth again when Damian suddenly ground to a halt in front of me. I nearly ran into him before glancing up sharply and skidding to a stop right behind him. When I looked past him, I realized why he'd stopped.

The path had expanded in front of us, giving way to a small field. To the left was another, larger path that headed back down a second, wider canyon. But to the right, rising out of the craggy mountain walls, almost as if it were made of the mountain itself — had it not been for the stunning glass windows — was a majestic building that could only be one place.

"I give you *Sì Miào Chán Wù*," King Osgand said, turning to face us and lifting his arms.

The temple where it had all begun — where the first sorcerers were created. The original source of power in our world, and Armando's obsession.

Damian reached back to take my hand in his, and together we stared up at the temple in awe. I could sense Rylan behind me, but I didn't turn and look at him. He'd been quiet the whole day, and I got the feeling he was battling with himself. When Damian had asked him to come with us, he'd actually refused, taking the king of Antion by surprise. But I'd seen the panic cross Rylan's face, and I knew the reason for his fear — Rafe could control him with any direct command. If it came down to Rylan protecting the king or the temple, and Rafe made it to where we were, he would become a tool for the enemy.

But he didn't speak up, and when Damian repeated his command that Rylan come, he agreed.

I didn't share his secret. It wasn't mine to divulge.

As I stood there, staring up at the beautiful temple, my fingers intertwined with Damian's, I realized I still hadn't told him my secret, either. He didn't know that I couldn't fight Rafe. And according to Akio, since I was no sorcerer, there was no way I would be able to break through his command as Damian had done. My only hope was that since my father had been a sorcerer, perhaps a hint of his power ran in my veins. But I knew it was an improbable wish.

"Damian," I said quietly, and he immediately turned toward me. "There's something I have to tell you." I swallowed hard, forcing my humiliation and shame down.

He waited expectantly, his eyebrows lifted in concern, when suddenly there was a strange sound from behind us — almost like a birdcall, but not quite.

King Osgand stiffened beside Damian, his head cocking with alarm. "That's the signal," he murmured.

"What signal?" Mateo asked from behind us.

King Osgand looked right at Damian when he answered.

"That sound means the Dansiian army has been spotted. They're almost here."

⇥ FORTY-THREE ⇤

WHEN WE WERE in his castle, King Osgand convinced
Damian to agree that the two monarchs would go to the
temple, along with their most trusted guards. It was the safest
place for them to be and also the most crucial place to defend, if
the Dansiians made it that far. We were to be the last line of defense
if necessary.

I didn't like being so far away from the front line of the
battle — and so far out of sight as well. We would have no idea
what was happening in the city or lower parts of the mountain up
here, except what was relayed through messengers. All we would
know was that if the fighting reached us, things were dire indeed.
I did find out that all of King Osgand's top guards were, unsur-
prisingly, some of the best sorcerers in Blevon.

"King Damian, if you'll come with me, I will take you in to
meet the *Rén Zhūsas*, as you should have done many years ago."
King Osgand indicated for Damian to follow him, but the King of
Antion didn't let go of my hand, turning to look down at me,
alarm in his eyes.

"Go on," I urged, squeezing his hand, then letting go. "I'll be
waiting out here for you."

He glanced past me, toward the valley we couldn't see, where Armando's army might have been swarming already, and then he took a deep breath. "All right. But I won't be gone long."

I nodded and watched him walk away as he followed King Osgand up the final incline of the trail and onto the ledge where the temple was built.

"Excuse me, Alexa, right?" An unfamiliar voice from behind took me by surprise, and I turned to see a Blevonese guard standing there. I hadn't looked at him closely until then, but when I did, my jaw fell open, and I couldn't keep from staring.

He looked so much like my father, it was almost as if I'd seen a ghost, though his black hair was streaked with white, he was even taller than my father had been, and his eyes were a dark brown, not hazel.

"Your father was Vito Hollen, yes?" he asked.

I nodded.

"I am Jiro Hollen — I am his cousin."

For the next hour, Jiro and I sat on a large boulder, ignoring the cold, and talked, sharing memories of my father, while the other guards, both Blevonese and Antionese — including Rylan — looked on. I'd never known that my father had other family in Blevon. I'd only ever heard briefly of my grandparents. I had met them just once as a baby, before King Hector took the throne and started his war between Blevon and Antion, so I didn't remember them at all. We'd never been able to travel to Blevon again, and they had died before my parents did.

"Jiro," I began slowly, after he'd finished telling me a story from their childhood, when they'd lived in the same village in the southern part of Blevon, near what he called "the endless waters." "Was my father . . . Do you know if he was a sorcerer, like you?"

Jiro's dark eyes were compassionate when he nodded. "Yes, he was. He and I came here together when we were of age."

I took a deep breath and squeezed my eyes shut as the simultaneous pain of realizing he'd kept such a vital part of himself a secret from me and the excitement at discovering that my theory had been correct washed over me. "He called me his *zhànshì nánwū*," I said quietly.

Jiro smiled. "He must have loved you very much."

I nodded. "I think so."

"And you must be very talented to have earned a nickname like that," he added.

I smiled back at him. "I like to think it was from all the years of training for hours and hours a day, not necessarily just talent."

Jiro inclined his head. "That is probably far more accurate."

Another noise sounded from down the canyon, this time a different one, more piercing, and Jiro immediately jumped to his feet, all semblance of amusement gone from his face, and in the place of a kind relative suddenly stood a soldier. He began to bark out orders in Blevonese, and I glanced around wildly, wondering what had happened.

"What's going on?" I questioned Jiro as Rylan stood up from where he'd been leaning against a tree and walked over to us. Mateo was a little farther up the trail, talking to one of the other Blevonese guards, and Asher stood just beyond them.

Before he could respond I heard another sound — but this time it was no birdcall. It was the echo of an explosion, somewhere

271

below, in the canyon. Snow sprinkled down on us from the tree-tops as the ground vibrated from the impact.

I stared down the canyon in horror and then spun to see the temple door pushed open and Damian standing on the ledge it was built on, his hand on the hilt of his sword, with King Osgand right behind him.

There was no time to wonder what he'd seen or experienced inside the temple as our eyes met across the distance, and I could see my own terror etched on his face before he composed his features into the mask I knew so well.

"Prepare to fight," King Osgand said in Antionese, stepping forward. "We must do everything in our power to protect what lies in this temple from the hands of those who would attempt to steal its power and doom us all. Even if it means giving our lives. It is better for a few to die than an entire people." Then he spoke again, this time in Blevonese.

Damian continued to look at me until another explosion sounded below us, this one even louder. I spun around, yanking out my sword and lifting it up with my icy fingers to await the battle ahead.

⧎ FORTY-FOUR ⧎

THE CAPE I wore covered the quiver of arrows and my bow, so when it became apparent that the enemy wasn't coming up the trail to where we stood waiting quite yet, I quickly used one hand to unhook the cloak and toss it onto the boulder beside me. I hadn't realized how warm it was keeping me until the frigid air bit right through my thin tunic and pants, making me shiver violently. Rylan moved up to stand next to me, and Mateo stood next to him, then Asher. The Blevonese guards also spread out across the small field; some had their swords out, and others had their eyes closed and heads bowed as though they were praying. Perhaps they were. Asking for help and strength from the Unseen Power that Eljin had told me about — the voice that had spoken to King Mokaro and his brother, Delun, all those years ago.

I could only hope that the promise the Unseen Power had made to King Mokaro would be fulfilled. That if the Blevonese sorcerers stayed true to the command to only use their power to help or protect, and to never delve into black sorcery, even if it meant losing their lives, that they would be strengthened and given even greater power in their time of need.

When another boom rocked the canyon, sending more snow drifting down from the trees above us, I glanced around at the ten

Blevonese sorcerers and the handful of Antionese guards who had come to the temple, and suddenly realized how woefully pathetic we seemed. We were all that stood between Armando and his goal.

But what he didn't know — or didn't believe — was that if his black sorcerers fought through us and breached the temple grounds, *every* sorcerer, Blevonese, Antionese, and Dansiian, would die. If what Eljin had told me was true, even if I managed to keep them from killing Damian in the fight that loomed in front of us, he would die anyway as soon as Armando's abominations entered the temple.

The sound of shouting echoed up the canyon, and I squinted to see men rushing up the trail toward us. At first I couldn't make out who they were — or even which kingdom they were from — but as they got closer, I recognized the Blevonese uniform on the first few men. And the man at the head of the group was none other than Borracio, the sorcerer who had led the Insurgi in Antion for years.

He glanced at me and gave me a brief nod as he ran up the steep incline toward us, but then he went right on past me to Jiro. The other Blevonese men and a couple of women behind him stopped a little way below us on the larger trail. And just behind them jogged a huge man with skin as dark as the night.

"Deron!" I cried out. I hadn't seen my old captain since I'd returned. When he heard his name, his head snapped up so that his eyes met mine.

I sheathed my sword and ran down to meet him halfway, shocking him by throwing my arms around his neck. He awkwardly patted my back, and I quickly let go to step back. He cleared his throat and gruffly said, "I'm glad you're alive."

"I am, too," I replied.

"But not for long, if we don't figure out how to stop them," someone said from behind Deron. When I saw that it was Jerrod, I wasn't entirely surprised. But then I remembered what he'd been like when I'd last seen him, stunned and full of remorse from accidentally killing another guard, and I decided I was glad he'd seemingly recovered enough to be pessimistic again.

Jerrod's tunic was singed on the edge of one of his sleeves, and when he noticed me looking at it, he glanced over his shoulder at the rest of the soldiers, guards, and sorcerers who were rushing up the trail to fall back and protect the temple.

"They've already made it this far?" I asked, though I knew the answer from the bleak looks on everyone's faces.

"It's a bloodbath," Jerrod said quietly. "There's too many of them, and they have so many black sorcerers. We had to call a retreat, or we would all be dead right now as well."

I glanced at Deron, hoping he'd rebuke Jerrod and give us some sort of hope, but he just stared forward in silent agreement. My stomach plummeted as fear gripped my heart with icy claws.

"We have to stop them," I said, making my voice firm, shoving my own worries down deep where I could hide them. "We will have the upper hand here. It's narrow, and we can climb the trees and pick them off with arrows. Who are your best shots, General?" I turned to Deron, and at the businesslike tone in my voice he snapped back to alertness and began to point out soldiers, barking their names and ordering them to climb the trees and use their arrows to take out as many Dansiians as possible.

The men and one woman he'd pointed to all scrambled to obey him, moving to different trees and starting to climb as high as they could go while still remaining in good range to pick off the Dansiians. I honestly didn't know if their arrows would be able to reach any of the black sorcerers who were heading toward us, because they could just use their fire to incinerate them, but at least it gave them focus and hope.

One of the last Antionese soldiers to rush up the path, her face streaked with soot and her arm cut and bleeding, was Tanoori. I wondered how she had gotten assigned to such a difficult location. She should have been put somewhere much safer, where there would have been little chance of fighting. In fact, I wished that she had chosen to go with the women and children to the southwestern part of Blevon, where she would have been completely safe.

But instead, she hurried up to stand beside me, trying not to wince in pain when she sheathed her sword.

"What can you tell me to help prepare us?" I asked.

"They're coming," Tanoori said, her voice shaking slightly. "They sent the majority of their soldiers to the city to fight, with a few black sorcerers, but the king and the rest of his black sorcerers headed directly for the canyon. Even with the Blevonese sorcerers, we couldn't stop them. There were too many." She shook her head, and her shaking got worse. I'd seen it before — she was going into shock. She'd probably never been in a true battle before, never seen people dying left and right.

"Come over here and sit down; put your head between your knees," I instructed, pulling her over to a large, flat boulder. She followed without protesting, and once she was doing as I said, breathing slowly in through her nose and out through her mouth, I returned to Deron and Jerrod. Rylan now stood with them as well. When I glanced up at the temple, Damian still stood on the ledge, watching us, his expression unreadable in the falling haze of twilight.

"How many are there?" I asked Deron, but he shook his head. "Your best guess," I added.

"Twenty? Thirty? There could be more behind them. All I know is that we were prepared to fight soldiers with maybe a few black sorcerers, and instead, they created this thick cloud of darkness around themselves and continually threw their abominable fire at us and forced us to retreat, killing far too many of my men without even trying."

"How far back are they?" I pressed.

"The last blast caused a landslide that blocked the trail, so hopefully that will hold them back for at least a little bit."

I knew, after having watched them destroy the massive wall between Antion and Dansii, that it wouldn't take them long to clear the path again. As if to illustrate my point, another boom shook the ground beneath our feet.

"We need to think of something that we can do to take out as many of them as possible before they can use their fire to kill us all. What weapons could we use? What trap could we set that would kill as many sorcerers as possible?" I asked, spinning to look down the trail. Then an idea suddenly struck me.

"Who here has the ability to cause an earthquake?" I shouted up at the Blevonese soldiers and sorcerers. Jiro and Borracio were talking together, but when they heard my question they both turned and looked at me curiously, as did many others. Damian's eyes narrowed, and I wondered if he could hear me from where he was standing. When he turned to say something to King Osgand and then began to walk across the ledge toward the field where we all stood, I motioned for him to go back, but he ignored me and continued forward.

"Why do you ask?" Jiro called, and I jogged up to where he stood, beckoning Deron and the rest to follow me. Tanoori had calmed down enough to stand up, and she came as well.

"Our only hope of defeating Armando and his sorcerers is to take out as many of them as possible before they can use their fire to kill us," I repeated myself.

"I agree, but how do you propose we do that?" Borracio asked, his keen eyes trained on me.

Damian strode over to where I stood and said, "Alexa, what's going on?"

I looked up at him and smiled. "I think I have an idea."

⊰ FORTY-FIVE ⊱

THE WAITING WAS torture — the anticipation and fear of what was to come. Would it work? Or would we all die in the next few minutes? I'd begged Damian to go back to the temple with King Osgand, but he'd refused.

"If I am to die today, I will do it by your side, not standing like a coward up there, watching my people fall before me," he'd said, staring down into my eyes and making me wish I hadn't stopped him last night. "Plus, I can help," he'd added.

He stood beside me now, so tense his shoulders were slightly hunched forward. I'd never seen him with anything other than perfect posture.

The booms and explosions continued at regular intervals for several long minutes. But then, finally, there was nothing but silence.

"Get ready," I called out quietly, and the warning was repeated swiftly across the line of sorcerers that stood waiting for the first sighting of the black sorcerers. My plan was simple, but if it worked, it would be very effective.

We all strained to see in the growing darkness as the sun began to dip below the western horizon. The sky was stained crimson and orange from the final rays of daylight — fitting colors for this day full of blood and fire.

And then I saw it — a flash of black weaving between the trees far below us, trying to stay out of sight.

A Dansiian sorcerer, still wearing the robes King Armando insisted they use.

Right when I spotted him, a quiet trill, like the coo of a song-bird, sounded. The signal for our sorcerers to ready themselves. Behind the first, many more began to appear. Soon, the trees would disappear for a stretch where the trail was surrounded by the sheer walls of the canyon on both sides, and they would have no choice but to come out in the open.

And that was when we would strike. When they were forced to reveal themselves and would most likely begin to attack us with their fire.

As I watched, the first black sorcerer stopped just before the trail narrowed and he would have had to come out in the open. He was waiting for the rest of them to catch up — to overwhelm us with sheer force and numbers.

I lifted my hand, signaling our sorcerers, including Damian, who were lined up to wait. I stood beside him so I could have a good vantage point on what was happening. Eight other Blevonese sorcerers had the ability to cause an earthquake, including Borracio and Jiro and a woman who stood next to my father's cousin.

The Dansiians stretched out in a line, a veritable wall of black robes, and behind them I could see even more men in robes. Black sorcerers facing off against all that remained of the sorcerers who refused to turn to blood and sacrifice to seek greater abilities. I sent up a silent prayer to the Unseen Power, or whoever else might be listening to help us, to fulfill the promise to give the Blevonese sorcerers greater power in their time of need. I wondered where the *Rén Zhǔsas* were — why they didn't come out to help us. Surely they had more power that we could have utilized? Maybe they feared our failure and stayed inside the temple as a last protection for what lay within its walls.

But then there was no more time to wonder or wish for help or pray for more power. The front row of black sorcerers lifted their hands as one, and identical flames burst up from their palms. They began to slowly walk forward as the fire they wielded grew larger and larger.

I kept my hand lifted. "Wait," I cautioned. We had to make sure as many of them as possible would be targeted.

"Surrender now," a terrifyingly familiar voice suddenly shouted from behind the line of sorcerers, echoing up the canyon, "or you will all die!"

"That's Armando," I whispered urgently to Damian. "He's here."

He turned his head sharply to look down at me and then snapped it forward again to peer into the oncoming line of sorcerers, searching for his uncle.

"Ready," I called out, louder now.

"I'll take that as a no," King Armando shouted, and then the sorcerers pulled their arms back to launch the writhing flames at us.

"NOW!" I shouted and then threw my arms out to brace myself as the ground began to shake.

Our sorcerers focused their aim right beneath the black sorcerers, only tearing apart the earth they stood on. With all nine sorcerers, including Damian, acting at once, the trail tore apart almost immediately, swallowing up the black sorcerers and their fire. They fell out of sight, inhuman screams filling the air. But one of them was able to hurtle his fire first before falling. It sailed through the air toward a section of waiting soldiers who dove out of the way just before it exploded against the hard ground near some trees, setting a trunk on fire. Someone shrieked in pain but there wasn't time to look over and see who it was, because the rest of the sorcerers and everyone else who had been behind their front line were running forward, leaping over the falling earth to land on the other side. We'd taken out a large number of the black sorcerers, but more were coming, and our sorcerers couldn't make the hole any wider without risking the entire trail collapsing and possibly setting off a chain reaction that would take all of us and the temple with it.

"Archers!" Deron shouted, and Jiro added his own shout in Blevonese as we all began to fall back, rushing to escape the reach of the fire that the remaining black sorcerers were conjuring up. Some of our sorcerers stopped and threw their hands out, knocking one or two of the black sorcerers down.

The whistle of arrows sounded as we turned and ran back to higher ground, where the rest of the soldiers and sorcerers awaited the fight. I heard one or two cries of pain as arrows hit targets, but not nearly enough. I stopped and, swinging my own bow over my head, I grabbed an arrow, quickly notching it, and spun around to take aim. The first black sorcerer I spotted was looking up at some archers in the trees ahead of him, lifting his arm to ready his unholy fire. I let my arrow fly, and it rushed through the air, hitting him straight through his eye, knocking him to the ground. The fire in his hand extinguished, unthrown. He was dead.

"Alexa!" I heard Damian's frantic shout, and I sprinted to catch up to him and everyone else trying to get out of reach of the fire that was exploding all around us. There were more screams and cries of pain as the black sorcerers hit some of our men. I didn't dare look back, terrified I would see someone I knew.

There wasn't much farther for us to go — the temple loomed ahead. We had to turn and fight.

I grabbed another arrow and stopped to turn back and try to take out another one of the enemy. But what I saw turned my blood to ice in my veins — Rafe was running toward us, sword lifted. He was easy to pick out because of the empty eye socket he had; only puckered flesh remained of what used to be his eye.

I took aim at him, hoping that I could somehow break through his command, but the instant I pulled the string back, confusion clouded my mind and I let the arrow drop down again.

"Alexa!"

The frantic shout of my name shook me from the haze to see Rafe grinning at me, his one remaining eye glinting. "Hello, Alexa," he called out. "I can't tell you how happy I am to see you here, so that you can protect me from harm."

I turned and ran, desperate to get as far away from him as possible, so that I wouldn't be forced to do exactly that — to protect him from my own people.

Another fireball exploded right next to me, knocking me to the ground and taking out several of our soldiers and at least one of the Blevonese sorcerers. I groaned and forced myself to my feet. I hadn't been burned, just bruised and shaken. But I'd dropped my bow. Rather than turning back to get it, I yanked my sword out as I finally reached Damian and Rylan, who stood together, gripping their own swords.

"We have no choice but to fight," Rylan said, his gaze meeting mine, and I could see the dread beating in my stomach echoed in the depths of his eyes. He'd seen Rafe, too.

I turned to look up at Damian for a moment, and then I spun on my heel and shoved my sword in the air. "For Antion!" I shouted, and then I raced back the way I'd come, straight at the enemy.

The nearest black sorcerer hadn't been expecting my attack, and when he saw me coming he tried to throw his fire at me, but his aim went wide when I cut to the inside of the trail. And then an arrow whizzed past me and went straight through his throat. He'd been distracted by my attack, and one of our archers had noticed. I rushed forward, plunging my sword into his chest and then back out again, making sure to finish the job. He collapsed to the ground, but behind him stood another man in a robe.

He didn't hold up a gloved hand — he wielded no flames. He gripped a curved sword in his left hand, though.

A decoy, I thought, and hurtled toward him, sword raised. He lifted the sword to parry my blow, and we began to fight in earnest. All around me, the sounds of battle echoed in the canyon. I saw a body swathed in black robes go flying past us and a Blevonese sorcerer rushing after him, one hand raised and a sword in the other, as our blades clashed together again and again. We circled and lunged, parried and feigned in a deadly dance. He was skilled but not as fast as I was. He got in a good swipe and nearly took a piece of my arm, but I managed to spin away in time, just as a fireball exploded right above us, singeing the backs of my arms. In my haste to avoid being impaled, I tripped over a burning body behind me. I quickly regained my balance and then barely got my blade up in time to block his next blow.

I went on the attack, pressing my advantage of speed by swiping my sword back and forth and back again, a flurry of movement, until he misjudged my next move and went to block a blow that wasn't coming — so that I was able to drive my sword through his other side. In and out. His eyes widened and then he collapsed to the ground, landing on his sword as his eyes rolled up into his head.

I looked up right as another fireball flew toward me, and I threw myself to the side, narrowly avoiding being burned again, then rolling a few feet across the hard, frozen ground, tearing my sleeve open and skinning my elbow. Someone held out a hand, and I looked up to see Tanoori. I quickly took it and let her help me up, and then together we turned to face what was left of the Dansiian horde. Soldiers and sorcerers fought all around us. Trees were burning and bodies littered the ground.

When I saw Rafe standing a few feet away, fighting one of the Blevonese soldiers, my mind suddenly went hazy.

I realized I needed to protect him.

I ran toward him, with Tanoori on my heels. Was she a threat to Rafe? I glanced over, but her sword was still at her side. No.

But the Blevonese soldier was. I lifted my sword and jumped in front of him, parrying his blow.

"Perfect timing," Rafe said. But I ignored him, fighting the Blevonese soldier for him.

"Alexa! What are you *doing*?" I heard Tanoori's question, and when I glanced over, she was lifting her sword, readying herself to fight Rafe. I quickly surmised that the Blevonese soldier was the greater threat, so I continued to fight him. I had to finish him off first, then I could deal with the second threat.

"Alex! Please, what's wrong with you! That's our man!"

The sounds of blades crashing echoed all around me along with Tanoori's shouts, but I had to focus on protecting Rafe. The Blevonese soldier was skilled, but he seemed hesitant to fight me for some reason. I had just managed to get past his defenses and strike a blow to his leg when a bloodcurdling scream made me pause.

I spun around to see Tanoori standing in front of Rafe, her arms hanging at her side, his blade run through her belly. The haze suddenly cleared and left me shaking with horror.

"Tanoori! NO!" I lunged forward just as Rafe pulled his sword back out, and she dropped to her knees, lifting one hand to the blood pouring from her wound. Her head turned toward me, and then she crumpled to the ground. I tried to rush to her side, but Rafe stepped in the way. "Tanoori!" I screamed. Her eyes lifted to mine, and she tried to say something, but blood filled her mouth, and then her eyes went blank.

"No!" I lunged forward again, but Rafe grabbed my shoulders and pushed me back, laughing at my frantic anguish.

It was my fault. It was my fault. She'd died because of me. Because of *Rafe*.

Fury boiled up in my veins like acid, and I raised my sword, wanting nothing more than to run him through, but as soon as I pictured doing it, my mind went blank again, and I found myself standing there, staring at him in confusion.

"Alexa! Get away from him!"

I turned to see Damian pushing his way through the fighting, narrowly avoiding getting hit by another fireball, heading right for me — and Rafe.

⊰ FORTY-SIX ⊱

No!" I SHOUTED, terrified that Rafe's command would make me hurt or kill the man I loved. "Go back!"

Rafe just started laughing, and then suddenly, his sword was pressed to my throat.

Damian lurched to a stop a few feet away.

Rafe shoved me at Damian, who reached out to steady me, but I jerked away, terrified of myself. The light from the fires burning all around us flickered across Damian's face and reflected the confusion in his eyes — confusion that turned to horror when they dropped to the ground where Tanoori lay.

"Come on, Damian. Let's play, shall we?" Rafe stepped up next to me and lifted his sword. "We have some unfinished business, you and I, seeing how you killed my sister."

Damian's expression hardened, and when he lifted his sword, preparing to fight Rafe, I, too, lifted mine. I couldn't let the king hurt Rafe. I had to protect him.

Damian lunged at Rafe first, but I stepped in front of him and blocked his blow with my sword.

Damian stumbled back, his mouth opening in shock, and then he shook his head. "He got to you," he breathed, as his eyes filled with a sudden, strange grief.

I took his moment of hesitation to my advantage and lunged at him. He managed to get a shield up in time to block me. But Rafe was there, on the other side. Damian wouldn't be able to hold us both off for long, even with his sorcery. Damian focused on fighting Rafe, only blocking my blows but never going on the offensive against me. The three of us circled one another, lunging and parrying while Rafe and I tried to get past the shield Damian kept throwing up to block our attacks.

"Alexa, you don't want to do this!" Damian cried out at one point, when I could tell he was tiring and losing track of both of us. We were wearing him down. "Alexa, I love you — please, stop!"

Something inside of me tilted at his words, a tiny tug of anger. But I was confused about who, or what, I was angry at. And then Damian swiped at Rafe again, and I remembered — I was mad at him for trying to hurt Rafe.

"Isn't she marvelous?" Rafe taunted the king of Antion.

"I love you, Alex. I fought back for you — I know you can do the same for me!" Damian turned toward me, and when his eyes met mine, I paused, confused and upset.

Hope flared in Damian's eyes when I hesitated. Because of his momentary distraction, he was a split second too late getting the shield up to stop Rafe's blade from slicing toward him. He threw himself backward, so that the blade missed the intended target of his neck and sliced deep into his arm instead.

When he cried out in pain, my insides turned to ice for one horrible moment. I stared at him, my heart pounding as Rafe lifted his sword again. Damian pressed his bleeding arm to his body and lifted his sword to deflect Rafe's blow with his other.

"Alexa, please! Remember who you are!"

I couldn't bear to see him hurt. Why couldn't I stand it? I was supposed to hurt him — to protect Rafe. But something was very wrong with him getting injured while I stood here watching.

Rafe had him backed up to a burning tree. Damian had to stop retreating or he would get burned. But instead of going for the kill, Rafe turned to me. "Would you like to do it, my dear?"

I stepped forward, gripping my sword with slick hands, my head pounding with confusion. When I came to stand next to Rafe, Damian let his sword fall to his side. His eyes met mine, and the empty resignation in their piercing blue depths struck me straight in the chest, a driving pain that made me want to cry.

You love him, a voice deep within me whispered. *You love him.*

"Alexa, finish the job!" Rafe urged beside me.

"I love you, no matter what," Damian said, and then he tried to smile at me as I lifted my sword, a heart-wrenching grief in his eyes.

For some reason, I suddenly remembered being in his room, when he'd tried to kill me. He'd fought back then. What had he been fighting against? I needed to remember. I *had* to remember. I shook my head, the pain excruciating now.

"Alexa, now, or I'm going to do it!"

"It's all right, Alexa. I love you. Just remember that. I forgive you, no matter what."

Damian's eyes met mine once more and I knew. I loved him. He'd fought back against Vera because she wanted him to kill me — but he hadn't.

I turned to look at Rafe, and hatred filled me. He'd done this. He'd turned me into his weapon. My head ached, pounding against his control. I forced myself to lift my sword, even though my muscles screamed at me to stop. Fear flickered across his face, and he took a step back.

"You will *not* control me," I growled, and then, as if I'd burst through invisible chains, his hold broke away from my mind, and this time when I lifted my sword to lunge at him, nothing stopped me. He barely managed to parry my blow.

Damian rushed forward and lifted his sword with his good arm.

"Rylan!" Rafe suddenly shouted, glancing left of me. "Stop them! RYLAN! Kill Damian — right now!"

I spun to see Rylan fighting a Dansiian soldier, one not wearing the black robes, but the moment Rafe yelled at him he stopped and turned to us, his eyes blank. He rushed forward, his sword lifted, aimed at Damian.

"Him, too?" Damian cried out, jumping back and lifting his sword to parry Rylan's attack.

And then Rafe lunged at me.

I turned to face him, my back to Damian's as we both fought for our lives. With Damian so injured, I knew he wouldn't last long against Rylan. I could sense him drawing on his power to block Rylan's hits with his shield, but he wasn't moving as fast as he should have.

"I will kill you for what you did to Vera — to all of us!" Rafe shouted, pulling my attention back to him as he rushed toward me, aiming to run me through, like he'd done to Tanoori. I made a split-second decision to rush at him, realizing that if I jumped out of his way, he would hit Damian from behind. I swung my blade down and then back up at the last second, hitting his sword to the side so that I could barrel into him with my shoulder without being impaled, and knocked him back. True fear crossed his face as I went on the offensive against him for the first time, holding nothing back. My blade flashed in the firelight as I swung it left, right, then left again. He blocked and blocked, but he wasn't fast enough — I quickly realized he was weak to the right.

"No, Rafe," I spat out, "*I* will kill you for what *you*'ve done."

And then I lunged to the left. The minute he took the bait I spun around as fast as I could, and he wasn't able to do anything except stare at me as my blade sliced through his right side, deep into his belly.

When I yanked it back out, he stumbled back a step. His sword fell to the ground from his limp hand as he stared at me, his one remaining eye slowly glazing over in shock. And then his mouth fell open, and he dropped to the ground, dead at last.

I spun around to face Rylan and Damian, praying they were both still alive. Damian held his sword up, ready to defend himself, but Rylan had stumbled back a step, shaking his head in confusion now that Rafe was dead, his sword dropping a few inches. Relief crossed Damian's face, and he relaxed slightly, pulling his injured arm against his body once more.

Neither of them noticed the black sorcerer standing further up the trail, lifting his hand, taking aim at the king with his fire.

"Damian!" I screamed, running toward them but already knowing I wouldn't make it in time.

Rylan and Damian's heads snapped up. Damian looked at me, but I saw Rylan turn and notice the sorcerer just as he let the fire go, directly at Damian.

It all happened as if time had slowed to a crawl. Rylan's head jerked back so that his eyes met mine. And then he leaped forward, throwing his body in front of Damian's so that the fireball exploded against him instead of Damian, blasting Rylan through the air, knocking Damian over. Rylan landed past him, rolling a few times, leaving a trail of flames before finally coming to a stop on his side, smoke rising from his body.

⊰ FORTY-SEVEN ⊱

RYLAN!" I SCREAMED. But the sorcerer wasn't done. He was already conjuring more fire. I lifted my sword and charged right at him.

Damian beat me to him, his face darkened with fury. He made the ground beneath the sorcerer shake so that the fire he threw at us went wide, hitting the side of the canyon instead. Then Damian thrust his hand forward, sending the sorcerer slamming back into a tree behind him. Damian rushed forward, slicing his sword down so hard and fast the sorcerer couldn't pull back quickly enough, and he chopped his arm clean off. But I'd seen what Iker could do with all that blood, and even as I thought about it, the sorcerer began to summon a dark cloud that swirled up around his body, hiding him and Damian from view.

I plunged right into it, swiping my sword down where he had last stood. The cloud burned my eyes and made my skin hurt, but when my blade met hard flesh, the darkness suddenly dropped away, leaving the sorcerer standing before us, my sword sliced through his shoulder, down into his lungs. I yanked it back out and, without even waiting to see if he fell to the ground or not, I spun to face where Rylan lay unmoving.

My sword clattered to the ground as I sprinted to his side. He had to be alive; he *had* to be alive. I dropped to the earth next to Rylan. His whole body was burned, some parts worse than others. I gently rolled him to his back, and he moaned.

When I saw his face, I sucked in a gasp that was a half sob.

"Alexa," he coughed, his mouth barely moving. I could see the agony in his eyes — the only part of him untouched by the sorcerer's fire. "Is . . . he . . . all right?"

I started crying in earnest when I realized he was asking about Damian. After everything, he had sacrificed himself to save the king.

I nodded, lifting my hand to hesitantly touch his charred face. He flinched, and I pulled away.

"No . . ." he groaned. "Pain . . . is all right. Die . . . in your arms . . ."

"*No*. You *can't* die," I sobbed. "It wasn't supposed to end like this. You can't leave me here alone."

All around us the sounds of the battle raged, but I didn't care as Rylan tried to lift a hand to my face. His arm shook, and he couldn't reach quite high enough. When I realized what he was trying to do, I bent down and held his hand against my face so he could cup my cheek. "You're not . . . alone," he whispered. "Love him . . . as I . . . loved you."

My entire body was shaking from the tears that seemed to rise from the deepest depths of my soul. I shook my head against his hand, not wanting to accept what was happening, and then I turned to kiss his palm. He took a shuddering breath. I could hear the fluid in his lungs.

Rylan's eyes filled with tears as he looked up at me, but then he lifted his head slightly, and his gaze moved past me. He whispered something, but I couldn't understand him. I leaned in closer.

He spoke again, a soft sigh. "Jude . . ."

His lips moved as if he was trying to smile, and then he went completely still. His hand dropped from my face, falling to the ground beside him. The light faded from his beautiful brown eyes, until they glassed over.

"No! RYLAN! *NO!*" I screamed again. A tidal wave of anguish dragged me down, until I bent so that I had pressed my face to his burned tunic, my tears running across his ruined skin.

And then Damian was there, dropping to his knees beside me, taking me by the shoulders and pulling me back. A loud boom shook the ground near us, but I didn't even flinch. Rylan was gone. He was *gone*.

"Alexa, we have to go," Damian said, pulling on me even harder, not even realizing he was echoing what Rylan had said when Eljin died. "I'm so sorry, but we have to go *now*. There are even more coming! I can't hold them off any longer. We have to retreat."

"We can't leave him!"

"If we stay here, we'll die, too!" Damian shouted back at me, tears in his eyes as well.

"We can't leave him!" I repeated, my entire body shaking uncontrollably.

"You're right," he agreed with me, and then he bent forward and scooped Rylan's body into his arms, even though he was severely injured himself. His wound gushed blood as he struggled to stand under Rylan's weight.

"Your Majesty!" I heard a shout and turned to see Deron running toward us, a wound in his side bleeding profusely. He was intent on his king and didn't see the soldier rushing toward him with his sword raised. I grabbed Damian's sword from the ground and ran forward, barreling past Deron and swinging the blade up to stop the blow that was aimed at Deron's head. The soldier spun to attack me, but I was so angry and hurt and devastated and ruined, I didn't care. I just attacked. I killed him as they'd killed Rylan. And Tanoori. And Marcel and Mama and Papa. I killed that soldier, and then I moved on to another and then another.

And then I saw him, standing far back from the fighting, watching it all unfold.

King Armando.

With a primal scream of rage, I streaked toward him.

His eyes widened, and then he broke into a smile, as if welcoming my attack. Another sorcerer stepped in my way, blocking the king from me. Before we could start fighting, a voice unlike any I'd ever heard before sounded over everything else — over the clashing of swords, the burning of fire, the cries of the dying, and the sobs of the living left behind — a voice that was somehow soft and yet so loud at the same time that it shook the ground. The black sorcerer's eyes widened, and he suddenly froze, dropping to his knees to stare at something behind me, horror etched on his face.

I spun around, to see everyone facing *Sì Miào Chán Wù*.

When I gazed up at the ledge where Damian and King Osgand had once stood, there now stood two men and a woman, all dressed in robes of white lined in gold and silver. All three of them had long, white hair, and even from here, I could see how bright their eyes shone in the darkness.

The *Rén Zhǔsas* had finally emerged from the temple.

⊰ FORTY-EIGHT ⊱

$\mathcal{T}$HE MAN WHO stood a little bit in front of the other two sorcerers spoke again, and this time his words pierced my heart with hope. Though I could hear the sounds of Blevonese when he spoke, for some reason I understood his words, as if their power transcended our languages, speaking directly to my heart.

"The people of Blevon have stayed true to the oath that the first sorcerer, King Mokaro, made to the God who granted us such power, and so the promise given him shall now be fulfilled."

The man lifted his arms, and the other two sorcerers behind him did the same. At first nothing happened. But then, as I watched in awe, a beautiful golden light began to pulse behind them, almost as if it came from within the temple — perhaps even from the waterfall of golden water it hid. The light spread out to encompass the three sorcerers, wrapping around them like a shimmering cloak. And then it continued to spread, rushing forward, turning into a river of molten gold, encircling the Blevonese sorcerers, cloaking them as well, before moving on to Damian, who still held Rylan in his trembling arms. The glow eventually encompassed everyone from Antion and Blevon, even me, creating a grid of glowing, pulsing light around the black sorcerers and Dansiian soldiers who remained. When it wrapped around my body, I felt strangely light — and empowered, as if it was healing me, taking away my exhaustion and my pain.

Once we were all encircled, the golden glow grew stronger until it was a blinding, shining light. Suddenly, that light shot straight up into the sky above us. Every head was turned up to stare at it. And then just as quickly as it had risen above us, the golden-white light rushed back to the earth, hitting the ground with a massive boom. In the blink of an eye, it exploded around us, blinding us all.

When my vision cleared, I could hardly believe what I was seeing. Every single black sorcerer who had still been standing now lay on the ground — dead.

"For their crimes, their souls shall be *Diūsh* forever more," the sorcerer declared.

Cheers erupted around me, but I couldn't bring myself to do anything except stare halfway across the field at Damian, holding Rylan, his arm healed. For Rylan, the *Rén Zhúsas* had been too late.

"But for you, King of Dansii," the sorcerers suddenly spoke all together, their voices rising until the ground trembled and my ears actually hurt, "for your crimes, you shall be cursed to suffer far more than death or becoming *Diūsh*. You shall be cursed to not only wander the Lost Paths for all eternity, but to suffer the pain you have made others suffer until the end of time."

I spun to face King Armando. For the first time since I'd met him, fear filled his eyes. But then his gaze dropped to me, standing only a few feet away, and his fear turned to rage.

"This is your fault!" he roared, and, yanking a sword out of a body next to him, he rushed at me with it lifted overhead.

Strengthened by the force of the brilliant light, I lifted my own sword and blocked his blow with a resounding clang that echoed over the suddenly silent canyon.

His eyes burned with the fires of loathing as he charged at me again and again, but I continued to deflect him until he began to tire. And then, with the firelight of the trees burning all around us flickering across our bodies, I charged at him, lifting my sword and swinging it around as hard and fast as I could. He stumbled back, the fear returning, but he was too late — and too slow. My sword drove through his flesh and organs, but rather than pulling it back out, I pressed it in even harder as I stepped closer to him so I could whisper, "Enjoy your eternity of suffering."

He tried to say something, but his words were only a gurgle.

I pulled out my sword, and he dropped to his knees in front of me. Not ever wanting to see him again, I turned and strode away, so that I only heard the soft thud of his body when he hit the ground.

It was over. He was dead.

They were all dead.

⊰ FORTY-NINE ⊱

ABOVE US, THE sky was an endless expanse of velvety black, with millions of stars spreading like glittering diamonds spilled across the dark canvas. Before I'd left Antion, I'd never seen so much sky at once; it was only visible in patches through the unbelievably tall trees and bushes that enclosed our kingdom in a lush canopy. But here, the sky was as incomprehensible as eternity, stretching on forever.

I stared at the stars, because I couldn't bear to bring myself to look down at the bodies that lay before me and those being buried elsewhere. I didn't want to remember that they were gone. That they'd been taken away to live up there somewhere, among the pricks of light in the sky.

Asher.

Borracio.

So many other soldiers and sorcerers from both of our kingdoms.

Tanoori.

Rylan.

Tears slipped out of my eyes to run down my upturned face.

I heard someone walking up to me, but whoever it was stopped a few feet away and waited silently. Finally, I squeezed my eyes shut and let my head drop. I wrapped my arms around my body and took a deep breath.

When I glanced over my shoulder and saw that it was Damian standing there, wearing clean clothes and his crown, the grime and blood of the battle washed away, the tears started all over again.

He stepped toward me without a word and took me in his arms. I clung to him, staining his clean tunic with my tears as my body shook from the sobs I'd been holding in for years. No matter how many losses I'd suffered, I'd always forced myself to go on, to bury my pain and grief. But tonight, there was no one else to fight — no more battles to prepare for.

We'd finally conquered the enemy; we would finally have true peace.

But the cost had been unbearable.

My entire family, almost everyone I'd ever loved or cared for, except for Damian, had been taken from me.

But the same was true for him, too, and when I finally pulled away, I realized I wasn't the only who had been crying. His face was streaked with tears as well.

Together, we turned to face the funeral pyres.

It had taken all night to bring the bodies down from the canyon and to put the wood together to honor our fallen, after the remaining soldiers from the Dansiian army had surrendered. Apparently, the golden light the *Rén Zhǔsas* had called upon had come all the way out of the canyon, into the city and valley beyond, killing the black sorcerers who had remained with the bigger portion of the army and terrifying the rest of the Dansiian soldiers into throwing down their weapons and surrendering. Many of them were even helping prepare graves for the fallen, apologizing for fighting against us, and claiming they'd had no choice.

I believed them.

The Blevonese were burying their dead, as was their custom, with the help of those Dansiians who were willing, which I hoped was the first step toward a lasting peace between all three kingdoms. But Damian had insisted we honor those we'd lost in Antion's tradition.

"It's time," Damian murmured, and I nodded.

He let go of me so I could step forward and say my final goodbyes. I went to Tanoori first, reached out to stroke back the hair from her cold face. It was my fault she'd died. She might not have survived the battle no matter what, but her death had been a direct result of Rafe's control on me. I bent forward to kiss her forehead, fresh tears splashing on her stiff face.

"I'm so sorry," I whispered. "I'm sorry I failed you. I hope that you and Eljin are together now. I failed you both."

I kissed her again and then made myself straighten and turn to face Rylan.

We'd wrapped his body in white sheets, to preserve the memory of him as he'd always looked, not as he looked now. When I stepped up next to him, my legs wouldn't hold me, and I dropped to my knees beside him, shaking with sobs. I reached over to put my hands on his, where they were crossed over his chest, my forehead pressed against his shoulder. I remembered his last word, his brother's name, and I fervently prayed that he was with his family again — that they were all reunited now.

"Thank you," I choked out. "Thank you for saving him."

I'd soaked the white sheets by the time I finally forced myself to climb back to my feet on trembling legs. Damian came to stand beside me, wrapping his arm around me and drawing me in to his side. He reached up to wipe his face as well.

"I owe him my life," he said after a while, his voice hoarse. "If you hadn't risked yourself to save him and bring him back to Antion, he wouldn't have been there last night to save me. I'm not sure I deserved that sacrifice."

I looked up into Damian's tear-streaked face, at his bloodshot eyes, which were still so beautiful, and it truly hit me for the first time. We'd both survived.

There was nothing and no one left to tear us apart, ever again.

"He told me to love you . . . as he loved me," I said. "In the end, he was happy for us. He truly came to love you, too."

Damian swallowed once, hard, his jaw clenched, and nodded. "I will never forget him — or his sacrifice for us," he finally said, his voice unsteady. "You were right to love him. He deserved it."

He wrapped his other arm around me, holding me close for a long moment. And then he drew back. "Are you ready?"

I reached out to place my hand on Rylan's one last time. I broke away from Damian to bend over and press my lips to his cheek through the sheet. "I truly did love you. Thank you for what you did." I kissed his cheek again and whispered, "Good-bye."

And then I straightened and turned to Damian. "I'm ready."

He signaled, and some servants who had stayed behind with the troops came forward, their lit torches ready. We stepped back, and as the servants lit the pyres one by one, I whispered good-bye to Asher, and Borracio — being buried elsewhere — and the others who had also fallen during the night. Flawed men and women, but loyal friends to the end.

The flames took hold quickly, rising up to consume the bodies, releasing their souls to rise to their final resting place. As the pyres grew, the rest of the Antionese soldiers and guards who had survived the battle, including Deron and Jerrod, formed a circle around them. Even some Blevonese came; Jiro, my father's cousin, and King Osgand was there, standing back from the crowd, paying his respects without interrupting.

"We will never forget those who fell here, and paid the ultimate price so that those of us who survived might enjoy the peace that we will now be able to establish." Damian pulled out his sword and lifted it into the air, in salute. "We shall always remember their names and speak to our children of their bravery, so that our children will tell their children, and their deeds will never be forgotten — nor their sacrifices."

The rest of us all pulled our swords out as well and lifted them up into the sky. Soon, the very first hint of the rising sun would begin to lighten the sky to the east, wiping away the stars, but for now, the only light was that of the fires, burning away the remains of those we'd lost.

"For Antion!" Damian cried, and we all echoed his cry. "For Blevon!"

"To peace!" I added, and he glanced over at me and then smiled.

"To peace," he cried, and everyone echoed him yet again. "At last," he murmured.

Just as he lowered his sword, the first ray of sunlight burst over the peaks.

He turned to me and put his arm around my shoulders. Together, we watched the flames burn away, until there was nothing left of our friends but ash. Everyone else had left by then, leaving us alone.

Finally, I turned away. I knew there were many more days, months, even years of mourning and grief ahead of me — but the words Lisbet had told me all those months ago, after I'd defeated Iker and had been struggling under the weight of guilt for Marcel's and Jude's deaths, rose back up. She'd told me that I was dishonoring their memories and their sacrifices by wasting the life they'd given me if I lived as a shadow, stuck in my sorrow and guilt. She'd helped me see that the greatest way to honor them was to live the best life I could — to find happiness again.

I looked up to the sky, and I was struck by the contrast of the darkness fading to blue as the sun slowly rose, bringing life and light back to the earth. The night came every day, stealing the sun's power and turning the world to black. But every morning, the sun rose again, bringing light once more, no matter how dark the night had seemed.

When I glanced up at Damian, that's how I felt. As if together, we were that tender, first ray of sunlight stretching out to try and dispel the darkness of the night. He was my light and my life.

"What are you thinking?" he asked, his eyes meeting mine.

I shook my head, not quite able to put it into words just yet. Instead, I stretched up to kiss him. I could tell he was surprised, but he quickly recovered and gently wrapped his arms around me, his lips on mine a tender promise of what was to come.

And behind us, the sun finally burst free of the mountains.

⊰ EPILOGUE ⊱

2 years later
Damian

W HEN I COME into our room, Alexa stands by the window, staring out at the jungle. I often find her like this, lost in thought. I know her mind frequently drifts to the past, not only to the memory of the many battles we fought, but also to all those whom we lost.

I quietly cross the room to wrap my arms around her from behind. Though she still complains about wearing the dresses I had made for her, I hope to convince her someday of how beautiful she looks in them. Not that I mind when she wears pants and a tunic. I'm not blind. But her swollen belly will prevent her from wearing pants for a while yet.

She wraps her arms over mine, twining our fingers together, as we look out the window, toward the new building that is almost complete — the sanctuary for the women, babies, and children still searching for homes or a place in our kingdom after the horrors of my father's breeding house and Armando's experiments in Dansii. After the rest of his soldiers surrendered to us, King Osgand and I agreed that we would jointly rule over Dansii until a new monarch can be placed upon the throne, one we trust to keep the peace. For now, we are still focused on rebuilding and healing the wounds all three kingdoms bear — inside and out.

The reconstruction of the palace is almost complete as well, which is a miracle considering the destruction we returned home to two years ago. Alexa had warned me about Armando's threat to burn his way through Antion, but I hadn't truly believed it possible, until we saw the devastation ourselves when we returned. Armando had not only burned his way through the jungle — he'd looted and burned down a large portion of the palace as well.

But the jungle is tenacious, and it has already grown back to its former lushness — all except for the trees. It will take many more years before the trees that were destroyed grow back. But for now, Alexa doesn't seem to mind as much as I do. She says she likes seeing more of the sky, that it reminds her to live the best life that she can to honor the sacrifices that were made so that we have this life to enjoy.

"Did you need something?" she finally asks.

"Do I need an excuse to come hug and kiss my beautiful wife?"

She turns in my arms, her pregnant belly coming between us. "You know I can tell when you're lying."

"No, you can't. I fooled you for years," I tease her. "But in this case, I'm not lying. You are beautiful."

Worry lines still crease her forehead, pulling down over her hazel eyes.

"What is it?" I ask.

She shakes her head and turns back to the window. "What . . . what if I'm not a good mother?"

"What?"

I spin her around to face me again, and she grimaces. "What do I know about taking care of a baby? When he gets old enough to hold a sword, then I'll be good for something. But until then . . ." She shrugs, and I have to smother my laugh, turning it into a cough. But she isn't fooled and slaps my arm. "I'm being *serious*," she insists.

"You will be an amazing mother, just like you are amazing at everything you put your mind to," I assure her, bending forward to kiss her once, twice. I mean for them to be brief, but she softens into my arms, and I can't resist her. Her mouth opens beneath mine, and I pull her closer, my fingers tangling in her long hair, which she wears loose today, hanging down her back. Finally, we breathlessly break apart.

"You know, that's what got me in this whole mess to begin with," she points out, her eyes alight with a teasing glint that I love almost more than any other expression she makes.

"I'm not entirely sure what you mean. Maybe you should show me, so I can fully understand."

She just shakes her head and puts one hand on her belly.

"Is she moving?"

"Yes, *he* is."

She guides my hand to where our unborn child stretches against her skin, pressing a hand or foot into my palm. "You know, I was thinking, when our daughter is born, we could name her after our mothers."

"Nialah Olara," she muses out loud. "Hmmm, I like that." She moves my hand lower, to where the baby has rolled and continues to move beneath her skin. "And if I'm right and it's a boy?"

She looks up into my eyes, still smiling. But this is the real reason I came to find her. I'd been sitting in my office, going through some missives from King Osgand and General Tinso, who was found bound in a Dansiian dungeon and who returned to his castle shortly after our victory. The loss of his son was a terrible blow, but he is holding up rather well, considering. He still has Lisbet and his nephew, Jax, who often go to stay with him so he isn't always alone in his big castle in Blevon — though they are returning soon, as neither of them can wait to meet the new baby, and they both want to be here for the birth. As I was reading through their messages, I'd suddenly thought of our baby — how he or she would be born into a world of peace, instead of war and bloodshed as Alexa and I had been. And I'd suddenly realized what we should name our son, if we are given a boy this time.

"I was thinking we could name him Marcel Rylan," I say quietly.

Alexa's smile slips as her arms curl protectively around her belly. "Marcel Rylan," she repeats in a whisper. "That's perfect."

I lift my hands to her jaw, tilting her chin up so I can look into her face. "Are you sure?"

She nods, and when she finally meets my gaze, I see the tears swimming in her eyes.

"I'm sorry, I didn't mean to make you cry." I gently stroke her hair back from her cheeks, my fingers brushing past her whole skin on one side of her face and the striated, scarred skin on the other. I know she is still embarrassed by her scars sometimes, but I barely even notice them. She is just Alexa, the woman I love — my wife, my queen. And she is beautiful, inside and out.

"They're happy tears — mostly." She smiles and presses a kiss to my palm. She turns back to the window, but reaches to take my hand in hers. "Do you know why I love seeing the sky so much?" she asks, confusing me by the sudden turn in conversation.

"No."

But then she tells me a story, the story of a girl who woke up scarred, inside and out, in this very room, years ago. And the words that a wise woman told her that helped her find her way back from the grief and guilt that threatened to consume her.

And as she speaks, we gaze out at the expanse of blue sky that stretches above the jungle we call home and the palace where we will raise our son or daughter, to be just as wonderful as their mother. A woman who can look out at the sunshine and see a new beginning.

The new beginning we created together.

⊰ ACKNOWLEDGMENTS ⊱

As I sit here, trying to compose my thoughts to write these acknowledgments, I find myself overwhelmed by emotion. It is going to be a bittersweet thing, leaving these characters and this world behind. What a journey it's been. An entire trilogy . . . I actually did it.

First and foremost, I must thank my Heavenly Father for the blessings in my life — for the beautiful family I've been given, and for the gift of writing He bestowed upon me. I can't imagine my life without this gift, without the words and stories that have always come to me. I'm forever grateful for that blessing.

To everyone who has helped make this dream, the dream of sharing my words with the world, a reality, I offer my deepest, heartfelt gratitude.

To my editor, Lisa, who remains one of the most lovely people I have the privilege of knowing. Thank you for believing in me and my words, and for giving them shape and bringing them to life. Thank you also to the incredible Sheila Marie — publicist extraordinaire. You amaze me. And the entire team at Scholastic — thank you for everything. The support, the excitement, the gorgeous covers, the kindness you've shown me — you truly are a family, and I thank you for letting me be a part of it. Donuts for everyone! (And maybe one of these times, I'll get to be the one to deliver them!)

To Josh — I can't thank you enough. None of this would be possible without you. I'm so grateful to have you in my corner. And of course, Tracey and the entire Adams Lit team. I am so lucky to be able to work with you all! Here's to many more adventures to come!

To Kathryn Purdie — *Defy* would never have left my computer if it weren't for you, and now look at it. All grown up, a complete trilogy. So grateful for you. And to all of my critique partners and author friends — thank you for always being there for me, for thoughtful feedback, and for understanding. It takes one to know one — and it takes one to truly get it. I'm so glad to have so many wonderful people who "get" me in my life.

To the bloggers, librarians, teachers, book clubs, friends, and family who have spread the word about these books, who have written me or called or texted or created fan art or posted a review — you are all amazing and I can't thank you enough. You are the icing that makes this journey so very sweet and wonderful.

Thank you to Ideas for Hollywood for the stunning trailer. I adore it.

To the musicians who inspire me and help me channel the emotions I need to write, thank you. As always, Hans Zimmer, and also James Newton Howard, Joseph Trapanese, and Alexandre Desplat. Your gifts help me use mine. And to Ellie Goulding, Imagine Dragons, OneRepublic, Bastille, Florence + the Machine, and Junkie XL. I love your music. Thank you.

To Robert and Marilyn — I'm so grateful to have such supportive and wonderful in-laws. Thank you for all of your help and excitement. It truly means a lot!

To Elisse — your support and enthusiasm and never-ending willingness to read and reread and talk about my books and plotting and revisions has made all the difference. Thank you so very much for everything. To Kerstin, thank you for always being there for me, for your generosity, and your excitement for my books. It means more than you know! To Lauren, I'm so grateful to have you for a sister and for all of your support over the years. I'm so glad you love my books so much! And thank you to Kaitlyn, too, for your support!

To Henri and SuZan — I couldn't have asked for better parents. Thank you for always believing in me and encouraging me to pursue my dreams. What a blessing to have you both in my life.

And to my beautiful children, Bradley, Gavin, and Kynlee. Thank you for your love and for putting up with me and this crazy ride you get to be a part of. You three are my everything.

Finally, to Trav. You are my sunrise, you are the light that banishes the darkness, and the joy in my life. Thank you will never be enough.

⇥ ABOUT THE AUTHOR ⇤

Sara B. Larson is the author of the acclaimed YA fantasy novel *Defy* and its sequel, *Ignite*. She can't remember a time when she didn't write books — although she now uses a computer instead of a Little Mermaid notebook. Sara lives in Utah with her husband and their three children. She writes in brief snippets throughout the day (while mourning the loss of nap time) and the quiet hours when most people are sleeping. Her husband claims she should have a degree in "the art of multitasking." When she's not mothering or writing, you can often find her at the gym repenting for her sugar addiction. You can find her at www.sarablarson.com.